P9-CES-843

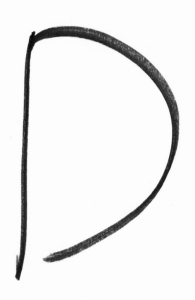

The Dire King

The Jackaby Series by William Ritter

Jackaby

Beastly Bones

Ghostly Echoes

The Dire King

The Dire King

A Jackaby Novel

WILLIAM RITTER

ALGONQUIN 2017

Published by
Algonquin Young Readers
an imprint of Algonquin Books of Chapel Hill
Post Office Box 2225
Chapel Hill, North Carolina 27515-2225

a division of
Workman Publishing
225 Varick Street
New York, New York 10014

Printed in the United States of America.
Published simultaneously in Canada by Thomas Allen & Son Limited.
Design by jdrift design.

LIBRARY OF CONGRESS CATALOGING-IN-PUBLICATION DATA
Names: Ritter, William, 1984- author. | Ritter, William, 1984- Jackaby series.
Title: The dire king / William Ritter.
Description: First edition. | Chapel Hill, North Carolina : Algonquin Young
Readers, 2017. | Series: A Jackaby novel ; [4] | Summary: In this conclusion to the
Jackaby series, the eccentric detective and his assistant Abigail Rook find them-
selves in the middle of a war between magical worlds.
Identifiers: LCCN 2017002941 | ISBN 9781616206703
Subjects: | CYAC: Mystery and detective stories. | Imaginary creatures–
Fiction. | Supernatural–Fiction. | New England–Social life and customs–19th
century–Fiction. | LCGFT: Detective and mystery fiction. | Paranormal fiction.
Classification: LCC PZ7.1.R576 Di 2017 | DDC [Fic]–dc23
LC record available at https://lccn.loc.gov/2017002941

10 9 8 7 6 5 4 3 2 1
First Edition

*For Mira and Helena and Leah and Gailian
and all the rest of the unready heroes growing up today,
who will open new doors in the course of their lives
that I did not even realize were locked in mine.*

The Dire King

Chapter One

To say that the house at 926 Augur Lane was not yet back to normal would be to grossly misrepresent the nature of the house at 926 Augur Lane. At its best, the peculiar property was an abode of the abnormal and a sanctuary for the strange.

The notion of premeditation did not appear to have been of any concern to the building's architects, the result of which was an eclectic edifice constructed using all manner of materials and styles. Its columns and cornices, balconies and balustrades all came at one another from unruly angles to form what ought to have been a hideous mess but was somehow beautiful instead. Still a mess, certainly, but a beautiful one.

From within, the house was more astonishing still. My

employer, private investigator R. F. Jackaby, was no average detective, and the proof was packed in every corner of his property. Eldritch mementos from countless curious cases filled the shelves; strange smells swept from his kitchen laboratory, wove through the crooked hallway, spilled into his overstuffed office, and tickled the spines in his lavish library. As I slid past the spiral staircase, I could hear from above me the familiar splash of wings on water, the echoes bouncing down from the duck pond on the third floor, where Douglas, Jackaby's prior assistant and current resident waterfowl, spent much of his time.

Strange as it all might seem, I had come to think of this place as my home. And then my home had been violated.

I stepped out the back door into the bright summer sunlight, past the pile of broken busts and shattered reliquaries Jackaby had pitched out of his office window as he had tidied up the wreckage during the past weeks. Our investigation had rattled a hornets' nest, and the hornets had sent giant monsters to rattle ours. Their intrusion had done irreparable damage to our statuaries and plasterwork, but even more to our sense of safety. We had done what we could since the incident. We had swept up the pile of crimson splinters that had once been our cheery red front door, plastered over the worst of the battered masonry, and scooped up the sea of broken glassware in the ravaged laboratory. But the damage had been done.

The house at 926 Augur Lane was not back to normal. It was not back to abnormal. It was wrong and it felt wrong.

I came to a stop and fished a hefty iron key out of my pocket. My only consolation was that the culprit behind the destruction was now our captive, locked up securely in Jackaby's supernaturally safeguarded cellar.

Morwen Finstern did not look very intimidating as I swung open the door and climbed down the steps into her makeshift prison. She was of average appearance, with strawberry blond hair hanging in tangled waves around her slender face. Her eyes were wide and sad, and I might have felt sorry for her if I had not known she was a malicious nixie, a shape-shifting creature responsible for the brutal deaths of countless innocent victims over the centuries.

"Shepherd's pie," I said, dropping the plate on the dusty table. "It's not very warm."

"I smell onions," Morwen said.

"I used extra."

"I told you yesterday, I hate onions."

"That's why I used extra."

Morwen's fingers flexed as though she might like to take a swipe at me. The slender chain around her wrist clinked softly with the motion. Tibetan sky iron, Jackaby had called it, enchanted by some manner of sorcery. I did not fully understand the artifact, but I could not deny its effectiveness. So long as the binding held fast, the nixie could take no action against her captor's will. This did nothing to improve her temperament, but it did render her more or less benign.

"I'm thirsty," she grumbled.

"There are a couple of grapes on the side of the plate. You can suck on those."

"Just a small glass of—"

"No." I had seen what Morwen could do with a little water.

"What's the matter? Afraid of little old me?" she jeered.

"Mortified," I replied. "Imagine what the neighbors would think if they looked under our house and found you skittering about down here. It would be almost as shameful as finding mice in the walls or mold in the attic."

"It's not your neighbors you should worry about finding me here," she spat as I turned to go. "The council is coming for me. My *father* is coming for me!"

"Well then." I stepped back up into the daylight, hoping that I sounded as dauntless as I wasn't. "I guess you had better finish up those onions before he arrives." As I clicked shut the heavy iron padlock, I could hear her muffled curses through the door.

Of course I was afraid. Morwen's unsettling intrusion into our home had been nothing compared to her father's trespasses. The self-proclaimed king of the earth and the otherworld had been inside my head. He had controlled me. It made my skin crawl to think of it—and it was far from over. "*The age of man has ended,*" he had promised. His specific intentions were inscrutable—but not a week passed during which we did not receive word of another unnatural episode or creepy creature emerging from the alleyways of New Fiddleham, and all of the threads led back to the Dire Council and their cryptic king.

For all the signs and portents, the king and his council might as well have been whispers in the wind. I found myself obsessing fruitlessly, lying awake at night, staring at the cracking plaster of my ceiling until the morning light crept through my window.

I took a deep breath and straightened my skirts as I crossed the garden. The king had trespassed in my mind, but I refused to let him take up permanent residence there. There was still work to be done. I trod around the side of the house, busying my mind with more productive tasks.

Jackaby's weathered wooden fence was inscribed all around with protective words and symbols, and the branches of his trees were hung with feathers and cords tied in intricate knots. The old willow's foliage had faded from bright green to pale gold in the past week, and leaves spun around me as I untangled a few of the wards that hung from their branches. I dusted off stone totems and pulled stray twigs out of the ring of salt that ran along the foundation of the house. As I watered the fragrant rosemary and the budding yellow witch hazel, I gazed up at the brickwork, noting the myriad symbols hiding in the masonry like sly old friends. There, by the eaves, was the eye of Ra, there, the hammer of Thor, and there, the seal of Solomon. I brushed my palm over a faded shamrock relief as I rounded the front of the house.

Hanging over the entry was the same wrought iron sign that had greeted me so many months ago when I first came trudging up the icy cobblestones of Augur Lane in that cold January of 1892.

INVESTIGATIVE SERVICES

PRIVATE DETECTION & CONSULTATIONS:

UNEXPLAINED PHENOMENA OUR SPECIALTY

Beneath this stood the detective himself, hammering in the final nail to rehang his horseshoe door knocker. The new door was a bit wider and sturdier than its predecessor, but it was already painted the same brilliant red. Built into the frame above it was a new narrow window as well—a single pane of frosted glass, into which were etched the words:

R. F. JACKABY

PRIVATE DETECTIVE

"Good morning, Mr. Jackaby," I said. "The new entryway looks lovely."

"Contextual relevancy," he said, although the words had to wend their way through a mouthful of spare tacks.

"Come again?"

He spat the nails into his hand. "The transom. Here, come closer."

I stepped up to the landing, and the frosted glass clouded over momentarily, clearing just as quickly to reveal a revised set of words:

R. F. JACKABY

MENTOR & EMPLOYER

"That's incredible!" I said.

"Bit of a special order. The limited clairvoyant effect is achieved through a psychic crystal suffusion in the glass. It senses the needs and expectations of each caller and generates a respective title. Come, see it from the inside."

I followed him in. The letters should have been reversed, but the transom read the same from within as it did from without.

"The house now knows what our potential clients really think of my services before we even open the door," he said. "I thought that might be a convenient forewarning, given a few of our most recent visitors."

"A wise precaution."

"Yes. I took the liberty of having them enchant it with a glamour-inhibitor charm, as well. I have no trouble telling who is what and what is who, but I thought you might appreciate knowing who you're dealing with. Now then, speaking of visitors," he said, depositing his hammer and spare nails casually into a drawer marked *Receipts*, "have you fed our unwilling guest this morning?"

"Yes, sir. And I locked up tight behind myself."

"Good. Checked the exterior wards?"

"Just now, sir."

"It's Tuesday. Be sure you leave a saucer of honeyed milk out for the pixies."

"Wednesday, sir. And I already put out fresh strawberries for the sprites."

Jackaby gave a satisfied nod. "Excellent. Get yourself ready, then. We leave within the hour."

"Yes, sir. Where are we going today?"

"Seeley's Square, and from there through the veil to see a king about a council."

"The king of the Annwyn?" My breath caught in my throat. A pair of blood red eyes burned in my memory. "Sir, we aren't remotely prepared yet!"

"What?" Jackaby said. "Oh, not that king. There are as many kings in the otherworld as there are kings on earth. As many bad kings and as many good, but there has never been one king to rule them all, in spite of what that nasty nixie's father says. No, no. It has taken some time, but I finally arranged a meeting with a king of a very different sort. If there is anyone in the Annwyn with a vested interest in protecting the barrier between that world and this one, it is the Fair King, Arawn. His emissaries will meet us at noon precisely to escort us through the veil-gate."

"I suppose at this point I shouldn't be surprised to learn you're friends with the magical king of the good fairies," I said. I occasionally wondered if I would ever wake up from my bizarre life in New Fiddleham to find I had really just dozed off on a pile of storybooks and scientific journals, and that I was back home in Portchester, still in England, where life made sense and fairy tales were fiction.

"*Friends* is not necessarily the term I would use," said Jackaby. "I am in Lord Arawn's debt. He presented me with the dossier of the Seer when I was a boy, just as he had presented it to the Seer before me. I would know nothing of the history of my gifts if it were not for–" Jackaby froze and looked up at the open door.

I followed his gaze to see a white-haired old man stumbling up to the landing panting heavily, his skin wan. He reached out to steady himself on the door frame, but missed, collapsing to his knees on the threshold.

Above him, the cloudy glass of the transom window was already clearing.

R. F. JACKABY

DESPERATE LAST RESORT

Chapter Two

The devil's come for me," the old man wheezed. "He's come for me at last!"

Jackaby knelt beside him, offering him a steady hand. "There are no devils here," he said. "Catch your breath a moment. That's it." His eyes narrowed. "Hold on, now—you're familiar."

"We have met, Detective," the man croaked. "The church—" But he collapsed into a fit of dry coughs.

Recognition dawned and Jackaby cocked his head, startled. "My word! It's Gustaf, isn't it? No, Grossman? Grafton!" The old man nodded weakly. "Father Grafton. Yes. Good God, you've grown old!"

"Sir," I chided.

"Miss Rook, allow me to introduce Father Grafton. We

last met—what was it—three years ago? When Douglas and I were investigating a rather grisly series of killings on the outskirts of town."

"Not my doing," Grafton managed. "The killings."

"No," confirmed Jackaby. "The pastor was doing everything in his power to prevent any further harm from befalling his parishioners. Made a good show of it, too. Of course, he was at least thirty years younger then." He whipped back to the old man. "Three decades in just three years? Have you been meddling with the occult? You know firsthand how dangerous that is! I'll have you know Douglas hasn't been the same since he left that church of yours!"

"Put the fear in him, did it?"

"A bit. Mostly it turned him into an aquatic bird."

"*D-dim hud.*" The man's eyes seemed to be having trouble focusing. He shook his head, blinking. "No magic. Not anymore." A patch of wispy white hair fell from his head and drifted to the floorboards.

Jackaby peered intensely at Father Grafton. "You're getting older by the second!"

Grafton nodded weakly.

"I don't understand." Jackaby peered into Grafton's ear and then took a sniff of his wispy hair. "I don't see any sign of a curse, no traces of paranormal poisons, no visible enchantments. Who did this to you?"

"Time," Grafton rasped. "Not much time." Wrinkles cut across the man's face like scars and milky white cataracts formed in his eyes. His shoulders shook. "*Harfau o Hafgan,*" he breathed.

"*Harfau o Hafgan?* What does that mean? Is that Welsh?"

"*Mae'r coron, waywffon, a darian,*" Grafton mumbled, his head drooping with each word–and then he lurched up so suddenly it made me jump. He clutched Jackaby's arm. "The crown, the spear, the shield. You cannot let him collect them. He has already taken the crown. The spear . . . it was destroyed, but I fear it has been remade. The shield . . . the shield . . ." He was gasping with each breath, his whole body shuddering. His eyes were wide and wild. "He trusted me. Now I have to trust you. The shield is in the Bible. The Bible of the zealot."

"The shield is in a Bible?" said Jackaby. "What Bible? Whose? Are you the zealot?"

"Not much time. The shield. In the Bible. You must stop–stop–*stopiwch y brenin.*" Father Grafton crumpled to the floor, and with one last rattling breath, he was still.

Jackaby delicately turned him over. Grafton's skin had gone as dry as parchment. The old man's body looked as though he had been mummified. I put a hand over my mouth.

"Is he–" I whispered.

"Quite," said Jackaby.

"How?" I gulped.

"It doesn't make sense." Jackaby scowled.

He stood and began to pace at Father Grafton's head.

"He wasn't charmed or hexed. There was a somewhat ethereal aura about him, but no more than I might expect from a man of the cloth. There's nothing about him that should have caused this! It's as though he was just taken by a sudden and inexplicable bout of old age. If I had not seen it happen—if I had only stumbled across him—I would say this was the corpse of a man who died decades ago of natural causes."

"What about *that* was natural?" I asked.

Jackaby shook his head, vexed. "Did you catch everything he said?" he asked.

"Yes. I think so."

"Jot it all down for our records, then. It seems we have been hired for another case, Miss Rook, and the good father has already paid us with his life."

We managed to maneuver the body inside before it could draw attention from the neighbors. I would like to say it was the first body that Jackaby and I had ever deposited on the old wooden bench in our foyer, or that it would be the last, but neither would be true.

"What should we do with him now?" I asked.

"I have a decent coffin in the attic that should suit the gentleman well enough. I'll just need to find somewhere else to store my encyclopedias." Jackaby paced the threadbare carpet. "We should search his church immediately. It's a smallish parish on the outskirts of the city. He said the shield was in a Bible. Whatever the shield is, I expect we'll find it there—and if the devil really is after Father Grafton, then I'd rather find it before he does."

"So much for meeting the fairy king at noon," I said. "I guess Lord Arawn will have to wait."

"Oh hell," Jackaby said. "No, I can't miss my rendezvous. The fair folk don't take kindly to social improprieties, and I can't afford to wait for another meeting."

"Well then, I'll go."

"Absolutely not. Arawn's emissaries expect me. They would never grant you the meeting without me."

"I mean I'll go to look for the Bible."

"What? Out of the question," Jackaby said. "The last assistant I sent into that church alone has been eating bugs and bread crumbs out of the grass ever since."

"I won't go alone; I'll bring Charlie." Officer Charlie Barker, formerly Charlie Cane, was the finest companion I could ask for on a job like this. In addition to being a top-notch and highly trained detective in his own right, Charlie was also—well—special. Descended from an ancient family of shape-shifters called the Om Caini, Charlie could transform at will into a powerful hound. He had saved my life and that of countless others, although he had been forced to live in hiding ever since his secret inhuman heritage had been revealed. A great affection had grown between Charlie and me—though his nature, the need to conceal it, and the pace of the unbelievable events unfolding around us made our situation . . . complicated.

"Charlie is on special assignment for Marlowe again," said Jackaby. "Left Douglas in charge of his dog and took off just before dawn this morning. Lord knows when the commissioner will be done with him this time—he needs all the help he can get. The whole of New Fiddleham is a boiling mess. I think I preferred it when Mayor Spade just pretended the supernatural didn't exist. Now he's causing more trouble than he's averting with his ludicrous witch hunt. Marlowe can barely keep up."

I couldn't entirely blame Mayor Spade. The nasty nixie in our cellar had spent the better part of the past ten years masquerading as Spade's doting wife, manipulating and using him all the while. The truth of this had not come gently to the mayor. His world had turned upside down overnight, and in the weeks since, he had launched his own personal crusade to set it right, with little regard to how he might set it wrong in the process.

Charlie had been covertly helping Commissioner Marlowe smooth out the prickliest situations caused by Spade's creature-catching campaign. It was thankless work, but Charlie was stubbornly noble, risking his hide for a city that would just as soon label him one of the monsters. His stalwart nature made him gallant—but it also made him absent, which did little to help me right at the moment.

"Why don't you send me?" Jackaby and I both turned to see Jenny Cavanaugh, the ghost of Augur Lane, hovering in the doorway. She was translucent, her edges wavering ever so slightly, her silvery hair floating behind her. The loathsome Morwen Finstern had taken poor Jenny's life over a decade ago, but Jenny had firmly taken back her afterlife. Around her neck now hung a pewter locket. Inside it was a simple inscription, *From Howard with love*, and a pinch of brick dust. Howard Carson had been Jenny's past. The brick dust was her future. By carrying with her that small piece of her home and the place of her death, Jenny had made herself free to explore the world once again in her ghostly form.

"It's too dangerous," Jackaby said.

"Then it's a good thing I can't be killed again."

At length Jackaby relented. "Grafton said the shield was in the Bible. Look for a Bible with a crest on the cover," he said. "Or perhaps one with something tucked inside. Just"–Jackaby met Jenny's eyes–"be careful."

Jenny smiled softly at the detective. "And you."

Chapter Three

M other had always told me that it was prudent to be prepared–although I imagine she would have preferred that I equip myself with spare silk handkerchiefs and sun hats and leave the silver daggers and vials of holy water at home. By the time Jackaby swept into my room, I had finished loading the pockets of my skirts with supplies and safeguards: a sprig of wolfsbane, a small talisman, a silver coin. The weight of my knife and scabbard on one hip was balanced by that of my leather-bound notebook on the other.

My modest collection was nothing compared to the walking arsenal of artifacts that was my employer. The overstuffed pockets of his long duster clinked and jingled, and he smelled pleasantly of cloves. "Ready, Miss Rook?"

"Whenever you are, sir."

"Then let's be off. Our carriage is waiting out front."

"You've chartered a driver for the trip?" Jackaby almost never summoned a cab if he could manage on foot.

"No," said Jackaby. "Didn't I mention? I have hired one on a more permanent basis. Well, semipermanent. Really quite temporary—call it a trial period. I retain the right to give her the sack as soon as the world is no longer in imminent peril. For the time being, it seemed convenient to retain reliable transportation."

I followed my employer down the spiral stairs, through the winding hallway, and out the front door. Waiting on the street was not a sleek black hansom cab, but an exceedingly battered one-horse vendor's carriage with the words *Dr. Emerson's Enervating Elixir–also good for cats!* written in peeling paint along the side.

"Who is Dr. Emerson?" I asked.

"A fellow whose tonic, it seems, did not sell well enough to merit the expense of his vehicle. He was willing to part with it for a reasonable figure."

A tall, dark woman stepped down from the driver's box. She was dressed in a neat black skirt and matching jacket with a prim bow at the neck of her crisp white shirtwaist, and she wore a rosy bonnet pinned up in the curls of her hair. Her shoulders were broad and her jawline hard, but she moved with all the grace of a dancer. I knew her at once. Miss Lydia Lee.

"Miss Lee!" I called out. "How delightful to see you again!"

"Likewise, Miss Rook. And very kind of you to say." Lydia Lee smiled a little nervously, tugging at the hem of her jacket. She opened the door and stood up straight like a proper valet.

"Thank you, Miss Lee," Jackaby said. "Up you go, Rook."

"Have you much experience working with horses?" I asked Miss Lee, climbing up the creaking step. Within, the coach smelled strongly of garlic and peaches. Behind our seats was a storage area, where a few empty bottles of Dr. Emerson's Elixir clinked about on the floor.

Miss Lee pursed her lips, looking less than confident as she clicked shut the door for us. "She'll be fine," Jackaby assured me. "The stable master taught her all about bits and bridles and all that business yesterday when we bought the old stallion off him. Miss Lee was of the opinion that she was woefully unqualified at first, but as I explained to her then, the best way to become qualified is to do. How's it coming along, Miss Lee?"

Miss Lee shrugged. "This old plug and I are getting used to each other, I guess," she said, giving the dappled gray a pat before she climbed back up to take the reins. "The Duke's only nipped at me two or three times this morning."

"Splendid progress. Seeley's Square, please. We have a king to question."

When we arrived at the vibrant park in the center of New Fiddleham, the clock atop the Stapleton building read five minutes to twelve. My stomach had begun to flutter with the anxious excitement that every new case with Jackaby seemed to elicit. Admittedly, the feeling may have been exacerbated by the fact that the Duke seemed unwilling to take the winding curves of New Fiddleham's streets at anything less than a full gallop no matter how desperately Miss Lee pulled at the reins. By the time we arrived, I was more than eager to step down from the coach and into Seeley's Square. Mr. Jackaby bade Miss Lee good-bye as I took a few deep breaths and regained my bearings.

The park before us was a beautiful expanse of green grass and healthy foliage. Butterflies fluttered about over the bushes and birds twittered in the treetops. A handful of businessmen took their lunches on park benches, and a woman pushed a stroller along the path while twin girls in bright petticoats ran circles around her.

Jackaby ambled away from all of them, heading off the path and through the less manicured brush toward a grove at the very center of Seeley's Square. I had not noticed it at first, but in the dead center of the park stood a cluster of trees that grew in an unnaturally tight circle. Jackaby drew to a stop in front of them.

"Is this where we will be meeting the . . . er . . . them?" I asked.

"I believe we are meant to enter the ring first," he replied.

I tried to peer between the trunks to see what might lie within, but no matter how I craned my neck, I could not seem to catch the right angle. The trees did not appear to be touching one another, but it was almost as though they kept leaning closer so that no matter where I peeked the inside of the circle was just out of view.

"How are we meant to do that?" I asked.

"Hm." Jackaby reached out a hand and touched the nearest tree. It responded by remaining a tree. Jackaby began to rummage through his pockets. "The Jericho doorbell is no good on a living wall. Magic beans would get us over the top and then some, but it seems rather a waste."

While he pondered, I strode around the perimeter of the grove. It was fifteen or twenty feet in diameter, growing with perfect geometric precision. "It's no good," I said. "They're just the same, all the way around the–" As I finished walking the full circle I froze. Jackaby had vanished.

"Sir?" I called. I hurried back the way I had come in case he had followed behind me. "Mr. Jackaby?" As I came to the front again I jumped. Standing where I had last seen my employer was a new figure, dressed in green. Over a pale olive tunic, he wore forest green robes that just brushed the tips of the grass. He stood with confidence, although his frame was slight and he stood no taller than myself. His hair was a tawny yellow, tucked behind pointed ears and hanging straight and long down his slender back.

"You accompany the Seer?" His voice was soft.

"Erm, yes," I said. "Yes, I am Mr. Jackaby's assistant. Abigail Rook. A pleasure to meet you."

"You may call me Virgule."

"Grand. Virgule. So, you're really a . . ." Even in the face of one I had difficulty accepting that this was an honest-to-goodness fairy.

"A liaison," he finished. "Your master requests your presence with him within the ring."

"Well, good. Shall we, then?"

"No." His expression remained flat. "You may bring no items with you that might do harm to the Fair King."

"Oh," I said. "Yes, of course." I removed the silver dagger from my pocket and presented it to Virgule.

Virgule took the knife. He slid it from its sheath and then back. He returned it to me. "This blade is of no consequence. It is not the offending item."

"Then what?" I emptied my pockets item by item, wondering how on earth Jackaby had managed to complete this process before me. I presented the vial of holy water, my notepad, the padlock key.

"There. Iron. Place the implement in here, please. It will be returned to you in due time." He gestured to a knothole that I was quite certain had not been there a moment before, and I deposited the key within it. "Now," said Virgule, "you may enter."

As I watched, he approached the wall of living wood

ahead of me, took a steadfast step, and was simply and suddenly inside the circle. The nearest tree abruptly became the farthest, leaving an obvious gap directly in front of me, as though the impenetrable barrier had been nothing but a trick of the eye all along.

I shook my head and followed, a lady of science and reason strolling into an impossible fairy ring.

The sounds of the bustling city all around us melted away. The grove was cool and shady, with a faint hint of vanilla and citrus in the air. Jackaby acknowledged me with a nod. He stood in the middle of the clearing, the light from the noonday sun finding its way through the circle of branches above us to bathe him in a column of golden light. All around him little flecks of pure white danced and spun through the sunbeams.

Virgule crossed the grass to stand beside another willowy figure. She wore robes of deep blue in contrast to Virgule's greens. Her hair was honey blond and her features were even more graceful than her counterpart's, save for a pearl white scar running from one high cheekbone down to the corner of her lips. She stood with a military bearing and an emotionless expression. "Seer," she said. "It has been many years."

"Thank you for granting us an audience," said Jackaby. "Miss Rook, allow me to introduce General Serif and Captain Virgule, emissaries to Lord Arawn."

"Charmed," I said.

"Not noticeably," said Virgule. "Is it a passive enchantment?"

Serif cleared her throat. "Whether we will escort you anywhere remains to be decided," she said. "Lord Arawn does not waste his time lightly on the tribulations of humans."

"He will have time for this," said Jackaby. "It concerns the Dire Council."

"The Dire Council has long been disbanded," she told him. "You're chasing shadows."

"One of those shadows is currently locked in my root cellar," Jackaby replied. "She killed a lot of innocent people before we put her there, and she wasn't working alone. Her father remains at large, and he has recently claimed dominion over the earth and Annwyn, which concerns both our homelands."

All around him, the little flecks of light in the sunbeams had begun to circle, orbiting the detective, gradually moving faster and faster.

"The Dire King," Virgule whispered timorously.

Serif shot him a cold glare. "Rumors," she said. "You have testified to nothing about which the Fair King is not fully aware."

"Your rumors have been leaving a trail of corpses across my city," Jackaby insisted. "And they've been recruiting from your side of the veil to do it. Redcaps, vampires, nixies."

Serif was impassive. "Your city is of little concern to us, Seer, and a handful of Unseelie nuisances are nothing that the Fair King cannot quell. If you have nothing further—"

The beads of white spinning around Jackaby suddenly collided at a single point, bursting into a brilliant, blinding flash. I shielded my eyes, and when I looked up again, blinking in surprise, an archway had opened in midair. It was rimmed with sparkling light, and beyond it I could see a room lined with heavy columns. Serif's words appeared to be caught in her throat. Virgule found his voice before she did. "Our master will see you now."

Chapter Four

The council room of Arawn, the Fair King and lord of the Seelie fae, was not bathed in golden light, it was not cool and airy, and it definitely did not smell of vanilla and gentle citrus. The room in which we found ourselves as we crossed through the portal appeared to be part of a medieval castle. The walls were hewn of massive stones and hung with heavy tapestries depicting all manner of humans and beasts engaged in war, in sport, and in activities that would have made my mother blush. Above us the columns gave way to vaulted ceilings that might have looked equally at home in a cathedral. A wide fire occupied most of one wall, and in spite of the cavernous space, the air was hot and heavy. At one end of the room was a terraced rostrum, like the pulpit of a church, and on this stood a tall throne embedded with gems that sparkled violet in the crackling firelight. The throne stood empty, but on either side of it sat twin hunting hounds, milky white with vivid crimson ears. They lifted their heads to watch us as we filed into the room.

A wide oak table stood before the dais, and around this two figures were seated, quarreling. Both wore brown robes and neither looked especially regal. "A trade embargo with the Northern Elflands won't accomplish anything," said the first, a dour fellow with round spectacles. His hair was tied in a no-nonsense knot at the back of his head. "Lord Arawn is well aware that King Freyr has no authority over the dark elves. We would only strain one of our strongest alliances. Appealing to the dwarves is the best way."

"You want to drive the kingdom deeper into debt to those filthy pit-breeders?" interrupted the other. He had a weaselly, angular face. "I'd almost rather see the stinking swarts keep robbing us blind than hand it over willingly to the ruddy longbeards."

"Leave us." The voice came from behind us. It was deep and firm.

There was no doubt in my mind, as I turned to see who had spoken, that I was now in the presence of royalty. Although Jackaby was taller, Lord Arawn seemed to tower over everyone in the room. His regal stature suggested that at any moment an artist might pop out from behind a pillar to finish up an oil painting of him. His features were graceful, but his frame was sturdier than those of his subjects, and his jawline was harder. His flaxen hair was topped with a polished bronze circlet, and around his shoulders was draped a cloak of deep, velvety purple clasped with a golden pendant engraved with a sunburst.

"My liege." Serif knelt. "The Seer begs an audience."

"Thank you, General," Arawn said. "I am aware. Please escort Ampersand and Kern to the aldermen's hall. They can conclude their discussion without me." The pair at the table had ceased their bickering and were already hastily packing up their papers. Serif bowed low.

"Captain." The king turned to Virgule as Serif and the others filed out. "You may oversee the veil-gate."

"Yes, my liege," said Virgule, positioning himself ceremonially beside the portal.

"From within the fairy ring, if you please," Arawn amended with a practiced calm.

"Yes, my liege." Virgule nodded and then stepped back through the glowing doorway into the grove in Seeley's Square. Behind him, the portal shimmered and then vanished with a faint pop like a soap bubble.

Jackaby and I found ourselves alone with Lord Arawn. The fire crackled away.

"Well," Jackaby said. "You and I have different taste in decor, but I can't argue with the entryway–a door like that gives quite the first impression. Nowhere to hang a knocker, though. Or a horseshoe."

"In a thousand years," Lord Arawn said, "that veil-gate has never been opened for a human. You may be the first mortals to ever cross through it."

"It is quite an honor, sir," I said. "Er—your majesty. It's quite an honor, your majesty, sir." I immediately wished I had remained silent.

"And what is she?" Arawn regarded me with detached amusement.

"She is my associate," Jackaby answered. "And she is generally quite sharp. Usually. Sometimes. She'll surprise you from time to time."

"I'm sure she will," said Arawn. "You humans never do exactly what one expects. I kept one in my castle for an entire year once."

"A human?"

"Yes. I let him wear my glamour and everything. He left to go be a prince of some petty kingdom in the end. A shame. I rather liked him."

"We're here on rather urgent business, I'm afraid."

"So I understand." Arawn sauntered toward the dais at the end of the room. "You have concerns about the old Dire Council?"

Jackaby nodded. "More than concerns. The council has risen again. They're active. My associates and I have managed to incapacitate a vampire and to nick a nixie at the heart of their ranks, but the Dire King remains at large, planning his next murderous maneuver."

Arawn turned lazily as he reached his throne. "Such an excitable species, you humans. So rash. There is no Dire King lurking out there."

"There is," I said. "I've seen him."

Arawn's eyes fixed on me as he slid into his chair. "Have you?"

I screwed up my confidence. "I've seen his eyes," I said, "glowing red in the darkness. He said that the age of man has ended, and that he is tired of waiting. He intends to destroy the barrier between the earth and the Annwyn and rule over whatever is left as king of both realms."

Unimpressed, Arawn reached a hand down and absently stroked one of his snowy white hounds between its crimson ears. "At any moment, there are almost certain to be a dozen scurrilous seditionists who *intend* to destroy my barrier, a hundred who *intend* to usurp my throne, a thousand who *intend* to see the age of man come crumbling to an end. Let the rabble continue to amuse themselves with their idle *intentions.*"

"It's only an idle intention until it becomes a reality," said Jackaby.

Arawn rolled his eyes. "It is an absurd fantasy."

Said the fairy king to a traveler with magic beans in his pockets, I thought, but I kept the observation to myself.

"You're being a fool." Jackaby took a step toward the dais. The twin hounds raised their milky white heads and their eyes narrowed. "Your veil is not impervious. Unseelie creatures have already slipped through the cracks—as I'm sure you're well aware. Innocent people are dying while you reassure yourself you're in control!" The hounds began to growl, and Jackaby drew to a stop, just a few paces from the king. "I'm at the heart of this now, whether you help me or not. More people will die. People I care about will die. Don't let your ego blind you. Don't wait for the veil to fall and for people *you* care about to start dying before you take this seriously."

"Very forward, Seer," said Arawn coldly. "You do not know your place."

"No, I don't. I've been told it's one of my most endearing qualities," Jackaby replied.

Arawn smirked in spite of himself. "One of your only," he said. "Yes, there are cracks in any wall. Cracks can be mended. What you're describing is something else entirely. It is laughable."

"Humor me, then. Please."

Arawn eyed Jackaby. "Very well, if it sets you at ease. Let us imagine the impossible. I will speak slowly. Do try to keep up."

Arawn gave a casual wave of his hand, and the heavy oaken tabletop beside me shuddered. Before my eyes, the surface rippled and rose unevenly, forming hills and plains and sprouting miniature wooden towers with paper-thin pennants.

"Anyone intent on destroying the barrier would need to subdue my army first," Arawn drawled.

As I watched, transfixed, miniature oaken figures rose out of the wood grain and snapped to attention, forming row after row of tiny soldiers.

"The Seelie forces are the most powerful army in this or any realm," Arawn continued, "and they have one sworn duty–to protect the veil. A rebel king would need to rally a legion equal to my own, the likes of which has never been seen. The Unseelie, unlike my forces, are the most capricious and unruly creatures in the Annwyn. Preventing even a paltry horde of these brutes from tearing each other apart would be nothing short of extraordinary, and mobilizing an entire army of them toward a common goal would be nearly impossible."

Chips and splinters had begun to peek out of the table-top, circling the oaken army like wolves in the underbrush.

"But I am humoring you," said Arawn dryly. "So let's take this preposterous pretense a step further."

The wolves attacked. Wave after wave of jagged monsters fell upon the soldiers. Toothpick javelins flew and wood-shaving shields crumpled. When the sawdust settled, the wooden army lay still. It had been a massacre in miniature.

"Supposing your would-be king could achieve the impossible and overcome my army, he still would not possess the raw power to bring down the veil. The magical potential required to unhinge the established enchantments holding the barrier in place would call for more focused energy than all of the strongest mages in my army could produce combined."

The table rattled. Inch by inch, the wolfish shards and broken soldiers began to slide along the surface. Concentric circles formed as the armies were dragged across the wood in opposite directions, the bristly horde spinning clockwise and the fallen soldiers sliding widdershins. From the center of these orbits rose a solitary figure. A tiny jagged crown sat atop its wooden head.

"Supposing it could be done," said Arawn, "unimaginable raw power would need to be focused toward a single goal, to be channeled through a single mind."

The rumble of the tabletop had become an unsettling hum. It made my teeth hurt. The tabletop began to splinter at the edges. Around and around the circles spun, faster and faster until, with a *crack*, the figure in the center exploded into a burst of wood shards. I shielded my eyes with my arm, and when I looked again, the table had returned to normal, its surface smooth and polished, minus one rough gouge in the center.

Arawn leaned back in his throne. "It cannot be done. The veil is safe. The Dire King is dead."

"Dead?" I said. "Then there *was* a Dire King?" Arawn's half-lidded eyes flicked in my direction.

"There *was*," he conceded. With slow, deliberate movements, the king rose and stepped down from the dais toward me. "Until there *wasn't*. Do you want to know what came in between?"

I nodded.

"Me." He drew so close I could see my own nervous face in the reflection of his circlet. "The Dire King was a formidable opponent, but he was outmatched. I have the wretch's crown in my trophy room," Arawn said. "Removed from his lifeless head as his corpse lay cooling on the field of battle. He's dead."

"His crown?" Jackaby's eyes flashed with a sudden thought. "I don't suppose you've ever met a fellow called Father Grafton?"

"The name is meaningless to me," said Arawn. "Is he a mortal?"

"Decidedly mortal. Downright *mort*," said Jackaby. "Shuffled off the old coil on our doorstep just this morning, as a matter of fact. He mentioned a crown right before he died. A spear and a shield, as well. He called them the *harfau o Hafgan*. Is that meaningless to you as well?"

Arawn's measured calm fell away, a look of genuine surprise taking its place. "The instruments of Hafgan," he said quietly. "I had almost forgotten that there was a time when he was called Hafgan at all. That name was once like thunder in these halls. Hafgan *is* the Dire King. Or he was. Those days are long past."

"And you're absolutely certain he's dead?" Jackaby asked.

"His followers and mine both watched me kill him. Yes,

I'm sure—as are a lot of other fair folk and oddlings from across the realm. The duel was a public spectacle, if you could call it a duel at all. It only took a single stroke to shatter his shield and pierce his heart. Ballads were written and paintings done. Most of them were awful, to be honest, but there isn't a fairy in my kingdom who does not know the tale."

Arawn gestured above our heads and I glanced behind me to see a tapestry hanging over the wide hearth. In it, a fair-haired figure with a bronze circlet and a purple cape stood gallantly in the foreground, his sword raised to strike. His opponent was wielding a spear of midnight black. Hafgan wore dark armor, and on his head was an obsidian crown, its edges tall and sharp and jagged.

"That crown," said Jackaby. "Did it have any special power?"

"Only the same as any. A crown is a symbol. It stands for authority, for the right to rule. There is great power in a symbol like that, as there is power in taking it." Something approaching a smile danced at the edge of Arawn's lips. "Would you like to see it?"

Arawn's pale hounds trotted at his heels like royal escorts as he led us through cool corridors and down drafty staircases.

"*The crown, the spear, the shield,*" Jackaby mumbled as we followed. "If you have his crown, what became of Hafgan's spear and shield?" he called forward to our escort.

"Splinters in the mud when I saw them last," Arawn replied. "I have no interest in a dead man's detritus. Ah. Here we are."

We had come to a heavy door set into an inner wall of the castle. It had no visible handle or keyhole, but as Arawn approached, it responded to his presence, swinging open noiselessly. The room beyond was less of a chamber and more of a long, wide hallway. Brilliant lanterns sparkled across the ceiling, and on every wall hung remarkable artifacts. My eyes slid from a silver arrow as long as a javelin, to a sword made of bright green jade, to a helmet made of beaten gold in the shape of a boar. Finally I looked to my employer.

Jackaby's eyes had lit up like a toddler's in a toy shop.

"Oh, Miss Rook—look at these! I do believe this is the actual club of the Dagda. Good heavens, the Dullahan's whip! Is that the eye of Balor over there?"

"That is the eye of Hagen," corrected Arawn languidly. "The eye of Balor remains in Balor's head, which can be found farther back in my collection. You will find relics here of dynasties stretching back to before the age of Llyr, before the age of Dôn, long before the age of man."

The lanterns flickered as we passed and I caught a flutter of movement. I stopped, squinting up at the bright lights.

"Coming, Miss Rook?"

I almost missed it, but just as I looked away again, a

flurry of delicate wing-beats swept the glass inside the lantern. "What are those?" I asked, catching up.

Arawn glanced where I was pointing. "You might call them prisoners of war," he replied. "Sprites and oddlings. They are the spoils of a conquest before my time."

"What? But they're alive! How long are you going to keep them locked up like that?"

Arawn looked nonplussed. "As long as I have need of light in my trophy room, I suppose. They serve a purpose here, which is more than I could say about their lives as free fae. Now, then. The Dire Crown is just past . . ." Arawn's voice petered off. He had come to a stop before a marble plinth. The podium stood empty.

"*He has already taken the crown,*" said Jackaby, drawing up beside him. "That's what the old man said."

The Fair King's jaw set, and his practiced ennui fell away.

"You were saying something about there being great power in a symbol like that," said Jackaby, "as there is power in *taking* it."

Arawn's eyes were glued to the empty plinth. "It is time for you to go," he said darkly.

"You helped me once," Jackaby said, "a long time ago. Let me help you now. Let us help each other."

"I do not need your help," Arawn answered through gritted teeth. He took a deep breath. "I have not forgotten your debt, Seer. I have not fallen so low, however, that I cannot manage my own affairs without calling on the help of mortal men."

"Your majesty, please," I implored. "The return of the Dire King affects us all. This affair is more than—"

"The Dire King is dead!" Arawn shouted. He composed himself, and when he spoke again it was in measured breaths. "Hafgan is dead. Stolen crowns cannot make kings of commoners."

"Someone is collecting the instruments of Hafgan," said Jackaby.

"Someone is *trying*, and someone will be found," snapped the king. "If someone is fool enough to brazenly trespass into my castle, then their capture will be all the more swift and their punishment all the more merciless."

The Fair King led us back up the drafty staircase and through the dim corridors.

"Don't underestimate them," Jackaby said.

"Don't underestimate *me*," Arawn replied.

He pushed open the door to his council room and we stepped back into the heat of the roaring fire. His hounds trotted to take their place on either side of the throne.

Serif had been waiting within. She hurried to her master's side and dropped to one knee. "My liege, we have just received news of the Valinguard."

"Excellent." Arawn continued forward into the chamber, and Serif rose to follow behind him. "Tell me. I could do with some good tidings."

Serif glanced at us, as though nervous to speak freely in our presence. "The Valinguard"—she swallowed—"have ridden together to the Mag Mell, my liege."

Arawn froze. He turned slowly to face Serif. "All of them?"

She nodded, almost imperceptibly. Her mouth twitched, pulling nervously where the alabaster scar met her lips.

"I see. Thank you, General." The king's face had become ashen. "I shall expect your full report after I have seen our guests out." With a distracted wave of his hand, Arawn reopened the shimmering portal back to New Fiddleham. A gentle breeze and the sweet smell of the grove in Seeley's Square wafted over us. Arawn turned to face Jackaby. "I . . . I have reconsidered. I think perhaps we might help each other after all, Seer."

Jackaby and I exchanged a quick glance.

"You have a reputation for finding things," Arawn continued. "You have made something of a career of it in your realm, have you not?"

"I am a private investigator, if that's what you mean," said Jackaby.

"Then privately investigate those cracks in my wall. Find them on your side, and I will repair them on mine. Help me to seal the rend, and I will consider your debt repaid."

"Who are the Valinguard?" Jackaby asked.

Arawn smiled weakly and did not respond.

"Where is the Mag Mell?"

Arawn drew a slow breath. "My envoys will be checking up on you. Good-bye, Seer."

Virgule straightened up as we emerged into Seeley's Square once more. The veil-gate closed behind us almost the moment we were through. "Lord Arawn is done with you?" Virgule asked.

"Well, you know how it is." Jackaby shrugged. "He might have wanted us to hang about for a cup of tea, but we have places to go, ducks to feed. Quite a talker, that king of yours."

Virgule scowled. "What did the Fair King have to discuss with a pair of humans?"

"Not certain we should divulge that information," I said. "A bit above Mister Virgule's pay grade, don't you think, sir? You're what, a first lieutenant?"

"I'm a captain." Virgule bristled, gesturing to his forest green robes, which were apparently indicative of his rank.

"Right," I said. "Yes, still—it's all rather inner-circle, top secret stuff, the things we were discussing with your king. I don't imagine you're allowed to know."

"Was it about the Dire Council?" Virgule asked. "Because I know all about the council. I even know about the last holdouts of their acolytes."

"Do you?" Jackaby raised an eyebrow.

Virgule nodded emphatically. "I was there when the Emerald Garrison raided Hobb's Hill. We flushed out a whole mess of sympathizers. I was the one to bring our report to the general."

Jackaby suppressed a smile. "Old news, Hobb's Hill. Our conversation with Arawn was of a much more sensitive nature. It would take a far higher clearance for you to know about, for instance . . . the Valinguard."

"The Valinguard?" said Virgule. "That's no secret! The Valinguard are Lord Arawn's most elite force. Every one of them is at least a twelfth-order magus, unparalleled in combat, subterfuge, and spellcraft. When the Fair King wants something important done right, he sends the Valinguard."

"Obviously all that." Jackaby made a show of dismissing the captain with a wave of his hand. "It's their latest mission that's so hush-hush. I've said too much. I really shouldn't . . ." He trailed off, and Virgule took the bait.

"I know about that, too!" he said, eagerly. "The rend! They're looking for the rend in the veil, right? The Amber Scouts couldn't find anything, so the Fair King got impatient and sent his Valinguard to find the rend and seal it immediately. They've been gone for weeks. That's not normal for them. We're all on alert to bring any news directly to Lord Arawn."

"Well," said Jackaby, "it seems you're not too far out of the inner circle after all."

Virgule looked pleased with himself.

"Although—don't tell Lord Arawn I told you about all that," Jackaby added. "I would hate for him to know that I gave away so much confidential information."

Virgule nodded graciously.

"Before we go," I said, "I don't suppose you know the fastest route to the Mag Mell from here, do you?"

Virgule stiffened, and he narrowed his eyes. "What did you just say?"

"The Mag Mell?" I repeated, wondering if I had said it correctly.

Virgule's expression darkened. "Is that some sort of threat? The Mag Mell is a fairy's ultimate reward. It is where the noblest and bravest of our kind go when they are dead. The fastest route to the Mag Mell"–he fixed me with a grim gaze–"is death on the battlefield."

A shiver tickled up my spine and set the hair on my neck on end.

"My associate was only joking, of course," said Jackaby. "Or trying to joke. Ghastly sense of humor, that one. Best to just ignore her, I find."

Virgule nodded sourly, still eyeing me. He escorted us out of the circle and over to the knothole in the tree, where I retrieved my iron key and Jackaby collected what appeared to be a few tinkling coins and a wrapped butterscotch.

"We need more help," Jackaby mumbled, half to himself, as we reached the edge of the park.

"It's bad, isn't it, sir?"

"It isn't good." He sighed. "Arawn's arrogance is going to get a lot of people killed. He thinks his defenses are unbreachable–yet someone nicked that crown out of the heart of his own castle. He thinks his army is unbeatable—but his most elite soldiers were just massacred."

"At least the king agreed to work with us in the end."

"He hasn't agreed to work with us, he's agreed to send us into the same trap that killed his best soldiers. His preliminary scouts couldn't find the rend, and his Valinguard just died trying. Arawn would rather let us blunder into the same fate than admit that he's out of his depth."

"So we're not going to go looking for the rend?"

"Of course we're going to go looking for the rend," said Jackaby. "And the crown, the spear, and the shield. There's too much at stake now to start worrying about little things like being brutally murdered."

Chapter Five

The Mason Street Police Station was busier than usual. The typically quiet detention hall was packed with haggard officers processing detainees. None of the uniforms even bothered with us as Jackaby pushed through the crush and made for the hallway to the rear. We wound our way through the corridors to the commissioner's office.

The dimly lit room was a sea of paperwork, atop which Commissioner Marlowe appeared to be keeping afloat by the sheer buoyancy of his enmity.

"Jackaby," he grunted as my employer rapped on his open door.

"Marlowe."

"Good afternoon, Commissioner," I said. "Please pardon our intrusion."

"Miss Rook. To what do I owe this"–Marlowe's eyes flicked back to Jackaby, who had begun conspicuously leafing through a stack of confidential reports–"this visit?" He took the stack from my employer and deposited it in a cabinet behind his desk.

"We may need to borrow a few of your boys," said Jackaby. "There is a–what would you call it, Miss Rook?"

"Cataclysm?" I suggested.

"A tad dramatic. But also accurate."

Marlowe's eye twitched. "Every one of my best men has worked double or triple shifts this week already. I have no intention of loaning out the few remaining hands I haven't already exhausted. But out of morbid curiosity, how many of my officers were you hoping to borrow?"

"Some," answered Jackaby. "Possibly *most.* Probably the whole lot, actually. How quickly can you get all of them assembled so that we can have a little chat?"

Provided proper tinder and dry kindling, Marlowe's expression could have been used to start a fire.

"Please, sir," I said. "We don't mean to make things more difficult, but I'm afraid it really is of the utmost importance that New Fiddleham be prepared for what's to come."

Marlowe turned to me with weary eyes. "And what is to come, precisely?"

I opened my mouth, but halted, trying to find a way to explain the whole affair that didn't sound like madness.

"Madness," Jackaby cut in. "Chaos and war and pande-monium. Have you read the Book of Revelation? A bit of that. More monsters."

Marlowe pursed his lips and placed his palms very slowly on his desk while we explained about the Fair King and the Dire King, about the Annwyn and the barrier, about the rend in the veil and about the end of the world as we know it. Marlowe listened.

When we were finished, he took a deep breath. "A year ago I'd have had you in lockup for wasting my time with an impossible report like that."

"A year ago, I think you did," said Jackaby.

"But a year ago my lockup wasn't already full to capacity with the subjects of impossible reports."

Jackaby tilted his head. "Come again?"

Marlowe nodded sourly toward the hallway. "You're not the only one hunting monsters these days."

"I knew Mayor Spade was on the hunt," Jackaby said as Marlowe opened the door to the holding cells. "But I underestimated the size of his net."

There were only three cells in Mason Street detention hall, two of which were now packed full of men, and the third full of women. Several more sad suspects sat waiting their turns in chairs across from the holding cells. None of them looked especially like criminals. One of the women in the far cell looked old enough to be my grandmother. She was wearing an apron still chalky white with flour. A pair of schoolboys huddled in the corner of one of the men's cells, sniffling. A man in oil-stained overalls sat on the bench beside them, shaking his head and sighing heavily.

"This is insane," Jackaby said. "I know Spade and his militia have been canvassing the city, but I thought they were like the butt of a bad joke the city was telling itself. I didn't think anybody was taking them seriously!"

"Nobody was," Marlowe said. "Public opinion had their whole operation chalked up to paranoia and superstition, until a couple days ago. The other shoe dropped when Spade's guys finally caught some kind of imp yesterday morning. Looked like a naked monkey to me. They're calling it the Inkling Devil. I'm surprised this is the first you've heard about it. They paraded what was left of the thing through the town on a stake. I've been doing managerial gymnastics trying to keep the rumors from throwing New Fiddleham into a panic, and Spade's boys are putting on a damned puppet show with a real-life demon."

"They killed it?" Jackaby's voice was even, but I could see the dark clouds rolling over his brow.

"Spade called it a matter of public safety. He said he was raising awareness, needed to show the people the truth. A real live dead demon gave teeth to everything Spade had been saying in all of his speeches and rallies. Now neighbors are reporting neighbors and landlords are ratting out tenants. This is just the crowd we've processed since last night." Marlowe waved a hand at the cells. "Spade wants every detainee thoroughly interrogated and documented. The paperwork is a nightmare. We'll have to start shipping them up to Crowley Penitentiary soon. There just isn't room enough in our jailhouse."

I surveyed the dejected lot. More than miserable, several of the detainees had suffered recent injuries—black eyes, bloody lips. A man toward the back was cradling his arm as though it might be broken, and behind him I could see a fellow whose face appeared to have been badly burned.

A portly officer with a walrus mustache was frantically filling out reports and signing paperwork for the latest batch of remandees.

"Mind if I have a little peek at those, Alton?" Jackaby asked as he slid the officer's clipboard off his desk and began to flip through the most recent arrivals.

"It's Allan," the man said. "Hey—I'm gonna need that back."

"It's fine," Marlowe grunted.

"Where is Snorri Schmitz?" Jackaby asked the room.

Manacles clinked as Mr. Schmitz waved a hand forlornly. He was a short, round-faced man. "This doesn't list any offense," Jackaby declared. "It just says he was accused of being half gnome!"

"You have to admit, he is rather on the stumpy side," mumbled the mustachioed officer. Snorri glowered at him. "But if you say he isn't, Mr. Jackaby—well, then I suppose you're sort of the expert." He looked to Marlowe to confirm this. Marlowe looked at Jackaby.

"What? Of course he's half gnome! That's not the point! Show me the law that says having human parents is a requirement for citizenship!" He flipped a few pages. "Stupid. Stupid. If that one were a changeling, those irons would be burning his skin. Stupid. And how about this? You're accusing this woman of witchcraft *and* devil worship? Well, which is it?"

"Erm, both?" Allan supplied.

"Oh, come on, Allan! You don't have to be an expert in the occult to work out the problem there. Who's the one person you need to believe in if you're going to worship the devil?"

"Er . . ." Allan's mustache bobbled. He looked to Marlowe for help, but the commissioner only raised an eyebrow.

"Care to take a crack at it, Miss Rook?" Jackaby turned to me.

"The devil?" I said.

"Right you are! If you're going to worship Old Scratch, you've got to believe in him in the first place, haven't you? Witchcraft is a belief system, Alton–"

"Allan."

"–and those who practice it believe in various gods, goddesses, and spirits. Care to take a stab at who's not on the list?"

"The . . . devil?" Allan guessed meekly.

"Now you're catching up! If you are going to make a lot of idiotic accusations, you might at least try to avoid making mutually exclusive ones!"

A door opened at the end of the hall, and two officers half dragged the sagging body of a thin man in a gray cardigan up to the door of the cell. Jackaby dropped the clipboard back on the desk and watched the procession shuffle up.

"Detainees will move away from the door," instructed the first officer, pulling the keys from his waist. The men inside did their best to squeeze back a few paces, and the prisoner was deposited within. His cell mates helped him limp over to the bench. His face was badly bruised, and he was bleeding from a cut just above his eye.

"Like I said," Marlowe grunted. "Thoroughly interrogated."

"What happened to that man?" demanded Jackaby.

"*Man* isn't quite the word for it," a familiar voice cut in. Mayor Spade himself had emerged from the doorway at the end of the hall.

The mayor wore a canary yellow waistcoat and a coffee brown bow tie. He stumbled as he stepped out, sending his spectacles sliding down his nose, and he nudged them back up. Spade might have been the least intimidating figure in the room, incarcerated grandmothers included. If one were to vandalize the portrait of a slightly stocky twelve-year-old boy by erasing his hair and scribbling in a beard, one would have produced a reasonable likeness of Mayor Philip Spade.

"It took us some time to coax the whole of it out of him," he continued, puffing out his chest proudly, "but we got the job done. Hello, Detective. Glad you could finally join us. I was beginning to wonder if my telegrams were going astray."

"I read the first few," said Jackaby. "I've instructed my duck to just file the rest directly under *P*. I left it to him to decide if that was for *politics* or *paranoia*."

"No need for that," Spade said, bristling. "Turns out we were right all along, weren't we? You might have saved us a lot of trouble if you had lent us your assistance sooner."

"I don't think you need my assistance to rough up innocent people."

"Oh, don't worry. We let the *people* go," Spade said.

Jackaby did not reply.

"Oh, come off it. Really. You and I are marching under the same banner, Detective. We've made a few mistakes, to be sure, but we're correcting as we go. I am making New Fiddleham safe again." He squared his jaw.

Jackaby looked unimpressed. "For whom?"

"For us!" Spade insisted. "For *people*!"

"There are at least a dozen sentient species represented in this chamber—so what gives you authority to decide which ones get to be considered people?"

"This is nothing," said Spade, his eyes twinkling. "You

should see what we've got locked up in the animal control office."

"Mayor Spade," Jackaby began. He took a deep breath. "Philip. This is wrong."

The mayor frowned. "Thanks very much for your consultation, Detective. I will take that under advisement."

"You can't—"

"You only think I can't!" Spade burst out. Beneath his beard, Spade's cheeks flushed. His eyes narrowed and he readjusted his spectacles. "You've built a life out of thinking I can't! You want a pat on the back and a nice reward every time you swat a bee for us, but all the while you've let the hornets build their nest in our eaves. I won't sit around waiting for you to play hero any more, Detective. You've been telling me for years that there are things hiding in the shadows of my city. Well, I believe you. I have found the things in the shadows, Mr. Jackaby, and now *I'm* the one turning on the lights!"

"Don't be asinine, Spade! You romanticize fighting oddlings the same way you romanticize a holiday in Spain. You make it sound like this grand exotic adventure—right up until you're there, complaining about the food and watching your neighbors hang their unmentionables on the line. They're just people!"

"Except they're *not people*! We're talking about magical creatures! Dangerous, unpredictable magical creatures, here in the real world!"

"Magic is just magic!" Jackaby threw up his hands. "It's not inherently special or strange or dangerous! It's everywhere! It's already all around you! If just being magical meant that something was dangerous, you'd have long since been killed by a butterfly, or a bubble, or an apple turnover."

"Those things aren't magical."

"Of course they're magical! Argh! You infuriating man! If a unicorn came and sat in the corner of your office every day, then by the end of the year you'd be hanging your coat on its horn. There *is* magic in your life! Not appreciating it does not make it any less magical. Yes, some of that magic is dangerous, but so are scissors and electricity and politics—and plenty of other completely human inventions!"

Spade's voice grew quiet, which somehow had the effect of magnifying his intensity. "Don't presume to lecture me, Detective. Redcaps. Werewolves. Dragons. I know very well that there are monsters in New Fiddleham. My wife was one of them. How many people did you let that nixie murder before you captured her?"

Jackaby considered this soberly for a moment. "Fight the monsters, then, Philip. Don't fight the innocent bystanders who happen to come from the same place. You're not afraid of magic, not really. You're just afraid of what you don't understand—and too stubborn to try understanding."

"I understand more and more, Detective," Spade hissed. "I know very well what I'm fighting."

"Do you really? Because based on this detainment facility, you appear to be winning the battle against bakers and mathematics teachers. What exactly do you *think* you're fighting? Biscuits and geometry?"

"What I'm fighting," hissed Spade, "is a war!"

The detention hall had gone eerily silent. Jackaby shook his head. "It doesn't have to be."

"This *is* war, Mr. Jackaby—make no mistake—and you find yourself dangerously close to the wrong side of it." Spade's voice had taken on a cold edge. "If you care at all about humanity, then stand with me."

Jackaby turned his gaze to the crowded cells, and then back to the mayor, his eyes rimmed more with regret than rage. "It is for the sake of our humanity that I stand against you."

Spade and Jackaby stood facing each other in tense silence for several seconds. At length, the mayor straightened his waistcoat and fixed Jackaby with his steeliest glare. "I'll be watching you very closely, Detective."

"I do hope so, Mayor." Jackaby nodded politely and spun on his heel. "You might actually learn something if you do."

Chapter Six

Jackaby did not speak as we left the building. We were three or four blocks away from the station house when Lydia Lee caught up to us, the coach rattling and clinking and the dappled gray horse stamping its hooves impatiently on the cobblestones. Miss Lee managed to convince the Duke to clop to a halt just ahead of us, and my employer climbed into the carriage wordlessly.

Miss Lee gave me an inquisitive look, but Jackaby finally broke his silence before I could explain. "Don't bother with niceties. Take me home, Miss Lee." He thought for a moment. "I'm going to need you to go to jail for me afterward."

"That is the second time a man's said those words to me," she replied gamely. "Although the last time I got flowers and a dance first, if memory serves."

"Bail," amended Jackaby as Miss Lee hopped back into the driver's box.

"They usually do, in the end," she said, sighing.

"What? Listen, I have a jar of banknotes in my office earmarked for bail. I'll bring it out to you as soon as we arrive. I need you to bring it to the processing officer at the Mason Street Station. He'll sort out the paperwork. Just sign where he tells you to. Ask for Alton."

"Allan," I corrected.

"I'm fairly sure it's Alton," said Jackaby.

"You want me to post bail for somebody?" Miss Lee called down as the carriage began to rattle on down the street. "I guess I can do that."

"Thank you," Jackaby called back to her.

"Who am I bailing out?"

"Everyone."

The carriage bumped along the paving stones for a silent stretch. "By *everyone*, you mean . . . ?"

"It is a rather large jar of banknotes," said Jackaby.

"Right," came Miss Lee's voice at length. "You're the boss."

"Sir," I said. "Are we sure about that? I mean, obviously the mayor has been wildly reckless, but you said yourself that those cells were loaded with nonhuman species. This is why we were there to talk to Marlowe in the first place, isn't it? Their world colliding with ours, and all the dangers that come with that? Wouldn't it be wiser to at least take their release on a case-by-case basis?"

"No," Jackaby grunted. "I refuse to treat them all like suspects. That legitimizes everything Spade is doing. It is a greater travesty by far to see the innocent punished than to watch the guilty go free."

"It's just a funny sort of situation, sir. The entire reason we were there today was to try to convince Marlowe that we need to be wary of the otherworld. It seems as though we left doing just the opposite. Are you at all worried? That some of them might be dangerous?"

"Oh, some of them are certainly dangerous. That gnomish fellow, for instance. Snorri. He used to run an illegal cockatrice fight out behind Chandler's Market. I've shut him down half a dozen times. He's done more than enough by now to deserve a hundred nights in lockup. That doesn't make it right. Not like this. We cannot make the world less awful by being more so ourselves."

"We do it by the book, then?"

"Precisely. *By the book.* Yes. Except that there isn't a book."

"Right. We do it by a vague but nevertheless tenacious commitment to the book that there isn't."

"That's why I like you, Miss Rook—you catch on to the subtle nuances so quickly."

Shortly afterward, with a tinkle of old liniment bottles, Miss Lee pulled the coach up to the curb in front of 926 Augur Lane. New Fiddleham was a much smaller city when one was in possession of a carriage.

As we trod up the front walk, Jackaby let out a thoughtful

"Huh." I followed his gaze to the transom ahead of us. It read, in clean, frosty letters:

R. F. JACKABY:
EXQUISITE FRUSTRATION

"Are you feeling exquisitely frustrated of late, Miss Rook?" he asked.

"I wouldn't put it as such, sir," I said. "I don't think that one's for me."

Jenny materialized between Jackaby and the bright red door. "Ah," said Jackaby. "Good afternoon, Miss Cavanaugh."

"I couldn't find it," Jenny said without preamble as we mounted the steps.

"What? Right—the Bible. It's fine. I'll see to it myself. That church is a long way off. It was quite ambitious for you to even consider the trip. I shouldn't reasonably have expected as much of you."

"I made it to the church just fine, thank you very much for your vote of confidence. Do you have any idea how many Bibles and psalm books and hymnals there are in a parish that size? You said to look for a shield, but none of them had anything obvious like that. If the shield is somehow inside one of them, it could be any of them."

"That's all right, you did your—" Jackaby began.

". . . So I just brought all of them."

The door swung open to reveal a small hillside of books heaped on the front desk.

"Hrm." Jackaby grunted. He stepped inside and began to dig through the stack, picking up battered old books and dropping them back onto the heap.

"*Thank you, Miss Cavanaugh,*" Jenny intoned behind him. "It was nothing, really," she replied to herself. "*I underestimated you, Miss Cavanaugh.* Oh, I was just happy to help. *You are special and precious to me, Miss Cavanaugh.* Please now, Mr. Jackaby, you're simply too much."

Jackaby paid her dialogue no mind, and appeared to have forgotten that anyone else was in the room at all.

"I'll just go fetch that bail money for Miss Lee, shall I?" I suggested, and excused myself.

I nipped down the hall to the office, grabbed the jar, and brought it outside. It contained upward of three hundred dollars in bills of varying sizes and clinked merrily with the handful of coins thrown in for good measure. Miss Lee's eyes widened as I passed it up to her. "How often does Mr. Jackaby need to make bail?"

"It comes up more frequently than you'd think," I said. "Thank you, by the way. I don't imagine most drivers get asked to go bailing out crowds of almost-humans from lockup in their first week on the job."

Miss Lee tucked the jar into a little compartment in her seat and turned back to me. "You know our boss is crazy, right?" she said.

"I picked up on that fairly quickly, too, yes."

"Well." She shrugged. "If a crazy man is the only man in this town who wants to give me honest labor, does that say something about me, about the man, or about this town? Maybe all three? Whichever it is, I'm not about to turn my nose up at the job. Besides, even if it's crazy, it's good work."

I nodded. "He might not have both oars in the water, but his course is sound."

We said our good-byes. The Duke neighed in annoyance as Lydia Lee coaxed him into motion, but soon she was on her way.

Jackaby was still engrossed in his examination when I came back inside. "Books. Books. Just books," he was muttering. Jenny was hovering by the window. I joined her.

"How did you manage it, by the way?" I asked. "All those Bibles, all across town? It is a remarkable feat."

"It looks more impressive than it is," she said, still not meeting my eyes. "I borrowed Jackaby's special satchel, the one that holds anything. The whole pile took just one trip. The real trick was keeping myself solid all the way home. That's the bit I'm really proud of–" She turned to face me. "Oh, Abigail, it was amazing. People *saw* me!"

"People saw you?"

"I was in disguise, of course. I wore my long coat and gloves, and I had that floppy white hat on, so they didn't see much, but still–people *saw* me and they didn't gasp or make a scene. Someone even mumbled *Good day* to me as

I was crossing the footbridge! It was exhilarating! I have never been so excited to have somebody see me—actually see me—and not care at all!" She glanced at Jackaby. "Although you would think I would be used to it by now."

"Jenny, that is absolutely amazing!" I said.

"It is, isn't it?" she said wistfully. "Just a little bit, at least? Oh, Abigail, I'm exhausted, I'm not ashamed to tell you. I had planned on setting my spoils out in nice triumphant rows when I got back, but it was all I could do to hold myself intact by then. Solidity is sort of like flexing a muscle, except the muscle is in your mind, and your mind is really just an abstract concept. I was basically flexing my entire body into existence the whole way home. But did it merit so much as a *Good job, Jenny* from that infuriating man?"

Jackaby surfaced from his perusal and looked up at last. His cloud gray eyes found focus on Jenny. From his expression, I couldn't tell if he had been following our conversation or not. "Completely unexceptional," he said. "Nothing at all in this batch. We will need to scrutinize them more closely, of course, just to be sure. Oh, and Miss Cavanaugh . . ."

She raised an eyebrow skeptically.

"You performed . . . quite adequately," he said, "despite expectations."

Jenny opened her mouth to reply, but then closed it again. Her face fluttered through a series of potential reactions. Finally she just threw up her hands and vanished from sight with a muffled *whuph* of air closing into the space where she suddenly wasn't.

"What in heaven's name was all that?" said Jackaby.

"Exquisite frustration, I believe, sir."

"Ah. Right." He slumped into the desk chair and began to fidget absently with the spine of one of the Bibles. "Miss Cavanaugh is a singular and exceptional spirit, you know."

"Only a suggestion, sir, but that is precisely the sort of thing you might consider saying when she is still present and corporeal."

"I worry about her."

"Sir?"

"I have studied ghosts, Miss Rook. I've studied ghasts and geists, spirits and spooks, and until recently I believed that I had begun to fathom the science of specters. I thought I understood how ghosts work."

"I think there may be a few things about this one you're still missing."

"More than a few," he admitted.

"So, ghosting is a science?"

"Everything is a science. Science is just paying attention and sorting out the rules already in place. There *are* rules governing the undead, to be certain. What worries me is that Miss Cavanaugh is no longer following them."

"She's just"–I searched for the right word–"growing."

"She is, and that's just it. Growth isn't how ghosts work. Dead things tend to do the opposite."

"That's good, though, isn't it?"

"It is good beyond anything I have ever dared wish for Miss Cavanaugh. Against all odds, she has a life, of a sort. A strange, impossible, beautiful, heartbreaking, terrifying life."

"What's so terrifying about it?"

"It is a life that should not be possible," he said. "It is a fragile ornament hanging from a tenuous thread. She subsists on borrowed moments, and they might run out at any moment."

"Of course they will, in the end. For all of us. That's what life is."

Jackaby eyed me. "I see my cheery disposition is rubbing off on you."

"Try to be happy for her, sir," I said. "And, if I may be so bold, stop keeping her at arm's length while you're at it. She's not a bauble you can wrap in silk and leave on the top shelf. She's chosen life. You can choose it with her."

"I'm not keeping her at arm's length!" Jackaby huffed.

"*You performed quite adequately, despite expectations,*" I recited.

"She did. That was a compliment." Jackaby frowned. "It is possible that I do not know how to talk to Jenny."

"Possible?"

"Probable."

"We'll work on it, sir."

There came a firm rap at the door, and I glanced up to see the frosted window form the words:

R. F. JACKABY:

CONSULTANT & COLLEAGUE

"It's Charlie," Jackaby said, his gaze penetrating the door. "Come in, Mr. Barker!" My heartbeat quickened. As the door swung open, I felt a flutter, and I privately admonished myself for being so childishly delighted just to see him. Emotions and foolish behavior are much easier to manage when they are someone else's.

Charlie was dressed in plainclothes; his recent assignments for Commissioner Marlowe had been strictly off the record. He wore a starched white shirt and a chestnut vest over pressed slacks and simple leather brogues.

"Miss Rook!" His chocolate brown eyes brightened as he saw me, and he crossed the room at once to sweep me into a warm embrace. I felt his chest rise and fall. I could hear his heartbeat. He smelled like cedar.

"That will suffice," Jackaby grumbled loudly from behind me. "Yes, yes. You are young and your love is a hot biscuit and other abysmally romantic metaphors, I'm sure. You do recall that you saw each other yesterday?"

Charlie pulled away but paused to brush a hand gently across my neck. His smile was tired but gratified. I straightened and tried to will the flush out of my cheeks.

"Normal people do occasionally express fondness for one another."

"Yes, fine. I'm familiar with the concept," he groused. "It's the bubbly auras and fluttering eyelashes that really test one's limits."

"My eyelashes do not flutter," I said.

"Who said I was talking about your eyelashes? Charlie has eyelashes."

"I apologize, Mr. Jackaby, for any undue fluttering on my part," Charlie said diplomatically. "I could use a little fondness right now. My day has been, on the whole, a deeply unsavory experience."

"Life, as Miss Rook and I were just discussing, is an unsavory experience."

"It doesn't always have to be," I countered.

"What are all these?" Charlie plucked a book of psalms from the unruly pile on the desk. "Have you two robbed a church since I left this morning?"

"No," said Jackaby. "Not personally. We had to delegate that task. Pilfering parish property has fallen to Miss Cavanaugh this week."

Charlie rubbed his neck as he dropped the book back on the stack. "Because if there's one thing New Fiddleham needs right now, it's a bit more paranormal petty crime."

"If it makes you feel any better," I submitted, "the pastor more or less asked us to. He was rather insistent that we should find something in one of his Bibles."

"You're certain he won't go storming into the station house tomorrow to tell the duty officer how he's been robbed by a ghost?"

I swallowed.

"Not unless he is one himself," said Jackaby. "He's dead."

"What?"

"Quite dead. He's up in the attic if you would like to check for yourself."

"Why do you have a dead preacher in your attic?"

"Because we found it easier to carry him up to the coffin than to maneuver it down to him."

Charlie looked suddenly very tired.

"Enough about our morning," I said. "You had a difficult patch yourself?"

"Yes. I have a new assignment," Charlie said. "It is not pleasant."

Jackaby studied Charlie more closely and raised an eyebrow. "We had a tête-à-tête with Mayor Spade just this afternoon. What does he have *you* doing? Harassing little old ladies? Insulting short people?"

"Examining a crime scene."

"Oh, yes? What merits a crime, then? Possession of pointy ears? Distribution of abnormally chewy dinner rolls? Eye color? Green really is gratuitously showy."

"Murder," Charlie answered, "in a public space. Under very odd circumstances."

"Oh." Jackaby swallowed. "Well, hrm. I suppose that

might be worth a follow-up, then. Best of luck sorting it out."

"I was actually hoping I might enlist some help to that end," said Charlie.

Jackaby shook his head. "As it happens, I am busy saving our entire world and the next one over from colliding together and raining death and destruction upon us all. So, while I appreciate your consideration, and I do love odd, I'm afraid I am otherwise engaged."

"Understood, sir," said Charlie. "But I was actually talking about Miss Rook."

Jackaby blinked. "You want my assistant?"

I blinked. "You want my assistance?"

Charlie nodded and looked at me a little nervously. He hesitated before elaborating, and when the words came, they came in a rush. "Time and time again, Miss Rook, I have discovered you to be a woman of superlative intellect and intuition. I have discovered myself to be better for your company. It is an imposition, I know— but I want you with me on this case. I always want you with me."

In the ensuing silence, I felt the flush of heat rising back to the tips of my ears. "That, Mr. Jackaby," I managed when I had found my voice, "is how you should talk to Jenny."

"Out of the question," said Jackaby, closing the office door behind him.

"Honestly, sir," I said, "I don't see why you're making such a fuss." We had excused ourselves to speak privately for a moment, leaving poor Charlie politely rocking on his heels in the foyer. The office was warm and smelled of sage and witch hazel, and the desk was littered with bits of twine and herbs where Jackaby had been preparing fresh wards. Douglas had burrowed into a nest of old receipts on the bookshelf behind us and was sound asleep with his bill tucked back into his wing. I had given up trying to get him to stop napping on the paperwork. "You're the one who told me that I shouldn't have to choose between profession and romance," I said.

"I'm not the one making a fuss. I don't care the least bit about your little foray into . . . *romance.*" Jackaby pushed the word out of his mouth as though it had been reluctantly clinging to the back of his throat. "If anything, I am concerned that you are choosing to make precisely the choice that I told you you should not make!"

"What? Wait a moment. Are you . . . jealous?"

"Don't be asinine! I am not jealous! I am merely . . . protective. And perhaps troubled by your lack of fidelity to your position."

"That is literally the definition of jealous, sir. Oh, for goodness' sake. I'm not choosing Charlie over you! I'm not going to suddenly stop being your assistant just because I spend time working on another case!"

"You might!" he blurted out. He sank down into the chair at his desk. "You just might."

"Why are you acting like this?"

He pinched the bridge of his nose. "Because things change. Because people change. Because . . . because Charlie Barker is going to propose," he said. He let his hand drop and looked me in the eyes. "Marriage," he added. "To you."

I blinked.

"I miss a social cue or two from time to time, but even I'm not thick enough to believe all that was about analyzing bloodstains together. He has the ring. It's in his breast pocket right now. He's attached an absurd level of emotional investment to the thing—I'm surprised it hasn't burned a hole right through the front of his jacket, the way its aura is glowing. He's nervous about it. He's going to propose. Soon, I would guess."

I blinked.

The air in front of me wavered like a mirage, and in another moment Jenny had rematerialized. "And if he does," she said softly, "it will be Abigail's decision to face, not yours. There are worse fates than to receive a proposal from a handsome young suitor." She added, turning to me with a grin, "Charlie is a good man."

"Yes, fine! But she has such prodigious potential!" Jackaby lamented. "Having *feelings* is one thing—I can grudgingly tolerate feelings—but actually getting married? The next thing you know they'll be wanting to do something rash, like *live together*! Miss Rook, you have started something here that I am loath to see you leave unfinished. You've started *becoming* someone here whom I truly want to meet when she is done. Choosing to leave everything you have here to go be a good man's wife would be such a wretched waste of that promise." He faltered, looking to Jenny, and then to the floorboards. "On the other hand, you should never have chosen to work for me in the first place. It remains one of your most ill-conceived and reckless decisions to date—and that is saying something, because you also chose to blow up a dragon once." He sighed. "Jenny is right. You could make a real life with that young man, and you shouldn't throw that away just to hang about with a fractious bastard and a belligerent duck." He sagged until his forehead was resting on his desk.

Hovering behind him, Jenny moved to put a hand gingerly on his shoulder. Her fingers passed right through him, and she bit her lip and withdrew the hand. Jackaby did not appear to have noticed the attempted gesture at all.

"When Charlie proposes," he said, looking up from the desk listlessly, "just remember that *not* making a choice is always an option."

I blinked.

"We're never *not* making choices," said Jenny softly from behind him.

"Charlie," I managed finally, "is going to propose?"

Jackaby nodded. "Marriage," he added. "To you. Have you been listening?"

I shook my head. Charlie and I had been on only half a dozen proper dates–and only if you counted situations of mortal peril as proper dates. The thought of having a whole life with him all to myself, instead of just stolen moments, felt like tripping over a floorboard and falling into a feather bed, disorienting and delightful. But I had never considered that more of Charlie might mean less of my life here on Augur Lane. Charlie was one of the only people in my life who supported, even encouraged, my commitment to this mad line of work. It was part of the reason that–

I swallowed. My head felt all hot and foggy.

It was part of the reason that I loved him.

I realized Jackaby and Jenny were both watching me closely.

"I–I'm going to go look at a dead body," I said, straightening. "I'm going to go find clues and interview witnesses. I'm going to go think very, very hard about murder and mayhem and monsters, because that's what I do."

Jackaby smiled. He looked like he was about to speak again, but I cut him off.

"And I'm going to go do all that with Charlie," I said. "I like saving the world with Charlie. We'll be back this evening."

Jackaby's smile wobbled, but he did not stop me as I stepped numbly out the door.

Chapter Seven

The streets of New Fiddleham felt less chaotic with Charlie as my escort. I had never known Mr. Jackaby to take the same route twice, and when he was at the helm, we always spun around so many times that I could never tell which way we had actually traveled or how far we had gone by the time we got there. Charlie and I moved purposefully, and we caught a ride on a public horse-drawn trolley for most of the trip north.

Jackaby had gotten me so flustered, I found myself wondering, for the first few blocks, if Charlie was going to kneel down at any moment, take a ring from his pocket, and ask me the question I was not fully prepared to answer. What would I say if he did? Would I throw my arms around his neck and cry *Yes* as the gray-haired couple ahead of us turned and made saccharine faces, or would I panic completely and throw myself sidelong from the moving cart in a fit of anxiety? Either option promised a long and awkward return to Augur Lane. Nervous as the notion made me, it was a strangely giddy nervousness.

We passed a building on Prospect Lane with the windows all boarded up. Charlie sighed. The words *US OR THEM* had been painted across the door in crude strokes. In the absence of tenants, the whole side of the building had been papered with notices. Spade's edict about "unnatural neighbors" was visible two or three times, along with the faces of a dozen persons of interest. The familiar etching of Charlie's face was visible in the mix. I winced.

The exciting bubble of a potential future popped as the reality of the past thudded back into my mind. Charlie had very publicly transformed into a frightening beast in the center of town last winter. New Fiddleham did not know that he had spent the rest of that evening saving their lives and mine by risking his own against the real monster. They didn't know that he continued to risk his life every day to keep their streets safe. They did not know that he continued to act the hero for them long after they had painted him the villain. The wanted posters continued to surface, in spite of Marlowe's order for them to cease.

If New Fiddleham was ever going to forget the ridiculous rumors about a werewolf in the West End, it wasn't going to be in the middle of this furor over all things paranormal.

"What are you thinking about?" Charlie said, breaking the silence.

I emerged from my thoughts and looked away from the sad building. "The way things change," I said, honestly. "It can be a bit overwhelming, that's all."

He looked over his shoulder at the wall as we clopped along and nodded solemnly. Suddenly, the little old couple in front of me looked less sweet and adoring and more like potential witnesses, just waiting for their chance to hop off the trolley and tell the nearest constable that the dangerous fugitive had been spotted. Would they recognize him from the posters? Oh–why were we out in public at all?

"You know," I said, "you don't owe New Fiddleham anything. You don't need to help them."

"Look," Charlie said as we clipped past Market Street. He was pointing at a man delicately painting enormous letters onto a broad window as we passed. *NONNA SANTORO'S*, it read, although the *RO'S* was still just an outline.

"That Italian restaurant?"

"Yes," he smiled. "They will be opening their doors for the first time very soon. Sweet family. I bought my first meal in New Fiddleham from that man. A couple of meatballs from a street cart were about all I could afford at the time. He's an immigrant, too. He's going to do well. His red sauce is amazing."

"That's grand for him, then," I said.

"I like it when doors open," said Charlie. "Doors are opening in New Fiddleham every day. It is a remarkable time to be alive anywhere, really. Do you think our parents could ever have imagined having machines that could wash dishes, machines that could sew, machines that do laundry? Pretty soon we'll be taking this trolley ride without any horses. I've heard that Glanville has electric streetcars already. Who knows what will be possible fifty years from now, or a hundred. Change isn't always so bad."

"Your optimism is both baffling and inspiring," I said.

"The sun is rising," he replied with a little chuckle.

I glanced at the sky. It was well past noon.

"It's just something my sister and I used to say," he clarified. "I think you would like Alina. You often remind me of her. She has a way of refusing to let the world keep her down." He smiled and his gaze drifted away, following the memory.

"Alina found a rolled-up canvas once," he said, "a year or so after our mother passed away. It was an oil painting–a picture of the sun hanging low over a rippling ocean. She was a beautiful painter, our mother. I could tell that it was one of hers, but I had never seen it before. It felt like a message, like she had sent it, just for us to find.

"I said that it was a beautiful sunset, and Alina said no, it was a sunrise. We argued about it, actually. I told her that the sun in the picture was setting because it was obviously a view from our camp near Gelendzhik, overlooking the

Black Sea. That would mean the painting was looking to the west.

"Alina said that it didn't matter. Even if the sun is setting on Gelendzhik, that only means that it is rising in Bucharest. Or Vienna. Or Paris. The sun is always rising somewhere. From then on, whenever I felt low, whenever I lost hope and the world felt darkest, Alina would remind me: the sun is rising."

"I think I like Alina already. It's a heartening philosophy. I only worry that it's wasted on this city."

"A city is just people," Charlie said. "A hundred years from now, even if the roads and buildings are still here, this will still be a whole new city. New Fiddleham is dying, every day, but it is also being constantly reborn. Every day, there is new hope. Every day, the sun rises. Every day, there are doors opening."

I leaned in and kissed him on the cheek. "When we're through saving the world," I said, "you can take me out to Nonna Santoro's. I have it on good authority that the red sauce is amazing."

He blushed pink and a bashful smile spread over his face. "When we're through saving the world, Miss Rook, I will hold you to that."

The rest of the journey was mostly silent, but the awkwardness had fallen away behind us. I leaned in, and Charlie put his arm around my shoulders while we rode. There were some adventures I could not have with Mr. Jackaby.

Our ride came to an end half a mile from our destination, and we walked the rest of the way to the Coolidge Gardens. Technically a public park, the gardens were no simple planter box of geraniums or patch of grass in the middle of a city. The Coolidge Gardens were big. They sat at the northernmost limits of the city, a sprawling three-acre plot situated atop a high hill that overlooked New Fiddleham. It was a manicured Eden of hedges, heathers, and hundreds of varieties of fragrant flowers, whose perfume rolled through the paths and hedgerows and spilled up over the high fence that surrounded the property.

Charlie led us discreetly out of sight of the policemen stationed at the front entrance and along the perimeter until we came to a very old oak tree growing against the border. The tree's lower branches had been trimmed back to accommodate the barrier, but its upper branches reached over the fence and hung just above the garden. With a quick glance back to ensure we had not been observed, we climbed up and shuffled along the sturdiest branch, dropping down to the soft turf on the other side as quietly as we could.

The walk from there to the actual site of the crime was downright idyllic. Walking with Charlie as the early evening sun came streaming over fields of forget-me-nots and rosebushes, I was beginning to feel that the universe was conspiring to set entirely the wrong atmosphere for the evening's purposes. Charlie, mercifully, still did not broach the topic of the ring even once on our journey. If he had intended to propose, as Jackaby had warned, then at least he did not seem inclined to do so on our way to a grisly murder site. Credit to Charlie for that.

We came around a fat pink shrub and I shuddered to a halt. Directly ahead of me stood another uniformed police-man. There was no hiding from him; if I had been any closer we might have slow-danced. He was familiar. I had seen him in the precinct a dozen times, reporting officiously to Marlowe. What was his name?

The officer looked as startled as I was, and then his eyes turned to Charlie. *Maybe he won't recognize him*, I thought, desperately. *Charlie was out of uniform—maybe the man would just take us for young lovers out for a walk in the park. Young lovers who had somehow failed to notice the armed police barri-cade at the entrance.*

"Cane," the man said.

My heart sank. Charlie *Barker* was just a man. Charlie *Barker* had no history beyond last winter. Charlie *Cane* was a dangerous fugitive.

"Lieutenant Dupin," Charlie answered. "How is Marie?"

"Walking already," said Dupin, his face softening. "Growing so fast. Calls me *Da*. She calls the dog *Da*, too, and the neighbor's cat, but I try not to take it too person-ally." He coughed and jabbed his chin meaningfully toward me, raising an eyebrow. "Who's she?"

"She's here with me," Charlie said.

"You mean she isn't," Dupin corrected. "Because you're definitely not here." He sniffed. "Well, then. Standing here, all alone as I am, I feel suddenly compelled to go investigate a noise I might have heard over . . . elsewhere." He gave me a civil nod, and then added: "Should anyone *not be here* while I'm away, they would do well to make their *not being here* brief. The chief investigator sent for the coroner's boys to collect the body an hour ago. They'll be along any minute now."

"Thank you," said Charlie.

Dupin gave Charlie a pat on the arm as he passed. "You have nothing to thank me for, Cane. You're not here."

I heaved an enormous sigh of relief. Commissioner Marlowe knew the truth, but I had assumed everyone else in the police department had turned on Charlie.

"Dupin seems nice," I said.

"He is an excellent detective."

"You don't think he's going to raise the alarm?"

"Whether he does or not, it sounds like we should be quick about it. Are you ready?"

When one is raised in polite English society, one does not expect to find oneself keeping a mental list of gruesome crime scenes one has visited—and certainly not to silently rank them by quantity of blood and horridness of smells. What one expects to learn is how to dance the polonaise and to make small talk with the viscount at Mother's garden party and to stuff oneself into an elaborate costume to be presented at court. All things considered, the murder scene was not so bad.

This section of the park opened to a sort of fresh-air amphitheater. The lawn sloped downward, bordered by lush hedges that defined the space and drew the gaze toward a simple stone stage at the center of the clearing. I could easily have pictured a pretentious poetry reading or a fancy wedding ceremony taking place there. Except that the last ceremony performed here had clearly been less fancy and more fatal.

The figure lying on the stage had been covered with a cloth, but I could see the outline of a man's body. There were candle stubs in an arc around the victim as well, all melted down to nothing. He lay on his back, his legs and arms splayed out as though posed for a rendition of the Vitruvian Man. I tried not to think too hard about the spots of red seeping through the cloth. I stepped closer. On either side of the body were broad patterns, as elaborate as lace embroidery, but drawn with pale yellow lines that had been scuffed and blown away in a few places.

"Cornmeal," said Charlie. "I made some inquiries downtown. The design is apparently called a veve. Madame Voile recognized it. She has a book about vodou invocations."

"Vodou?" I said.

"That's what she said. Doesn't explain the rest, though." Charlie gestured to the trees that formed a sort of natural backdrop to the theater. The nearest trunks had each been marred by rough carvings. One had been etched with a pentagram, another with a hexagram, and the one in the center with a sort of cross with a loop at the top. I recognized it as an Egyptian ankh. Jackaby had one or two of those among his relics back home. He had told me they stood for life and death. My mind tried to catalogue the symbols. Pagan, Judaic, Egyptian. What was the pattern?

Some sheer fabric had been draped from their branches as well. It rippled in the gentle breeze behind the stage. The scene was sinister, to be sure, and obviously tragic, but somehow the weight of it felt hollow. I should have been revolted and frightened and overwhelmed—I should have felt at least some distant cousin of the emotions that had left me reeling the first time I saw a dead body—but I wasn't. I felt something else, instead. It was a subtler sort of unsettling, like a mosquito hum in the back of my mind. Perhaps I had begun to grow numb to the macabre, or perhaps it was simply that the stage for this latest murder was a literal stage, but I found myself curiously unmoved by all the paranormal paraphernalia and supernatural set dressing. What troubled me now was that it felt somehow irritatingly familiar, like a morbid moment of déjà vu.

"His name was Steven Fairmont," Charlie said quietly. "Thirty-five."

"Has anything been changed since the body was first discovered?" I asked, trying to remember what sort of questions Jackaby would have thought to ask.

"The cornmeal has gotten spread out, but otherwise it looks about the same."

I walked up to the edge of the stage. The cloth had been folded back to reveal the man's hand. Just below the wrist, I saw that his arm had been cut. A red, angry symbol had been carved into his flesh–a circle, underscored by a wider half circle with a straight line down from there, bisected halfway down like a cross. My old Classical Mythology courses came drifting back to me. It was the symbol of Hades–or maybe Hermes; I could never remember which was which.

How did the symbol of a Greek god have anything to do with vodou invocations? How did vodou have anything to do with ankhs and pentagrams? The buzzing hum in the back of my mind persisted. *Think, Abigail.* What was *odd* about the scene? Well, other than *everything*, of course. How did all the odd fit together?

It didn't.

"You have to believe in Old Scratch if you're going to worship him," I said, thinking aloud.

"Old Scratch?" Charlie asked.

"Something Mr. Jackaby mentioned back at the station. All of this is wrong. It's lazy. There's no reason for someone who believes in vodou spirits to also invoke Hades. These symbols all contradict each other. They're like a hackneyed vignette of the occult from the cover of an insipid dime novel."

The hum in the back of my mind suddenly became a clear note. I had read that insipid dime novel. It had been titled *The Arcane Assassin* or some such. Now I realized why this all looked so familiar! The body, the candles, even the fabric billowing eerily in the wind: the last time I had seen all this, the scene had been rendered in a dramatic woodcut on a bent cover; the details had been poorly defined, but the staging was identical. In that particular installment, if memory served, the naive young protagonists were captured by a dreadful demonic cult. I remembered being disappointed that the big human sacrifice scene didn't actually go the way it appeared in the etching. If the cover artist had been trying to prove that he had no real personal experience with unsavory occult practices, then he had succeeded. No, I thought, no self-respecting Acolyte of Evil would invoke the dark forces with such heavy use of sheer curtains.

"So," said Charlie. "What do you think?"

"I think," I said, considering the scene before me, "that this is all fake—it's just a façade. Someone wants us to believe there's a lot of mystical hokum going on, but it's all just for show. We've been reading the book by its cover."

"But why go to all this trouble?"

"That's a good question." I shook my head. "But none of it is real."

"That body is real enough," said Charlie.

We glanced back at the stage. The cloth that had been

shrouding the corpse lay in a stained, ruffled heap on the ground. It was quite empty. Mr. Fairmont was gone.

"Where–" Charlie began.

"Do you ever grow tired of unexplained phenomena?" I asked Charlie numbly. We both approached the stage. "Because I do. I grow very tired of unexplained phenomena. I would enjoy a perfectly logical and reasonable phenomenon just once. Just one case."

"No you wouldn't," Charlie whispered, sniffing the air as his eyes scanned the clearing.

"Oh, no?" I said. I nudged the rumpled shroud with my toe. "And what makes you so sure I wouldn't?"

His eyes caught mine, and there was a glint of admiration in his glance. "You're here."

I spotted it before Charlie did. I almost missed it at first, there in the shadows of the closest tree, the one marred with the ankh. The hunched figure standing at its base was facing away, nearly hidden in the shadows and partially shrouded by the billowing draperies. He was not holding still, exactly–I might have spotted him more easily if he had been perfectly still–but he was rocking ever so slightly. The motion was both natural and not completely human, like branches bobbing in the wind or clothes swaying on the line. Almost hypnotic.

I pointed, and Charlie gave a mute nod. He moved a step closer to the man. "Hello?" he said at last. "We see you there. Show yourself."

That was when the thing that had once been Steven Fairmont turned around. All of the horror I should have felt upon seeing the man's body lying dead flooded my senses at the sight of him up and moving. Terrible things had been done to Fairmont's body. Things that I will not recount. The man's injuries were grievous, but they did not bleed. What fluids did escape the wretched creature's wounds were the consistency of molasses and moved with its same sticky slowness. He continued to rock ever so gently, his eyes unfocused and filmy. The quiet hum in my skull had been replaced with a mad jangling of alarm bells. For all his rhythmic motion, the man's chest was not heaving. I watched it, fixated on it, holding the air in my own lungs until I could not contain it any longer. Fairmont was not drawing breath. The dead walked.

Chapter Eight

That dime novel, the one with the spooky cult and the unrealistic rituals on the cover, had not mentioned the living dead. It had concluded, as I recall, with a miserly old man from up the lane being unmasked and the whole affair being chalked up as a showy attempt to frighten away superstitious neighbors all along.

The thing beneath the trees was not wearing a mask. It was barely wearing its own skin.

"Mr. Fairmont?" Charlie called out, cautiously. "Can you hear me?"

The grisly face snapped up, milky white eyes fixing on Charlie's voice. The corpse's whole body seemed to shudder as it tensed.

"We are here to help," Charlie said soothingly. "Can you tell us who did this to you?"

Fairmont's sallow brow furrowed into a fierce scowl, and pale lips peeled back as the mutilated corpse bared its yellow teeth. It snarled wetly, a sound more like that of a rabid dog than of a man.

"We are not your enemies, Mr. Fairmont," Charlie continued.

"I don't think that's Mr. Fairmont any longer," I whispered.

Not–Mr. Fairmont leaned forward hungrily, its tortured muscles rippling for a moment as though straining against an invisible bond. In the next moment it was as if that bond had snapped. The corpse erupted forward. It was not running so much as it was falling, only barely catching itself with each stride. I staggered backward, clutching at my pockets to retrieve the silver dagger with which I hoped I might defend myself. Charlie positioned himself ahead of me, holding out his open palms, still trying to assuage the horrible creature. The wet, wheezing snarls only intensified as the cadaverous figure struggled up over the raised stage and back down on our side, lurching and swaying, but pressing ever toward us.

Charlie threw off his coat. "Stand down," he yelled at the thing, but his optimism for a peaceful resolution was clearly draining fast. He pulled his suspenders off his shoulders hastily, preparing for the inevitable. "This is your last warning." Charlie's face darkened as the stubble along his jaw began to spread.

With the ravenous creature almost upon him, Charlie transformed. The corpse threw itself forward and a powerful hound met the thing in midair. Charlie, in his canine form, was no scrawny stray. Imposing muscles pumped beneath a coat of tawny caramel and rich chocolate brown fur. His front paws slammed into the corpse at its sternum, whipping the disfigured figure backward like a rag doll and slapping it onto the hard ground. Fairmont's head hung at an unnatural angle on its neck.

Charlie growled low, baring his fangs.

The corpse reached a hand up to its own head and reset its neck with a sickening crack. Charlie barked, and I sincerely hoped he had no intention of actually biting that decaying carcass. The creature that had once been Fairmont balled its pallid fingers into a fist and hammered Charlie hard on his neck. Charlie was not braced for the first blow and bore the full brunt of it. The second he was prepared for, and he caught the corpse's arm at the elbow. His fangs sank into the sickly flesh, but the wretch barely seemed to notice. With its free hand, the thing drove a ruthless blow into Charlie's chest, spinning the hound off him and into the grass. They both staggered to their feet.

Charlie dropped something to the ground with a heavy thump. He had taken the dead man's arm with him. He shook his shaggy head, smacking his canine lips and looking both dazed and thoroughly disgusted.

The thing's milky eyes refocused on me. With renewed ardor, the creature lumbered at me, its one remaining arm reaching toward me. I fumbled frantically until I had the dagger free of its sheath, and then I whipped it straight at the monster's head.

I am not a marksman, although I had found more cause of late to practice. Contrary to my customary athletic style–which is haphazard and graceless at best–my knife spun through the air directly on target, lodging itself with a satisfying thunk squarely in the creature's jugular. I could not have replicated the shot with a hundred more attempts if I had tried. For a fleeting moment I allowed myself a modicum of pride in my own skill. The reanimated corpse of Steven Fairmont was harder to impress.

I felt the creature's cold, dead fingers graze my neck as I threw myself out of its grasp. Had the thing still been in possession of both arms, my maneuver would have been too late. It stumbled and spun, correcting its balance after the near miss as I tumbled out of the way and back to my feet.

Charlie was at my side in an instant, growling and bracing himself for a second encounter.

"Watch your end, Ned!" a voice said suddenly, breaking through the bushes to the creature's left.

"Yeah, yeah. I've got it," came another voice. Ned's, I presumed.

The snarling corpse turned its head crookedly to look toward the new voices. I cursed. The coroner's men.

"Stay back!" I yelled.

It was too late. Carrying the front end of a wooden litter, a skinny young man of no more than twenty stepped into the clearing. He froze, face-to-face with the abomination. The creature's grotesque visage locked on his, my dagger still jutting out of its neck.

"Oi! What's the idea?" The other man's voice came from behind the bush, and then the gurney was shoved forward, and the terrified Ned with it.

Charlie bounded forward in an instant, but not before the corpse clutched the petrified Ned by the hair and buried its yellow teeth into the poor man's throat.

Charlie slammed headlong into the monster, sending them both rolling across the grass until they crashed into the pillar at the head of the row. Above them, a sculpture rocked back and forth—a hefty urn overflowing with stone fruit. Charlie managed to gain the upper hand a second time, pinning the savage corpse at the base of the statue. The creature thrashed and growled, blood dripping down its chin and head, which was propped up at a sickly angle at the base of the pillar. For all its frustrated fury, it would have a more difficult time dislodging its captor with only one arm. The litter lay discarded in the grass behind them. I swallowed hard. Ned was dead.

The man who had been at the other end of the litter,

a heavyset fellow in a battered longcoat, let out a scream that startled the ravens from their trees halfway across the gardens. He turned and fled, his footsteps pounding away as he put as much distance between himself and the ghastly scene as possible.

The creature gargled an inhuman moan of discontent. I watched, helplessly, as the unholy corpse pummeled Charlie's neck and chest, driving the occasional kick up into his gut. Charlie weathered the blows valiantly, but the corpse showed no signs of tiring. It did not even seem to notice when its head cracked hard against the bricks as it struggled.

I clambered around as quickly as I could to the far side of the pillar. Bracing my feet against the dense shrubbery as best as I could, I reached high above my head and pressed against the urn on top. "Get ready to move out of the way!" I yelled. Charlie looked up for just an instant, and then let out an involuntary yelp of pain as the creature belted him across the jaw.

With great effort I could only just tilt the heavy statue an inch or so forward. It wobbled when I released it and settled right back into place. I cursed again. I had no leverage.

I heard Charlie whine piteously. Fairmont's remaining hand had grabbed a fistful of his fur just below his ear and was shaking the hound's head viciously. I leapt down clumsily and pulled my skirts free of the useless bush. "Hold on!" I yelled. I sprinted across the clearing and grabbed hold of the discarded litter. Trying very hard not to look at the life-less Ned lying beside it, I dragged the wooden gurney back across the grass. Propping one end against the heavy statue, I found purchase on a cluster of marble grapes spilling mer-rily out of the top of the urn. Another yelp from Charlie, and I saw a tuft of chocolate brown fur tossed aside as the creature's arm drew back for another blow.

"Now!" I screamed.

The corpse thrashed. Charlie rolled away. I heaved against my end of the litter, and the statue tipped. For a fraction of a second the urn seemed to hang in the air, weightless, and then it dropped. The head that had once been Steven Fairmont's lay directly below it. The two met with a wet crunch.

I staggered out from around the pillar. The body did not move. Not a finger twitched. The upturned urn had buried itself several inches into the soil where the thing's skull had been. All around the impact crater was a dark, sickly some-thing I dared not think too hard about. I breathed. Charlie panted. We stared at the corpse, which was lifeless once more. The smell was atrocious.

"I think," I huffed, "it might be over."

Charlie limped back toward the stage to retrieve his clothes. I cautiously retrieved my knife and cleaned it on the grass, keeping a wary eye on the corpse until Charlie returned in his human form. He stepped back to my side shortly, pulling his coat stiffly over his shoulders.

Footsteps sounded behind the hedgerows.

"We should go," I whispered.

Before either of us could act on my advice, Lieutenant Dupin appeared around the corner, staggering at once to a halt. He had a pistol drawn already, and his eyes widened as he surveyed the mad scene. The voices of his fellow officers were closing in.

Charlie did not run. His eyes moved from the mutilated Mr. Fairmont to the savaged Ned. "It isn't over," he said somberly. "Fairmont was the weapon, not the wielder. We still don't know who did this."

Dupin stood agape. He turned to face Charlie. The gun in his hands trembled. The voices of the agitated officers behind him grew closer.

"We will report to Marlowe everything that happened here," I assured the officer. "Charlie is not responsible for any of this. Please, you need to believe me."

"Go," he gulped.

A minute later, we were clambering along the low branch of the oak tree, and in short order we were back on the road into New Fiddleham. Neither one of us had spoken a word as we had retreated through the gardens.

"I should not have asked for your help," Charlie said at last.

"I think we can plainly see that you should have," I said. "You can't seriously have expected to handle a thing like that all on your own—someone's found a way to give the rotting dead the will to live. Good news, though: I do believe we've reached that special level of odd that Jackaby cannot possibly decline to investigate. You don't have to go it alone."

"I am fortunate that I did not tonight," he conceded. "Thank you for being there for me." His fingers brushed mine as we walked side by side, and I slid my hand up to hold his arm. He smiled shyly.

"I'll keep saving you if you keep saving me," I said.

Chapter Nine

When I was seven, I became terribly ill and developed a severe fever that lasted for days. My father recalls the incident as though I had nearly died, while my mother recalls the event as though I had done it on purpose to get out of piano lessons. My own memory of it is, perhaps, less coherent than my parents', but it remains with me to this day. At the height of my delirium, as my nanny pressed cool washcloths to my forehead, I lay on my bed with a parade of horrifying visions swimming before my weary eyes. In retrospect, that vivid fever dream may have been just the thing to brace me for the scene that awaited Charlie and me upon our return to 926 Augur Lane.

"No!" Jackaby's muffled bellow came from the other side of the door as we mounted the steps. "Take that out of your mouth! Put that down! That is an apotropaic wand carved from Egyptian ivory during the—and you've broken it. No! Don't sit on that! Oh, for heaven's sake."

I opened the door. To say that the crowd within was pressed shoulder to shoulder would not do justice to the assortment of bodies occupying Jackaby's foyer. The tallest among them, a hunched giant, could have put his head through the ceiling if he had stood fully upright. A tight group of very short men huddled around the umbrella stand scarcely came up to my waist, although their pointed violet hats nearly doubled their height. There were smaller creatures still, a few of them barely more than twinkling balls of light that fluttered around a lithe, angular woman with twigs in her hair—although I was not sure if I should count those ones as bodies in their own right, or if they were more adornments of hers. There were people with beards and people with gills and one with a face that my eyes refused to focus on no matter how hard I tried. Jenny was there as well, making an effort to shoo a small cloud of pixies away from the more fragile relics on the shelves. I could see by the red clay shards on the floor that she had not been successful in keeping them from toppling a Grecian urn. The motley mob stood, stooped, or flew shoulder to knee to belly button all around the cramped chamber.

"Please! If you would all simply stop moving!" Jackaby yelled. "Oh, Miss Rook—where in God's name have you been?"

"We–" I began.

"Riveting. Please make yourself useful, would you? Douglas and Jenny and I have been coordinating temporary placements for everyone until I can sort this all out." He waved us to step forward. I had to squeeze past the little men in violet hats, who kindly shuffled into a tighter huddle. The giant grumbled something in an accent that sounded a bit like French and a bit like a grizzly bear growling from the bottom of a very deep well.

"You heard me!" Jackaby spun and pointed a finger up at him. "I said *temporary* and I meant it! You're not staying!"

The giant shrugged glumly and his shoulder blades scraped the ceiling.

Jackaby turned back to us. "What in heaven's name took you so long?"

"Don't get cross with me. A man rose from the dead! His corpse literally stood up at the scene of the crime! He attacked us! I had to sort of . . . squish him."

"It's true," said Charlie.

"What color was its hair?"

"What?" I said. "What sort of question is that? What does it matter what color his hair was?"

"It never hurts to narrow things down. The West African 'zombi' is typically black-haired, while its Haitian variant can be any hue. The 'draugr' from Scandinavia, on the other hand, is frequently redheaded, and also typically boasts a full beard. Was your dead man bearded?"

"No. I don't think so."

"He was a brunet, I think," Charlie offered. "Why? Which ones are worse?"

"Oh, there's really no difference between them beyond the hair," Jackaby said. "Never hurts to be precise, though. Whatever he was, no good ever came of the dead rising."

"I'm going to pretend I didn't hear that," Jenny called from across the crowded foyer. "Hey! Get off that lamp! Oh—I hope you burn your wings, you little brats!"

"Sir," I said, "may I ask, where did all of these"—I hesitated—"*people?*"

"*People* will do."

"Where did all of these people come from?"

"The first batch came from the station house. The rest have been trickling in as word reached them in the more distant pockets of New Fiddleham's supernatural community."

"Might I suggest offering them the third floor to spread out a bit?" I said, as something silvery zipped and darted around my head, swimming through the air like a fish through water.

"We did," Jenny called over her shoulder.

"It got crowded up there," Jackaby added grimly. "And the centaurs do not associate peaceably with ipotanes, which is ironic, considering how much they have in common. Hey, you! Aziza! I see you there. Kindly do not shake out your pipe onto my Bibles!"

This last he directed to a hairy little man with jet-black skin who sat atop the pile on the desk. He was not much taller than the books on which he perched. Aziza nodded understandingly and then proceeded to tip his pipe onto a copy of the King James anyway.

Jackaby took a deep, steadying breath. "We're working on quadrants. Bipedal versus quadrupedal, trooping versus solitary, truculent versus, well, *less* prone to pitch a battle ax through a laboratory window." He glared meaningfully at a stocky, bearded fellow by his elbow, who at least had the decency to shuffle his feet and look abashed. "Your room is currently housing avian anthropoids, by the way. You may need to wash your bedsheets later."

"Why are they all here, sir?" I asked.

"Spade," grunted Jackaby. "Miss Lee liberated Spade's detainees per my request, but Mayor Spade was none too happy to see them go. According to a few of the first arrivals, he was downright livid. He apparently tried to block their release, but Marlowe stepped in on their behalf. That might have been the end of it, but Spade wasn't about to let me walk away from this without making my life harder. He added an amendment to his original edict then and there, a clause granting the 'undesirables' one sanctuary in the city—one alone. The word went out hours ago. Care to guess which building he decided to declare an official paranormal refuge?"

"You're kidding."

"That's right. This is me kidding. I'm knee deep in gnomes because I'm just so much fun at parties. Hey! I saw that! No biting your fellow refugees! We've been over this!"

"I had no idea New Fiddleham was so diverse," said Charlie, peering around the room in awe. "I always thought there were very few of–us."

"That would be the glamour inhibitor," said Jackaby. "I put it in for Rook when I had the door redone. It will wear off in a bit, but when they passed through the entryway it temporarily rendered their guises null. You are seeing them as I see them–as they really are. Well, except for the null." He nodded toward the man whose face I couldn't seem to focus on. "One can *never* see a null as he is, because strictly speaking, a null *isn't*." The null waved at us sheepishly from the corner. I think.

"I cannot say that I am comfortable with your system," Charlie mumbled. "Some of us have good reason to keep our identities to ourselves."

"Did you get the impression that anybody in this room was *comfortable* at the moment, Mr. Barker?" Jackaby asked, his eye twitching just a little. "They were warned–they came in anyway. Well, some of them did. Half a dozen had inhibitions about the inhibitor and decided to favor secrecy over sanctuary. Thank goodness they did. We'd be overrun."

"You really think we can keep them all safe?"

"No!" A hint of manic laughter crept into Jackaby's voice.

"Not remotely! I can scarcely keep *you* safe, let alone babysit every satyr and siren in the city! I can't exactly turn them out, though, can I? Not with the mayor's thugs patrolling the streets."

"I think it's good," I said. Jenny turned to me with skepticism in her eyes. "I know this may not be ideal, but they need help. That's what we do, isn't it? We help people. I'll sleep better tonight knowing that we did what we could."

Jenny shrugged. "You do remember that there are bird-folk nesting in your bedchamber?"

"I will suffer less discomfort knowing that a lot of innocent people don't have to go home tonight to find hunters waiting on their doorsteps."

"No, that's true," said Jackaby, nodding toward the entryway. His expression had suddenly lost a degree of happiness that it did not have to spare. "They will find one waiting on *ours*."

The entire assembly turned at the sound of the door thudding open and a booming voice erupting from the doorway. "Hot damn! Ain't you all a sight!"

I felt a lump drop to the pit of my stomach. Second only to the actual giant in height, Hank Hudson was a mountain of a man, dressed in thick hides and heavy boots. His left arm ended just past the elbow, concluding with a curved metal hook, like a storybook pirate. Hudson was a friend and an ally, but he was also an expert hunter with a taste for paranormal prey. Sometimes his paranormal prey got a taste for him, too. That hand had gone into the gullet of a fifty-foot dragon the last time we had met.

He stood in the doorway with a smile spreading from one end of his bushy auburn beard to the other. "How come I wasn't invited to yer shindig, chum?" he called over the crowd to Jackaby. "You know I like me a rare breed!"

Chapter Ten

With Hank Hudson in tow, Jackaby wound through the crowded house. Jenny abandoned her efforts to preserve a small statue of a man with a bird's head and swept after them, and Charlie and I followed close on their heels.

Jackaby's personal library was not as large as the public libraries I have known, but walking into it, I still found myself greeted by thousands of volumes, a collection full of rare and obscure works unrivaled by anything I had ever seen. My employer's shelving method was maddening, to be sure, with books organized completely illogically, although Jackaby insisted they were set according to supernatural potency and color of aura. My eyesight being limited to prosaic things like light and color and items occupying actual physical space, his methodology was less than help-ful—but still, Jackaby's library was a marvel. I breathed in the scent of paper and leather and binding glue as we filed inside.

There was something else in the air today. Something musty with a hint of axle grease and copper. I could tell that Charlie had caught the scent as well, and I followed his eyes to a band of mottled gray-green creatures loiter-ing around the alcove window seats. They were about the height and build of muscular eight-year-old boys with gan-gly arms and ill-fitting clothes. Each of the sinewy little men carried a weapon. These ranged from a bandolier of daggers to a massive blunderbuss that looked more like a small cannon in the hands of the diminutive figure.

"Chief Nudd." Jackaby gave a civil nod to the goblin in the center, who was wearing a black top hat with a spray of cardinal feathers tucked neatly in the band.

Nudd tipped the showy hat and gave me a glance. "Ye've kept yer new Douglas around, I see. Have nae gotten 'er turned inter a bird or anyfin' yet. You goin' easy on thiss'n?"

"Mm? Oh, yes. Miss Rook is hale and whole."

I nodded. "I was dead for a short while, but that was weeks ago. Very kind of you to inquire, Mr. Nudd."

He smiled up at me with all his jagged teeth, a goblin's most affable expression—which was, as far as I could tell, indistinguishable from a goblin's most menacing expression.

"Do pardon us," Jackaby said. "I just mean to have a quiet

word with my associates. The house is a bit more . . . occupied than I generally prefer."

"Know the feelin'. Yer bookroom is fair an' all, but th' twain keeps watchin' me, and all them nimmies is righ' unsettlin' after a time."

"Twain? Nimmies?" I glanced around. "I didn't see anyone else in—oh my!" A woman's face, which had moments ago appeared to be carved into the side of one of the heavy bookshelves, leaned forward and blinked out at us with eyes like glittering sapphires.

"Oh, that is a bit off-putting, isn't it," said Jenny. "Is that what it's like when I come through a wall unannounced?"

The nymph peered at her mournfully for a few seconds and then turned to Jackaby.

"You're not wearing the hat I made for you," she said in a whisper like the wind through leaves.

"Erm, yes. No. I am not, actually. There was an incident."

She sighed and rolled her eyes before falling backward, melting into the woodwork entirely.

"Wood nymphs," said Jackaby.

"Not a real cheery lot, them," observed Hudson.

"In retrospect, a library is a rather somber locale for their kind. A bit like housing a man in a graveyard. Well, a bit like housing a man in a graveyard in which his people's bones have been mashed to a pulp and reconstituted into slim sheets, onto which one has scribbled a lot of silly words with pictures of monks and satyrs in the margins."

Even with unexpected guests coming out of the wood-work, the library was still an oasis of calm. I had always found it comforting—so long as I did not allow my curiosity to draw me back into the Dangerous Documents section. Something indescribably eerie lay in those foggy depths at the end of a mazelike series of bookshelves. I much pre-ferred keeping to the front of the library.

"All right, then, straight to the back," said Jackaby. "We need to talk."

"Secret meetin', then?" Nudd said, scrambling away from his horde to join us. "This yer trusted few? Inner cir-cly sorta thing, nae? A'righ'. I'm wit' ye. 'Bout time ye took command."

"What? No," Jackaby said. "I'm not assuming command of anything. God knows why, but these fools are hardy enough to keep my company even in the face of this mess, so I simply intend to put their foolhardy company to good use."

"Aye. Tha's the inner circly bit."

Jackaby shook his head. "Come on, then."

We followed through tight corridors filled with an inex-plicable fog of dread until they gave way to an opening entirely enclosed by bookshelves, with just enough space for a single oval reading table. The table had a small oil lamp in the center, which Jackaby lit. There were only two chairs, but there was room enough for four or five to stand around the table comfortably. The six of us did our best.

"So, this is the Dangerous Documents section." I glanced at the spines and scrolls around us. Some were sealed with iron clasps and heavy locks; others had been chained directly to their shelves. Those that sat freely seemed to have edged away from their more intimidating colleagues.

"Yes," Jackaby said. "Don't worry, they won't bite. Well, none of the ones on that end, anyway. You can take a look, but nobody do anything colossally ignorant like read them out loud. Or let them read you out loud."

"Okay," said Hudson, scratching his beard with his hook. "Care to tell us why we're here?"

"I have no idea why you're here," said Jackaby. "I understand why the fairies and sprites and the other oddlings have come—they're here for my protection, what little of it I have to offer. You're human, though, Hank. You were in no danger. You could be anywhere right now, so why *are* you here?"

"It don't take an expert to read the signs, chum. Things ain't right. You got a way of makin' things right, and I aim ta help. Last time I got involved, it was me who made 'em wrong in the first place—so if you're fixin' this, I'm fixin' to fix it with ya."

"You know we're with you, too, sir," I said. Charlie nodded.

"It's only recently I've been able to go out into the world again," said Jenny. "I'm certainly not letting somebody go destroying that world before I've had a chance to enjoy it."

"What about you?" Jackaby turned to Nudd.

"My horde's got one foot in this world, t'other foot in th' Annwyn. Bin feelin' th' tremors shakin' both sides fer a long time noo."

"But your horde is seeded hundreds of miles away. Spade wasn't about to find you any time soon, and even if he had, as you say, you've got one foot in the Annwyn. You could always escape to the other side long before he posed any threat. Even if the worst came to pass, even if the earth and the Annwyn tore each other apart—you owe no allegiance to either faction. You could stand to the side until the dust cleared. So why seek me out? There's no profit in joining the fray."

"Nae. An' it wouldn'ae be our firs' time pickin' o'er the dead after a battle. I'll take no shame in it iffin' it comes tae tha', neither, but there's profit in protectin' an investment. We's invested."

Jackaby raised an eyebrow. "Invested in New Fiddleham? Brigand or not, you sound almost sentimental."

Nudd gave a barking laugh. "Gotta lotta contacts in this city, t' be sure—but it's nae New Fiddleham we's invested in."

Jackaby looked confused.

"I believe he means you, sir," I said. "Everyone in this room is invested in you."

Jackaby looked deeply uncomfortable as the room quieted, heads nodding in agreement.

"Even him?" Hudson broke the hush. He pointed up to the shelf behind Jackaby. A man not more than six inches tall, his body covered in dust brown, woolly fur, sat at the top, dangling his feet casually off the shelf. He looked a bit like a mild-mannered chipmunk and an accountant fused into a single body. His face was round and rosy, bordered by downy tufts of hair around his ears and a stubbly beard that circled his chin.

"Ah," said Jackaby. "That little fellow is an . . . actually, I don't know." He turned his head this way and that. "I don't know you," he told the creature.

"Humans don't," it said. Its voice was small and unassuming.

"No, I mean, I don't believe I've even read about you, which is—I must say—rather uncommon. You have an exceptional aura, though, has anyone ever told you? Unrestrainedly brilliant. A rather zoetic bluish-red. But not really red, though, is it? Nor blue. What are you?"

"Half of what I once was," said the creature humbly. "More than you will ever be," it added quietly.

"Ach, watch yerself. 'Tis a twain," Nudd interjected. "Powerful strong magic, th' twain, but beholden tae none but they's own. Unseelie as they come."

"It's an Unseelie fairy?" I said, taking an involuntary step backward—directly into Hudson. He steadied me with a hand on my shoulder.

"Unseelie. Seelie. Old words," said the twain, softly.

"They don't mean as much as they once did. War changes things."

"Some things don't change," said Jackaby. "And this isn't a war! Not yet. Not if we can help it."

"You're hesitant," said the twain. "Good. But this war began a long time ago. You have already seen new casualties, housed the refugees, met the generals on the front lines."

Jackaby's brow knit. His hands were clenched at his sides.

"I'm curious," the twain replied. "When you finally decide to join the fight, will you know what you are fighting for? Choose carefully. The spear grips the hand, as the saying goes. How will you plan mankind's victory against the otherworld when you're asking for advice from the undead and goblins?"

"Oi!" Nudd cut in. "'Tis nae goblins tha' drove all these twallies outta their holes an' inta this'n. It's humans ye need tae watch out for. Goblins ye can trust."

"With all things save one's coin purse," the twain said, evenly.

"Oi! Mind yer gob. Goblins pay their debts. We're nae the cheats, here. Humanfolk, now there's a den o' snakes."

"Izzat so?" Hudson raised a bushy eyebrow.

"Aye. My horde built a tower once. Human with big fat pockets wants a tower right in the center of New Fiddleham, right? Wants it a hundred stories tall from ground tae gables—a hundred human stories, mind ya, nae goblin stories. Tha's twice as big! But we built it, all the same. Done! Greasy munter refused to pay!"

"You built a tower in the middle of New Fiddleham?" Hudson asked. "A hundred stories high?"

"Oh, aye. Fine bit o' craftsmanship, too."

"I been to every corner of New Fiddleham," said Hudson. "There ain't no hundred-story towers around here."

"Ach, ya daft humanfolk na'er use yer nappers. Got ta think like a goblin. Couldn'ae build a tower what rose up into th' sky in th' middle o' a big city wi'out raising all kind o' unwanted attention—so we just flipped th' plans. Goblins is clever folk. Ground is still ground, gables is still gables, we just built th' thing down instead o' up."

"You built . . . down?" I said. "You mean you dug it into the earth? How is that a tower and not a tunnel?"

"Ach, tha's easy." Nudd grinned with all his pointy teeth. "It's got windows."

"If you don't mind," Jackaby interrupted. "What are you really doing here?" he asked the twain.

"Watching," it replied with a shrug. "Waiting."

Nudd snarled something that did not sound like respectable discourse, even for a goblin, and added, "Dinna trust a twain."

"Well," said Jackaby, still addressing the twain, "make yourself useful or make yourself scarce."

"Scarce as scarce can be," said the twain, his gaze hollow.

"I am the last and the only." And in a blink he was suddenly gone. Jackaby's eyes darted around the room, and then he scowled. It was his grudgingly impressed scowl.

"Instantaneous transtemporal dislocation," he said. "No incantations or powders. You weren't kidding. That's serious raw magic."

"Told ye," said Nudd. "Dinnae need charms or curses, them ones. No fiddlin' wi' chants or spellbooks. If they wants summat ta be, then it be. Give me th' jeebies. Ye only ever see a twain at th' big times."

"Big times?" said Hudson.

"Aye. Big times. The beginnin' times. The end times. Times fra' which history don' bounce back again." There was a collective moment of silence in the library. "Iffin' we got a twain on our side, 'tis nae a good sign. An' iffin' we've go' a twain against us . . ." He let the sentence die off.

"Well. Let's hope he's on our side then, shall we?" said Jackaby. "We find ourselves on the precipice of a war we do not want to fight. The question is, how do we avoid it?"

"No," I said. I found myself suddenly the center of attention. "He was right. The war is already here. The precipice on which we find ourselves is that of a choice we do not want to make." I took a deep breath. "But we cannot afford to avoid it. Either we engage the Dire King on our own terms now—or we allow him to engage us on his."

I felt my voice quaver in the hush of the library, but I continued. "Mayor Spade thinks he is making a stand for his city. He's paranoid, but his fear is not unfounded. The Dire King brought the battle to New Fiddleham. Spade is allowing fear to drive him to hatred and injustice, which means that the Dire King is already winning the first battle. When the veil weakens, when the Annwyn begins to cross over into the earth, the otherworlders will be met with Spade's hate. That's exactly what the Dire Council wants. The first battlefield isn't a place; it's a point of view."

Jackaby pursed his lips silently. His gaze darkened. He did not disagree.

"Mayor Spade is fighting a war," I went on, "but he's been fighting it blind, and so have we. The Dire Council has been so much cleverer every step of the way. Every time we thought we had won a battle, we had only helped stoke the fires of their growing war machine. Remember my first case with you, sir? What do you know about redcaps?"

Jackaby blinked, finding himself unexpectedly in his element. "They survive off the fresh blood of their victims. Typically found in the ruins of castles. Very solitary, anti-social creatures."

"And where did we find ours?"

"Running for political office in the middle of a vibrant metropolis," he answered.

"Right," I said. "How long did the council expect a redcap to last in the public eye before his bloodlust got the better of him? He was a pawn. He was meant to be exposed. They wanted the spectacle."

Charlie winced. "And I gave it to them. When I transformed in the square."

"That was nothin' to the spectacle I gave 'em," Hudson added mournfully. "Them transformin' critters they set loose on those high society folks. They was lookin' to cause trouble then, too. You almost had that one under wraps until I bungled it for everybody. Instead of a couple creepy critters in a swanky party, we wound up with a full-grown dragon screamin' outta the sky." He waggled his hook by way of illustration. The hand he didn't have was a harsh reminder.

"I'm the one who floated straight into the mayor's own house and tore a hole through his wall catching that nixie," Jenny added. "Spade was horrified. I saw his face. I didn't even care. It just felt good to feel strong for once. That was what put him over the edge. If anyone tipped the scales toward public panic it was me."

"It's not a competition," I said.

Jackaby groaned. "Although if it were, I think we all know who would be winning it. I've devoted my adult life to drawing attention to the dangers of the supernatural world all around us." He grimaced, clenching his eyes shut. "All those times Marlowe hushed up my cases to avoid alarming the public, he was actually right. An alarmed public is precisely what the Dire King wants." He leaned heavily on the table. "I begin to feel I may have been remiss in hiding those banana slugs in Marlowe's desk drawer. And for drawing that monocle and mustache on his portrait in the station house. And for taking out that newspaper advertisement in his name, requesting donations of foreign cheeses be sent to his home address."

"We've all played into the council's hands," I said.

"I've nae played inta any hands," Nudd said.

"Fine. Yes. We've all played into his hands, with the exception of Mr. Nudd," I amended. "What matters now is that we take the initiative. We can't keep fighting the battles they lay out for us."

"The shield," said Jackaby. "We may be too late to beat them to Hafgan's spear and crown, but we still have a chance with the shield. We even have a clue that they don't. We just have to figure out what *in the Bible of the zealot* means."

"I was thinking of Morwen," said Jenny. "She's our best route to manipulating the Dire King the way he's manipulated us. If it's a battle of minds we're fighting, Morwen has the information we need. She knows where to find the rend, and I would wager she knows where the crown and spear are as well."

Jackaby nodded. "Agreed. We research the shield and interrogate the nixie. What else?"

"Reinforcements?" suggested Charlie. "I don't relish the thought of the six of us up against the world. The worlds."

"Good. Information, interrogation, and collaboration. Plans are always best with a rhyme scheme. All right, then. Miss Cavanaugh and Miss Rook, I want you to interrogate

Morwen tomorrow. You two have the most experience with her to date. Watch her, though. She's slippery. Mr. Barker and Mr. Hudson—first thing in the morning I want the two of you to call on everyone in town we can trust. Summon as many as you can for a meeting here the following evening. Marlowe may not be able to spare any of his men, but not every warrior wears a uniform. Mona O'Connor might be a good place to start. The woman has proven herself a fair hand at triage under tricky circumstances. Anton, the baker on Market Street. Little Miss—you'll find her at Madame Voile's."

"Little Miss? No," I said. "You can't invite a seven-year-old girl to help you fight a war, even a psychic one."

"Little Miss can locate the dead," he said. "That is a talent that may prove vital in ensuring the world still exists come her eighth birthday. Corpses are apparently rising in New Fiddleham, and our own resident ghost brought down the only member of the Dire Council we've actually managed to capture. The dead may well turn the tide for the living in this fight. So, yes. Little Miss."

"Wha' aboot me?" Nudd asked.

"You trade in a lot of expensive goods, old friend—but what have you always told me is worth the most?"

"Unicorn kidney?"

"What? No. The other thing."

"Muthern's love?"

"No, no, no. Information."

Nudd's face blossomed in understanding. "What is it ye want the knowin' of?"

"I want to know about Hafgan's shield. Anything you can tell me–and I need to know if anyone else has been looking for it."

Nudd slapped the table. "Dinna worry. I'll put the horde on't righ' quick. We ha' eyes an' ears all o'er the earth an' the Annwyn." His face rippled in an unpleasant convulsion that might have been a conspiratorial wink. "Kin trade a lot o' information for a jar o' eyes an' ears. We'll get yer shield."

"What about you, sir?" I asked.

"You two investigated an occult crime scene and encountered an actual specimen of the living dead–all without *me*. I am not too proud to admit that I'm a shade envious, but I am also not naive enough to think it was an isolated incident. If the undead are walking the streets, then I shudder to imagine what else might be out there. I would prefer to be on the advance guard this time, not waiting to hear about it secondhand. Before my home became a mythical motel, my sources had just informed me that there are at least five more crime scenes in the city right now brimming with unusual activity. I will start with those."

"Wait, back up. There's dead folks walkin' around the city?" Hudson said. "Shouldn't this've come up a little sooner?"

"That's it, then." Jackaby heaved a heavy sigh. "Get some rest, everyone. Tomorrow, it seems, we begin one of those days from which history may not bounce back again."

Chapter Eleven

I awoke the next morning coughing and spluttering, until I managed to dislodge a downy feather from the back of my throat. A lady with the head of a pigeon glanced at me from the vanity and then went back to preening. Four large geese had made themselves comfortable by the window. I wasn't sure what was supernatural or human about them. They had looked at me with pronounced disdain when I came to bed last night, but in my experience, such is the temperament of all geese.

A pair of avian women was dozing in the corner. Those two looked like harpies to me, but I had not worked up the confidence to ask them to either confirm or deny this. Their faces were stunningly beautiful, with features that could have been carved by Michelangelo framed by flowing hair, but from the neck down they had the bodies of over-large birds, akin to a falcon or an eagle. Fully extended, their wings would have spanned from wall to wall in the bedchamber. They had introduced themselves last night as Alkanost and Sirin, but for the life of me I could not remember which was which. The one on the left had raven black feathers and a sour countenance, and her counterpart had dove white plumage and a bright smile. The lighter of the two had been delighted to learn my surname, although seemed mildly disappointed when I told her that, no, to the best of my knowledge, there were no literal rooks in my ancestry.

I dressed quickly and stepped out into the hallway, closing the door gently behind me. A smell like freshly baked bread and spices wafted through the air, decidedly unlike the usual smells I had come to associate with mornings in Jackaby's house. I trod with great care down the spiral staircase. A family of a dozen Cornish spriggans had camped out there, one on each step, and a moon white miniature pony was snoring at the foot of the stairs. The pony waggled its scruffy ears as I hopped over it.

I heard voices and nudged open the squeaky door to Jackaby's laboratory. I found myself facing a man made out of living fire. He was bare chested with billowy trousers tied by a cord around his flickering waist, batting Jackaby away from a pan of something that smelled sweet and lemony. Jackaby scowled like a scolded child.

I blinked as my tired eyes tried to focus on the fiery figure, but the smokeless flames that defined his body wavered like a mirage in the desert.

"Leave it!" the man said. "It must simmer now, until the dough is thick." His voice was a deep baritone flavored with a rich Arabian accent.

"You've got to stir it," argued Jackaby.

"I know how to make *kunafah*," said the man. "It will not burn. I am good with fire." He chuckled warmly.

"Good morning, sir," I said, announcing myself.

"I'm really quite handy in the kitchen, myself," Jackaby insisted, ignoring me. "And as this is my abode–"

"Perhaps it would be best to let the gentleman cook, sir," I said. "It does smell lovely, whatever it is." I could not remember the last time Jackaby had prepared something for breakfast that did not end up melting its own pot or lodging itself in the wall.

The man of fire turned and gave me a broad, charming smile. "You should listen to the woman," he said. I found myself mesmerized. It looked as though beneath his surface was a core as black as coal, but his skin was a living white-blue flame. "Please," he said graciously, "help yourselves before you go."

Jackaby bristled, but snagged a piece of flatbread from a mouth-watering spread already laid out on the counter. I selected one as well. It was still warm and soft, and it smelled buttery and fresh. I took a nibble. And then I took two more from the stack before jogging out the door after Jackaby.

"Thank you!" I called to the man.

He winked back at me.

"Hmph. Jinn," Jackaby said as I joined him in the hall-way. "Insufferably stubborn lot."

"That was a jinni?" I said. "As in, from a magic lamp?"

"No, that was a jinni, as in, from the Lower Inkling District. Third Street. He's a machinist. Formerly of the Arabian Desert, I suppose, but he has lived in New Fiddleham peacefully for as long as either of us has been alive. Calls himself Shihab currently, but I imagine he'll have to change that once or twice a century for the sake of the census man."

Charlie emerged from the washroom just ahead of us. He was freshly shaved, although his eyes betrayed how little sleep he had gotten during the night.

"Oh! Good morning, Miss Rook, Mr. Jackaby," he said.

"I thought you had gone with Hudson," Jackaby said.

"I was just on my way to meet him," Charlie answered. "He should be bringing his cart around. I'm very glad to have caught you before I go, though."

"Lovely timing, Mr. Barker," I said. "We can see you out."

"Actually, if the detective does not mind," Charlie said, timidly, "I was wondering if I could speak to you alone for just a moment first."

"Mm-hmm." Both of Jackaby's eyebrows climbed up his

forehead until they were hiding in his tousled bangs. He let his eyes dart between the two of us suggestively for a moment, and then waved me off. "Fine. I have matters of my own to attend to. Try not to raise the dead while you're alone this time, will you?" He stalked off in the direction of his office, leaving me to walk the winding hallway with Charlie.

"Something you wanted to discuss with me?" I asked. Charlie did not speak at once. I noticed his fingers fumbling absently with his vest pocket and my throat suddenly felt tight. In spite of my mother's best efforts, I had grown up more prepared to answer a reckless call to adventure than to answer the sort of question that comes from a nervous young man fidgeting with a ring in his vest pocket. He did look awfully sweet.

"You spoke very eloquently last night," he said. "About choices. About not avoiding them until it is too late. I have something to ask you—and I do not wish to wait until it is too late."

"Yes?"

"I–I have been thinking a lot, lately," said Charlie, holding the door for me as we stepped into the foyer. The desk within had been shoved aside to make room for the now-slumbering giant, whose gentle snores made the windows rattle. The gnomes in their violet hats were sitting in a circle by his arm, playing a game of dice. "I've been thinking about the future, should we have one," Charlie continued. "I have been thinking about . . ." He stumbled. "My . . . family."

"Charlie," I said, reaching a hand out to his faintly trembling arm.

"KAZIMIR CAINE!" roared a deep, rumbling voice. A man dressed in black furs with a thick salt-and-pepper beard had been slouched on the battered waiting bench. He launched himself upright abruptly, startling the young woman sitting next to him.

Charlie froze. The man lunged at him, and I wondered for a moment if the big brute was going to take his head off, but then there was a patting of backs and Charlie was returning a vigorous hug.

"Uncle Dragomir!" he said, pulling out of the bear hug. The girl on the bench had risen as well. She had dark, curly hair and wore a long traveling cloak. "Alina!" As Charlie hurried to embrace her, the resemblance was unmistakable; this was Charlie's sister. "What are you two doing here?" Charlie asked, looking delighted but dumbfounded. Alina's eyes dropped and she swallowed hard.

"The question is, what are *you* doing here?" Dragomir's voice was heavy with Slavic syllables. I had grown so accustomed to Charlie's subtler accent, it was easy to forget sometimes that his was largely Americanized. "We've heard things. There is talk of trouble on the rise. I had no idea it was this bad."

Dragomir sneered as he glanced around the room. One

of the gnomes had apparently gotten either a very good roll or a very bad one, and his kinsmen erupted into a flurry of discontent. The giant snorted and rolled over in his sleep, sending the gnomes scrambling to get out of his way.

"I cannot say I am surprised. Even as a pup, you were always causing trouble. Your father had such hopes for you, even after you left. And now little Kazimir, son of the great Suveran of the Om Caini, has fallen in with this lot. Rousing quite a rabble, as I hear it. You are living up to your name, aren't you?"

"What is that supposed to mean?" I said, but Charlie shook his head, abashed.

"It means," Dragomir said, glaring at me, "that I keep the peace. It is my job in our family. I am the—how do you say—arbiter. Kazimir does the opposite."

"Charlie isn't the one causing this mess," I rebutted, "and neither are we. Charlie is a peacekeeper as well. He's a policeman."

"Why do you keep calling him such a ridiculous name? What kind of name is *Charlie* for the heir to the House of Caine?"

I chose not to point out that Charlie had adopted a different surname as well, as of late. "We're the ones trying to help, sir," I said. "My employer and I have spoken to Lord Arawn. He keeps the gates between our world and the Annwyn, and he will soon be alerting the leaders of his neighboring kingdoms."

"Don't lecture me on things you do not understand, child. Arawn doesn't need to tell his neighbors anything." Dragomir's voice was confident and proud. "The otherworlds already know all about your hole in the veil. It is the topic of every trader and traveler between the realms. The Om Caini have good ears. We know how to listen."

"Well, that's grand, then. Jackaby will be glad to hear it," I said. "We could use the support. There is an organization at work called the Dire Council. They are the ones responsible for the rend; we're sure of it. We've nullified a few of their number, but we are still trying to track down the Dire King."

Dragomir looked unimpressed. "That's not how the story is going in the otherworlds. Word among the elves and dwarves is that humans are preparing to invade the Annwyn. They say the rend came from your side of the veil. They are saying that the humans have grown bold."

"What?" I said. "That's ridiculous!"

"Is it?" said Dragomir. "You should tell that to the refugees cowering in this house. The kingdoms of the Annwyn are not happy about you humans right now. They're not happy with Arawn, either. They are saying that the fair folk aren't strong enough to hold the barrier any longer. They are saying that the fair folk used to have powerful leaders. Hafgan was strong. They are saying Hafgan could've held the barrier."

"That's utter lunacy!" I said. "Hafgan's acolytes are the ones trying to tear it down!"

"That's not how I hear it. Anyway, it doesn't matter. The Om Caini are neutral. We stay out of politics. If I did choose sides—which I won't—then you might not like the side I choose, girl."

"This isn't about politics, Uncle Dragomir," Charlie pressed. "It's about principles. It doesn't matter what side you're on; the Dire King is a hateful, dangerous force—and if he is not opposed, he will bring death and destruction to *all* sides. The earth and the Annwyn are going to tear each other apart."

"I sometimes wonder if that would not be for the best," said Dragomir coldly. "A culling. A flood, like the old days. Tomorrow's forest grows stronger for yesterday's fire, does it not?" He huffed. "This is not our war. We're leaving, Kazimir. We only came to fetch you and be on our way. Come."

"What?" Charlie and I both managed at the same time.

"I can't leave now," said Charlie. "Tell my father—"

"Your father is dead," Dragomir barked. Charlie froze, speechless. Slowly his expression crumbled. Dragomir ground his teeth and closed his eyes. When he opened them again, his voice was softer. "Your father is dead, and your people need you—or have you spent so much time with humans you have forgotten your loyalty?" He narrowed his eyes in my direction.

"I know what it is to be loyal." Charlie stood his ground. "And I have spent enough time with humans to know what it is to be honorable, as well. I loved my father, but the House of Caine is not even a house—not any longer. Maybe it was once. But now—" He looked down, pained. "I am tired of running away from the world, Uncle. I swore an oath to this city. This is my home to protect. My peace to keep. I can't abandon them now."

Dragomir gave a gravelly sigh. "I warned your parents about you when you were still small. I saw it in you even then. I am only grateful they did not live long enough to see you turn on your family like this. It would have broken their hearts."

"That's enough!" Alina spoke out at last. "Both of you! Some peacekeepers you are. You can't see each other for five minutes without snarling at each other's throats."

Dragomir sneered. "Let him have his way. We will tell our people that their wandering Kazimir has chosen *this* over his own family. Come, Alina. We are done here."

"No." Alina stood rooted to the floorboards. "I lost my father—I am not leaving without my brother."

"Alina, he's right," said Charlie, delicately. "It isn't safe for you here, not now. You should go back with Uncle."

"No. Not without you." She crossed her arms and sat back down on the bench.

"Alina," Dragomir commanded. "You will do as you are bid!"

"You are not my father," she said. "And you are not the Suveran, no matter how much you might wish it. I did not travel halfway around the world to watch you two yap at each other and then turn around and go home with my tail between my legs."

Dragomir's shoulders rose and fell and he took several slow breaths. "You two are too young to know your own stupidity. I was not much older when your father and I faced the torches and pitchforks in Belgrade. You are not the first of our kind to give them a chance, Kazimir. Our people will never be safe around *them*."

Charlie looked down miserably.

"You stood by Father's side then," said Alina. "Let me stand by my brother's now."

"Argh!" Dragomir shook his head. "You are so much like your mother! I forget sometimes how stubborn she could be. Always so . . . so . . . How do you say . . . ?"

"Dogged." Alina gave him a sly smile. "I will be safe, Uncle. My Kazimir is here. I will bring him home. He will listen to me."

Dragomir allowed himself a hint of a smile. He waggled a finger at his niece. "Dogged," he said. "Yes, you are. Fine. See if you cannot make the idiot pup see reason. I wash my hands of the both of you."

In spite of his bluster, before he left he cupped Alina's head in his hands and kissed her forehead. *"Ai grija de tine,"* he whispered. He straightened his furs haughtily and pulled open the door, pausing once more before he stepped through it. "And you." He jabbed a finger at Charlie. "Don't be so stupid."

"Who's stupid?" The sound of Hank Hudson's voice made Dragomir jump. He spun as the trapper mounted the front step right in front of him. "Oh, hey, nice coat. That bearskin?"

Dragomir bristled and pushed past the trapper without reply.

"Ray o' sunshine, isn't he?" Hudson jabbed a thumb at Dragomir's retreating figure. "Well, you ready to hit the road, Chuck?"

"Chuck?" said Alina with a sour face.

"Charlie," I said.

"His name is Kazimir Caine," said Alina, watching the trapper with leery eyes.

"News to me," said Hudson. "*Charlie Barker* suits our boy just fine." Hudson patted Charlie firmly on the back. Charlie winced.

"Barker?" Alina raised an eyebrow.

"It is necessary," Charlie said. "And . . . I sort of like it."

"So, who's the little lady?" Hudson asked. "Friend of yours?"

"This is my sister," Charlie said.

"Okey-dokey. She stayin' at the house, too?"

"She really should not." Charlie turned pleadingly back to his sister. "Alina, you can still catch up with Uncle Dragomir—"

"I did not just ride in the belly of a great stinking ship for weeks to go chasing after Uncle Dragomir," she said. "Are you so eager to leave me again?"

"No, no, it's not that." Charlie looked miserably conflicted. "We are in the middle of something very important. Look, if you are going to stay, then stay here at the house. The city is . . . not itself lately. I need to go out for a while, but this house is safest, for now. More or less."

"Do mind the spriggans on the staircase," I said. "And the Dangerous Documents section. And avoid the whole north wing of the second floor. In fact, maybe it's best if you just stay with me. I would be happy to show you around."

Alina looked at me as though she were deciding whether to swat at me with the heel of her boot or catch me under a drinking glass and shoo me outside. "I am not staying here with this woman," she said.

"This woman is Abigail Rook," Charlie said. "And she is my—my friend. I would trust her with my life. In fact, I have. Very recently. Miss Rook, may I formally introduce my sister, Alina."

"A pleasure," she mumbled, casting me a smile that could wither daisies.

"I'm sure we'll get on splendidly," I said, trying to sound cheery. "I'll take you to see the duck pond; that might be nice."

"I have seen duck ponds."

"Ours is on the third floor," I said through gritted teeth. "And there are centaurs. Have you seen that?"

"Ipotanes," corrected Jackaby, bustling into the room. "The centaurs were relocated to the back garden." He was stuffing his arms through the sleeves of his battered old coat.

"Oh! Mr. Jackaby, I would like you to meet–" Charlie began.

Jackaby glanced up. "A fellow Om Caini, yes, I see. Very close genetic line. Sister?"

"Er–yes. Alina, this is Mr. R. F. Jackaby, he–"

"–is off to ensure that the streets of our fair city are free of the wandering corpses of the undead," Jackaby finished. "Sorry, Miss Lee is already waiting for me. I really have no time for all that *How are you? I am fine, thanks. Here's another inane question. Here's an equally banal reply. Charmed. Delighted.* nonsense."

"They're called niceties, sir," I said. "People say them."

"They're stupid. And people are stupid." He paused at the front door. "Come to think of it, the word *nice* used to mean stupid, so I suppose that's apt."

"Good-bye, Mr. Jackaby," I said. "Do be careful."

"Right." He tossed open the door. "Don't forget to feed the pixies and to interrogate the murderess in the cellar. Oh, and the azalea could use some watering."

And then he was gone, the cheery red door banging shut behind him.

"We oughta be goin', too, chum," said Hudson. "I got the horses waitin' out front."

Charlie nodded. "If you will not return home with Uncle Dragomir, promise me you will wait here at the house until I get back?" he implored Alina.

"Where I am safe, you mean?" she said. "With the humans and the giants and the—what was that about a murderess in the cellar?"

Charlie cringed. "Yes, with those. I'll be back this evening," he said. "And then we will talk. Like we used to." Charlie leaned in and put his forehead against Alina's. "I promise."

Alina sighed. "Go, then. I will wait for you. I have plenty of practice."

Hudson pulled open the door. Charlie slid away from Alina and turned to me. "Miss Rook," he said, his eyes looking agonized as he hunted for the words to fill the awkward pause.

"We'll have our time," I said, putting a hand to his chest and hoping I was telling the truth. "Be safe."

Charlie stepped out into the daylight, and Hudson gave us all a quick wave as he closed the door behind them.

Chapter Twelve

By the time I finally found myself plodding across the back garden to interrogate Morwen Finstern, my patience for contrary company had been worn threadbare. In spite of my best efforts, the tour I had given Alina had quickly become a long, sullen march punctuated only by sighs and peevish observations. Jenny had caught up with us and suggested I give the girl a chance to be involved rather than simply kept out of the way, to which Alina had agreed without enthusiasm. Happy to take anything short of patent disgust as a glowing endorsement, I consented, and so we made our way toward the cellar together.

I drew the iron key out of my pocket as we approached the cellar door. The ipotanes paid us no mind, grazing casually on the ivy and the drooping azaleas. As I drew my key toward the heavy iron lock, I paused. There were voices coming from within. Morwen's I recognized at once, but then there came, very softly, another voice. It was muffled, indistinct. Morwen's followed it. "I will," was all she said.

"Why are you waiting?" asked Alina, behind me. She was holding a plate with a bruised apple and a slice of leftover *kunafah* I had thrown together as today's rations for the nixie. I would not typically have wasted such exquisite fare on our unwilling guest, but Shihab had not produced anything unpleasant enough to fit the bill, and with Alina in tow, I did not feel up to cooking an entire meal just for the sake of its being awful. On the other hand, that particular slice of pastry had fallen on the floor earlier, which made me feel a little better about feeding it to Jenny's killer.

"Shh. There's someone else in there," I whispered. "Jenny, do you think you could peek inside before I open the door?"

"The cellar is safeguarded." She shook her head. "The wards that Jackaby put up against evil spirits work just as well on me, I'm afraid."

"The direct approach it is, then." I jammed the key in the lock and pulled open the door.

Morwen sat alone in the pool of light, squinting as we climbed down into the clammy cellar. "Lunchtime already?" she said. "More overcooked onions, I assume?"

"No onions this time. Just a little dust and scruffy pony hair," I said. "Who were you talking to?"

Morwen smiled. "Wouldn't you like to know?"

"Yes, I would. Which is why I asked."

Morwen ignored the question and glanced between the three of us. "It's good you brought the whole entourage—there's safety in numbers. Wouldn't want an innocent little girl tied to a chair to hurt you, now would you?" As she said it, Morwen's features fluidly shifted, making her look even younger than Alina, blinking up, doe-eyed and pouty-lipped. "I'm ever so frightful, aren't I?"

"Nobody is impressed," I said. I was, a little. After all, watching a shape-shifter transform before your very eyes is a mesmerizing spectacle, even if the woman behind the face is a monster—but I wasn't about to admit that to Morwen.

Morwen shrugged, her features rapidly aging to settle back into her usual visage. "Not impressed, perhaps—but I have got you nervous, now, haven't I? You should be. My father has already sent for me." Morwen smiled wickedly.

"Really?" I said. "He seemed much more interested in picking up some new accessories than in rescuing his daughter. Did you hear he has a shiny new hat to go with his spear?"

"The Dire Crown is not a hat," said Morwen. "It is a manifestation of his power and glory."

"Do you know what I think?" I replied. "I think that now that he has the whole set, he doesn't need you at all. It was the shield that really tied the ensemble together, don't you think?"

Morwen sneered. "Your lies are pitiful. He doesn't have the–" She caught herself.

"Doesn't have the shield yet?" I finished for her. "No, I didn't think so, but it's nice to have that confirmed. I do appreciate your being so candid today."

"You don't even know what you don't know," she hissed. "I will kill you last, I think. You'd better tell all your little friends to sleep with one eye open."

"Like ducks," I said, casually.

Morwen faltered. "What?"

"Ducks sleep with one eye open. Douglas does, anyway, so I guess I don't need to tell him to. Mr. Jackaby doesn't tend to sleep much at all, and when he does it's with his third eye open whether he likes it or not, so that's him covered as well. Jenny–well, you know very well that you couldn't harm Jenny even if she ever did sleep. Which reminds me," I added conversationally, "do you remember the last time you threatened everyone? And then she hit you?"

Morwen glowered at me.

"With a bathtub?" I added, helpfully. "Through a wall?"

"It rings a bell," Morwen growled icily.

"It certainly rang yours," Jenny added.

"Get your kicks in while you can," Morwen said. And then she did something thoroughly unnerving. She smiled. It was the absolute confidence of it. The only other person

I had ever seen who could maintain such unflappable calm while chained up as a prisoner was Mr. Jackaby. On Morwen, the attitude was far more ominous. "I will be out of here by morning," she added.

"You sound awfully sure of yourself for someone who's been peeing in a hole in the dirt all week," said Jenny.

"Aw. Don't get all sentimental just because you're going to miss me, *Jennybean*," Morwen taunted. "I might just have to take a . . . *souvenir* to remember you all by. How about your new friend here? She's cute, isn't she?" Morwen's strawberry blond curls rippled and darkened, and suddenly she was looking up at us with Alina's face. "The council could make good use of you, little girl."

Alina staggered back a step, shaken, and the apple rolled off the plate and into the corner.

"Or how about the other one." The nixie turned her eyes on me. "That dog-boy who keeps trotting after you? What's he called again?" She wavered, and suddenly Charlie was sitting before us. "Mees Roook," she mocked. The face was spot on, but her voice talents were lacking something when it came to impersonating men. "Don't let the beeg bad neexie take mee!"

"You're not going anywhere," I said evenly. "And you're not taking anyone with you. Now, you're going to tell us–"

The plate clattered suddenly on the ground, flaky pastry sliding to one side, and Alina rushed up the stairs and back out into the light.

"Alina, wait," I called.

"Something I said?" Morwen grinned wickedly.

I glanced up at the doorway and back at Morwen. "We'll finish this later."

We found Alina in the garden, slumped at the foot of the weeping willow. The centaurs had edged away toward the side of the house, and the garden was peaceful and quiet.

Jenny hovered beside her. "Alina," she said, soothingly. "You can't let Morwen get to you. She likes to wriggle under your skin until you're not yourself anymore."

"Why?" Alina shook her head. "I don't understand!"

"It's just the way she is. She—"

"Not the nixie. I don't care about the nixie. Why is my brother part of this?" She looked up at me, her eyes more angry than afraid. "She said it—Kazimir goes trotting after you. Why?"

"She was only being spiteful," I said. "Charlie and I help each other. Nobody is trotting after anyone."

"I've seen the way you look at him. This is your fault, isn't it?"

"My fault?"

"Why don't you leave him be? Kazimir is not like you! He is not one of you! He deserves better than . . . than . . . than *this*!" She threw up her hands. "Our father was Suveran—do you even know what that means? It means Kazimir is heir to the House of Caine! He is born to rule our people, not to play lapdog to some human cur."

I ground my teeth. "Charlie *chose* this! Charlie chose *me*. If you really love your brother, maybe you should stop hating the world that he has chosen to be a part of. What do you have against humans, anyway? You're half human yourself!"

Alina shook her head in disgust. "You have no right to define me. I am Om Caini. You know nothing of our history and nothing of our heritage."

"Is it your heritage to pick on human beings every chance you get? Because I'm beginning to know a little something about that."

"How dare you! My people chose peace. Humans broke that peace. Do your children not learn about that in human school? No, I suppose they teach you all lies about noble human heroes defeating a race of lowly dogs instead, do they?"

"Erm, neither?" I said. "I don't think I've ever met anyone besides Charlie who has ever even heard of the Om Caini. Well, Jackaby. But he knows about everything. Most of New Fiddleham thinks your brother is a werewolf. They've heard of those."

Alina wrinkled up her nose. "Of course they have. *Idioti*. Still, better a werewolf than a human. At least wolves open their eyes."

"Then open mine," I said, as gently as I could. "I'd like to know. Really. How did humans break the peace?"

She regarded me dubiously. "How much do you know about the days before the veil?"

"Until a few months ago," I admitted, "I was not aware there was a veil at all, let alone that there was a time before it. Please tell me."

She shook her head. She still looked cynical, but a little less disgusted, in spite of my ignorance. "This is basic history," she said. "Pups in our tribe know it before we know how to read. Millennia ago, when the veil was new, all of the noble races divided. Those who lived by magic were given the Annwyn. Those who lived by toil and earnest work were given the earth. Those who walked the line were given a choice. And so it came to be that the world was split in two."

"Does that mean the Annwyn used to be physically connected to the earth?" I asked. "Like, another continent?"

Alina rolled her eyes. "More than connected. They were . . . ugh, you are too simple to understand. Here, I will show you the way we show the littlest whelps. Cross your eyes. Like this. You see two of me? Yes? Two trees? Two everything? You see the world split into two worlds. That is how the Annwyn was divided from the earth."

"Oh," I said. "I think I understand. They're really the same physical space, only one side got all the magic bits and the other kept all the mortal bits."

"Yes . . . but also not the same at all. Remember, this

is how we explain it to the simple children. The details are . . . beyond you."

I bit my lip diplomatically.

"After the divide, my people remained on earth. We trusted men, held dominion alongside men. We were loyal allies. Their quarrels had always been with the magi and the fair folk, not with those who walked the land by their side, and so our kingdoms were united, for a time. There was trade, there was sport, there was courtly respect—but humans are only ever satisfied to be victors."

Her eyes grew cold again.

"My ancestors watched as our people were slaughtered during the first of the Breed Wars. They packed their things and fled from their ancestral homes, fled from their own kingdoms, but there was nowhere for them to run. In each new country they were met with greater hostility. We are nomads now. The Om Caini are strong. We have made a good life out of what we were given, but we have not forgotten our past. We have learned to be guarded. We have learned the worth of human promises."

"Human beings can be horrible," I conceded. "Monstrous. But there are good people, too, if you really look. People who make the world better. This city is full of . . . of doors opening. Charlie taught me to see that. I cannot take away what was done to your family, but please try to see what Charlie sees. He sees hope. He believes in this town. He has seen it at its very worst, but somehow he still believes. He sees a future for us here, together." Something unexpected stirred inside me as I put that into words.

"You still don't get it," Alina said, pushing herself up from the roots of the willow. "*This* is not Charlie's future! This isn't some silly human story about star-crossed lovers! Kazimir cannot stay here. Charlie may not have a throne and a castle to come home to, but he is no less a king. You have no idea how much it grieves me to watch him, my brother, Suveran of my people, running errands for an arrogant human fool and his insignificant assistant. You selfish humans would have a noble king as your lowly servant? How can you let him lower himself to this? Does it make you feel powerful? Does it make you feel proud? Our people *need* my brother. Why won't you let him come home?" And with that she stalked off hotly toward the house.

"Charlie *chose* this!" I yelled after her. "Nobody is keeping him against his will!"

"Because that would be unthinkable," came Morwen's muffled voice from the cellar.

"Oh, shut up." I slid down against the tree.

"Give her time," Jenny said, drifting slowly to my side. "She's young, she's headstrong, and she's overwhelmed in a strange new world. Sound familiar?"

"I wasn't so bullheaded when I got off the boat," I said. "I was *nice*."

"It sounds to me like that girl has spent her whole life being taught to keep her guard up. It's not her fault. It will take more than one uncomfortable afternoon around the house to bring it down. Be patient. Charlie loves her, doesn't he?"

"He does," I said. "I can't imagine why. She's a nightmare!"

"Why don't you take your own advice, then, Abigail. Try to see what Charlie sees. He's not such a terrible judge of character, you know." Jenny gave me an encouraging wink. "He did choose you, didn't he?"

Chapter Thirteen

Out of respect for my employer, Chapter Thirteen has been omitted. Accounts of these hours can now be found in the Dangerous Documents section, but only if you really know where to look.

Chapter Fourteen

As the day wore on, the mythical menagerie of creatures pervading our house had begun to settle into their own idiosyncratic routines. The ladies of a feather sharing my bedroom flocked together to the duck pond after lunch for a quick birdbath. The satyrs alternated between sneaking up to peep at them through the bushes and slipping into the library to harass the nymphs. Several swarms of spriggans, pixies, and other wee folk had found their way into the walls by midafternoon, which kept the passages a bit less crowded but generated a near-constant chittering, skittering sound that occasionally ended in eruptions of plaster. By early evening, Chief Nudd had returned with a few members of his horde and they had joined the gnomes at their dice game in the foyer.

In addition to the steady stream of the furry, flighty, and fantastical, I was also pleasantly surprised to greet a few familiar human faces. I had been checking on Shihab when I heard Hank Hudson's voice in the hallway.

"Mr. Hudson," I said, stepping out to greet him. "You're back. Lovely. Is Charlie . . ." I glanced up and down the hallway.

"He an' that sister of his skedaddled upstairs to have a little chat. Said he'd be back down soon. Jackaby around?"

"Ah, of course. No, he's still out, but we're expecting him any minute. Did you two meet with any support while canvassing the city?" I asked.

"Loads!" Hudson said, brightly. "Surprising amount, actually, along with one story after another about stuff ol' Jackaby had personally done to save a shop, or soothe some ailing granny, or rescue some kidnapped baby. Yer boss sure keeps himself busy, don't he?"

"He's not a fan of sitting still," I agreed. "Ah, that may be him now. If you'll excuse me."

The front door closed as I came around the corner. It was not Jackaby, but Lieutenant Dupin. He was off duty, but still wearing his uniform and visibly nervous.

I thanked him for coming and finally shared with him the full details of Steven Fairmont's unholy rise from the dead, as well as Charlie's and my part in putting a stop to the creature. Dupin listened attentively, looking solemn and a little wan by the end.

"I know it sounds like lunacy," I concluded, "but there you have it."

"Lunacy has become reality in New Fiddleham of late," Dupin sighed. "Thank you for your report, Miss Rook, and for your service. Will you tell Detective Cane—or Barker, or whatever it is now—will you tell him that there are still officers like me who have not lost faith in him as one of our own. Marlowe may not have put his support in writing, but he has his own sort of inner circle. Some of us are still loyal to his command over Spade's. We will heed the call when you need us."

"You can tell him that yourself if you would care to wait," I offered. "He just nipped upstairs. I'm sure he won't be long. Why don't I just put a kettle on?"

Dupin smiled regretfully. "Your hospitality does you credit, Miss Rook," he said. "But I think, perhaps, I have overstayed my welcome as it is."

I glanced behind me to see what he was talking about. The gnomes and goblins were glaring daggers at Dupin, and I could see several pairs of eyes peering out from the doorway that led to the rest of the house. None of them looked welcoming.

"Good night, Miss Rook, and good luck."

"Oh, for pity's sake," I scolded the house after he had gone. "He's on your side. You've got ears, haven't you? He wants to help."

The sleepy giant sat up, which brought him to a modest

looming rather than a full towering. He opened his mouth and rumbled something that sounded like a pride of French lions growling at each other from within the depths of a deep cave.

"Come again?"

"He said yon copper was nae much help when they was lockin' up grannies an' babes in irons," Chief Nudd said. Violet hats bobbed behind him as the gnomes nodded their agreement. "Ye kinna blame folk for bein' a mite skittish 'round a uniform."

I scowled. "No, I suppose I can't. But we can't meet prejudice with prejudice, either. Like them or not, we will need all the help we can get."

Another friendly face arrived shortly after Dupin had let himself out. Hatun walked like royalty in her rags, nodding amiably to the various figures around her. She was a woman with a unique view of the world—a view at least partially shaped by her perpetually shifting residence. Hatun had no house, but all of New Fiddleham was her home. She looked out for her city, and for everyone in it, from the wealthiest citizen in the tallest building to the lowliest troll under the darkest bridge. Truth be told, she preferred the company of the troll.

Hatun was met with a much warmer reception than the policeman had been. Though it probably should not have come as a surprise, I was taken aback by just how many of our paranormal lodgers seemed to know her by name, and how thoroughly unfazed she was by their appearances. Jackaby had once explained that at different times, Hatun saw the same world that everyone else saw, or the world as it really was, or the world as it really wasn't. It was hard for Hatun to be certain which version was real at any given moment, so she had learned to appraise reality flexibly. In addition, as I had experienced firsthand, Hatun sometimes saw the world as it was *going* to be–which I found to be by far the most unsettling.

Hatun promptly sat herself down on the bench in the foyer and took out a pair of knitting needles already hung with a mess of wool–or rather she took out one knitting needle and what appeared to be an ice pick with a cracked handle–and began to knit and purl away merrily while an unruly pile of assorted colors spilled out of her floppy satchel like drunken, flamboyant spaghetti.

"It's lovely to see you again, Hatun," I said.

"Miss Rook. Hope your boss is happy. I keep clear of waiting rooms, as a rule," she said. "No hospitals. No dentists. I haven't sat down to have a proper wait in a proper building with a proper roof and everything for nigh on two decades now. Hope he appreciates the lengths I go to. You can tell him I'm here."

"I'm afraid Mr. Jackaby is away just at the moment," I said. "He should be back shortly–but I should tell you, he's rather busy making arrangements for some very urgent matters–"

"Of course he's busy." Hatun cut me off, finally looking up from her knitting. "That's why I'm here. You look very pretty in that frock, by the way, dear. Orange really is your best color."

"Oh, erm, thank you. It's . . . it's green. Why did you say you were here?"

"That young fellow and the great big hairy one who smells like dried meat came around earlier, and they told me all about the meeting."

"Oh, of course. Misters Barker and Hudson. Yes, I'm afraid the big meeting they're organizing is set for tomorrow evening. Tonight there will only be a handful of us getting ready."

"Handful suits me, dear. Never been a fan of big crowds, anyway."

"Oh, erm, I don't know if Mr. Jackaby really intended for—"

"Jackaby doesn't ask for help," she said. "Not like this. I've known him a lot of years. He accepts it from time to time, usually when everything else has slipped through his fingers or blown up in his face, but he has never reached out for it like this before. Never."

I opened my mouth and then closed it again, not sure how to respond to this.

"He's scared out of his damn mind," Hatun cussed. "And he should be. He's the only person in this whole city people can turn to when they're facing something bigger than they know how to wrap their brains around. I'm not stupid. If he's grasping for straws, then whatever this is, it's bigger than him."

"It's not good," I admitted. "But I am still hopeful."

"No you aren't," said Hatun, waving the needle as though she were swatting the words away like fruit flies. "Hoping is a thing that other people do while people like you are rolling up your shirtsleeves and getting to work. I know. I'm like you, Miss Rook, and I am rolling up my sleeves, too. I'll be joining you folks tonight, thank you very much, and I will not be waiting around for the pretty version that you've trimmed up with a nice bow for the crowd tomorrow." She turned back to her wool, and the clicking resumed.

Jenny drifted up behind me. She would never have shown herself to a visitor under normal circumstances. "Let her stay," Jenny said. Hovering gracefully beside the bench, she turned to Hatun. "I'm sure Mr. Jackaby would be honored to have you with us. Thank you."

"Hey. I know you." Hatun squinted her eyes. "You used to go walking by the park with that handsome Carson boy, didn't you? Used to see you out and about almost every day. What was it, five years back?"

"More like ten," said Jenny, softly.

"You look different." Hatun peered at the translucent figure hovering in front of her. "Were you less dead back then?"

Jenny's eyebrows rose. "Erm, yes. Much less."

"That's what it is, then. Yep, I knew I remembered you." The needle and ice pick resumed their clicking. "So. You been well?"

"Have I been well, since before I died?" asked Jenny. "Well. I've had a few ups and . . . downs."

Hatun nodded amiably. "I expect so."

"Make yourself comfortable, Hatun," I cut in. "Mr. Jackaby should not be much longer. I'll just go and put the kettle on."

"Don't fuss over me, dearie," Hatun said, leaning back as she clicked away. She gave a glance to the corner as Nudd and his horde cackled and the gnomes shook their stubby little fists and grumbled. "Go mingle with your friends. I think that handsome fellow over there is making eyes at you."

I glanced where she was looking. "I don't think so," I said. "Also, I believe that one might be a lady. Although it is hard to tell with goblins. I think the males have less hair. Or more hair? Anyway, I'm spoken for. I've been going with Charlie Barker, remember."

"Which one's Charlie again?" Hatun asked. "Is he the one who killed all those people, or the one who can turn into a hedgehog?"

"Into a hound. And he hasn't killed anybody."

"Oh, well, he sounds nice, then." Hatun's knitting dropped into her lap. "Just mind the . . . the . . . the blade."

"The blade?" I said.

Hatun didn't answer at first. Her eyes were out of focus and she looked as though she were trying to look through a heavy mist. A tingle rippled up the back of my neck. I had seen that look before. "The blade," Hatun said, hollowly. "The black blade, the spear. Not the spear–the Seer. Under the blade, the Seer–oh!" She winced as though struck. "The Seer falls. The Seer is lost." Her head sagged.

"The Seer is lost? What do you mean lost? Jackaby's lost?"

"Hmm?" Hatun lifted her head. "What's that you lost? Got to be more careful, dear. That's why I keep a spare one tucked away in my stockings, just in case."

"Mr. Jackaby!" I said. "You were just talking about Mr. Jackaby!"

"Was I?"

"Please try to remember," I implored her. "How is Mr. Jackaby going to be lost?"

"You're talking a lot of nonsense. Jackaby is right there."

I spun. True enough, Jackaby had just walked through the front door. Lydia Lee was behind him, looking rather jumpy as she closed the door.

"Honestly, Miss Rook," Hatun chided, resuming her knitting. "Can't go around saying all sorts of silly things. People will start to say you're crazy."

The Dangerous Documents section was officially crowded beyond capacity. Jackaby stood at the head of the table, and I slid in on his right. Hudson shuffled in next to me, then

Jenny, Chief Nudd, Lydia Lee, and Hatun. Hatun sat in one of the only chairs and Nudd stood on the other. Charlie slid in apologetically just as Jackaby was getting ready to speak. He squeezed in at the far end, between Miss Lee and Nudd.

"Thank you all for coming again," Jackaby began. "Let's not waste time. To begin with, I would like to reassure everyone that, while there appears to be an upswing in paranormal activity on the whole, there do not appear to be any further walking corpses in New Fiddleham, which we can all agree is a very positive first step."

"Walking what, dear?" Hatun asked. She had pulled out her little project and was untangling a knot of wool on the table.

"Ah," Jackaby said. "Nice of you to join us, Hatun. No cause for alarm. Charlie and Abigail yesterday encountered a small abomination: an undead fellow who had risen from the grave to feast on the living. Nothing fancy. Only took one victim. You will all be happy to hear that Ned Short is still dead, by the way. I checked. Twice. By *happy*, I mean *sad*, of course—but the good news is that his steadfast necrosis seems to confirm that this strain of postmortal reanimation is neither a viral nor a transferrable phenomenon. That is to say—we can't catch it. Which is, you know, quite good on the whole."

"That's something," Jenny agreed.

"Well, what about the rest of you?" Jackaby glanced around the circle. "Reinforcements?"

"We've put the word out," said Charlie.

"I 'spect we'll see a lotta folks tomorrow night," Hudson added.

"Good." Jackaby looked at me. "Any luck with your interrogation?"

"Some," I answered. "Not much, I'm afraid. The council is definitely still looking for the shield, though."

"That brings us to you, then, Nudd." Jackaby addressed the chief. "Have your goblins learned anything about Hafgan's shield?"

"Aye. We learned tha' lookin' fer it is righ' bootless. Yer definitely nae th' only one tryin'."

"Did you learn who else has been making inquiries?"

"Aye, but tha' hardly narrows it doon. Everyone. *Huntin' Hafgan's shield* is such a time-honored tradition among th' Unseelie, it's apparently a sayin'."

"Like an idiom?" I said. "You mean they say *hunting Hafgan's shield* the way we say *a fool's errand* or *a wild goose chase?*"

"Thassit. Idiom. But why wouldja chase a goose?" Nudd wrinkled up his nose. "Geese is terrifyin'."

"Yes, yes. We can all agree that geese are the worst of birds," said Jackaby. "So, everybody wants to find the shield and nobody knows where to look. We have learned nothing. This leaves us with slightly more haystack and still no needle."

"I did find oot a little summat aboot yon spear, though,"

Nudd added. "When Hafgan was the Dire King, 'e 'ad a spear made for 'im as black as pitch, with a crown as dark as nigh', right? Well, after he lost th' legendary battle wit' Arawn, they say th' spear was shattered to pieces. Hafgan's toadies collected up the pieces after an' had 'em reforged."

"Father Grafton did say it had been broken and remade," Jackaby recalled.

"But 'ere's the interestin' bit," Nudd pressed on. "So, th' spear is still aroond—only 'tisn't a spear at all any longer. When it was recast, it was recast as a sword. They calls it th' black blade."

I choked. "Did you say *the black blade*?"

I glanced at Hatun, who was blithely tying off the end of her yarn, apparently satisfied with her—whatever it was. Her finished project appeared to be a somewhat less disorganized pile of colorful wool. She tucked the ice pick and the needle back into her floppy bag.

"Thassit. Issa thing o' legend among the smithies in' th' underlands."

Jackaby and I locked eyes.

"That slippery nixie!" Jackaby slapped the table. "Morwen had the black blade all the time! It's in my office right now! With all our infuriating fruitless searches and dead ends, we've had one of the instruments of Hafgan all along! No wonder we've gotten under the Dire King's skin! We didn't just take his daughter—we put ourselves one step ahead of him without even knowing where our feet were!"

With much bumping of elbows and treading on toes, we spilled out of the corridor of bookshelves. Jackaby took the lead, pulling open the door to the library and nearly bowling over a woman who stood outside. She was dressed in blue robes, and she had honey blond hair and an ivory scar that cut across one cheek.

"Serif?" Jackaby said when he had recovered his footing. "What on earth are you doing . . . on earth?"

"My Lord Arawn has requested a report of your progress," she answered stiffly. "I am here to collect it. Your duck let me in."

"Excellent timing!" Jackaby's unfiltered enthusiasm made the corner of Serif's lip twitch where it met the scar on her cheek. "Because while your Lord Arawn has been misplacing instruments of Hafgan, we have been placing them. We've secured Hafgan's spear!"

Serif followed him as he swept past her and into his office, the rest of us hurrying after. There, on the bookshelf, right where Jackaby had left it, Morwen Finstern's black blade . . . wasn't. The shelf was empty. The sword was gone.

Chapter Fifteen

T he sword . . . the spear–" Jackaby stammered.

"The spear grips the hand," said a very small voice. All eyes spun until we locked on to an unassuming little lump of hair sitting in the corner of the bookshelf. The twain rolled itself up to sitting. He was as physically intimidating as a boiled potato, but something about the diminutive fellow gave me the shivers.

"You are in alliance with a twain?" Serif put a hand to the hilt of her sword, her body suddenly tense and battle-ready. "Whose side are you on?" she demanded.

Jackaby held out a calming hand. "This is not an alliance. This is"–he turned back to the little figure on his desk–"I'm not certain what this is. *The spear grips the hand.* You said that before."

"It's from an old poem," the twain said.

"I know it," growled Serif. "I've heard it said that Hafgan wrote it himself."

"He didn't," the twain said. "The Dire King never bothered with poetry, but he liked it. It was probably his minstrel, Pughe. That one was always good with words."

"I'm sure he was. Where is my blade?" Jackaby asked.

The twain sighed. "It's yours now?" he tutted. "Shame."

"Ach, did'nae I tell ye?" Nudd burst out. "Ne'er trust a twain! Where's yer wee partner, then, twain? Off givin' th' blade to th' Dire King hisself?"

"She is dead," said the twain, flatly.

"His partner?" I asked.

"A twain always has a partner," Serif confirmed. "They are born together. Bonded."

"Thass where th' name comes from," added Nudd. "They's always twain, ne'er a single. I don' trust him a brownie's breath. Twain don' jus' die. Not alone. They's near enough ta immortal, them."

"It is true," the twain said.

"How'd she kick it, then?"

The twain offered Nudd a hollow gaze. Not empty-acorn-shell hollow; it was the sort of hollow gaze into which one might drop a pebble to gauge the distance to the bottom and then never hear it land. "She gave up her life," the twain said at last, "in the service of our most venerable ruler. She believed in him. I believed in him. She had given him much already. He needed more power, and so she gave him power. She crafted tokens to focus his will and channel his might."

"Tokens?" Jackaby asked.

"A crown, black as midnight. A spear, black as pitch." The hairs on the back of my neck stood up. "They were not enough. In the end she gave herself."

"You," I said, taking a step backward, "you serve the Dire King?"

"Know'd it!" Nudd pounced. He slammed into the book-shelf headfirst, his hands slapping together on empty air. The shelf gave way and Nudd collapsed to the one below it, which gave way in like fashion, until Nudd was deposited gracelessly onto the floor in a slough of loose papers and curios. His top hat slid across the floor.

"No. We followed *Hafgan*," said an unperturbed voice behind us. We all spun around. The twain was sitting cross-legged on top of Jackaby's heavy safe. "We *made* the Dire King."

"Explain," demanded Jackaby. "How did you make the Dire King?"

The twain seemed to regard the command with detached interest.

"It is the most sacred act of their kind," Serif filled in. "They can live practically forever, or they can give their life to another."

"When we cease to be," the twain said, nodding, "it is

so that a worthy life may burn all the more brightly, or so that one that has been snuffed out before its time may be rekindled."

"You can raise the dead?" Jackaby's eyebrow shot up.

"We can." The twain nodded. "And not in the shallow pantomime of life that you have seen in your world of late. We bestow real vitality to the body, mind, and soul. It is our ultimate sacrifice. Our greatest gift."

There was a flash, and Serif's sword was suddenly slicing through the air toward the twain. I blinked.

And the cold night air bit my cheeks and my shoes sank down into the sod. I gasped. Serif's sword lopped the azalea bush in two and she toppled into the grass. There were exclamations from the rest of our party as we took stock of our surroundings.

The twain had deposited us all, unharmed, in the garden just outside the office window. The little furry figure hopped onto the sill and regarded us from behind the glass.

"It is going to be different." The twain's voice was a soft hush, but I could hear him as easily as if he had whispered directly into my ears. "War changes things." And then the window was empty and we were standing in the cold.

"Unfathomable cosmic potential," Jackaby muttered, "and he used it to shunt us twenty feet away."

"At least now we know what side he's on," I said. "They can sacrifice themselves to bring the dead back to life, and he said his other half gave herself to Hafgan. The same

Hafgan whom Arawn killed. The twain must be the reason the Dire King has risen! They're the reason this is all happening again!"

"Hate ta interrupt," Hudson said. "But I don't suppose one of you folks left yer cellar open like that?"

We looked across the garden.

Jackaby muttered to himself as we hastened toward the cellar steps. "We couldn't have five minutes pass without things getting worse?"

We reached the doors and Jackaby inspected the lock. "It isn't broken," he said. "It's unlocked. From the outside. Wait here." He stalked down the steps and returned a minute later holding the sky iron chain. It had been sliced into pieces. "The bad news is, she's gone," he said. "And worse, she has the black blade."

"Is there good news?" Miss Lee asked.

"Well," Jackaby answered gamely, "karmically, I would say we're due for an upswing on the pendulum of fortune. That's almost good news."

"That's not good news," Serif said, crossly. "That's just a very wordy way of saying it's all bad news."

"It's worse," Jenny said. "She promised to take someone with her."

"That's true," I confirmed. "She told us she would be free by morning, and she threatened to take . . ." My eyes shot to Charlie. "Where is Alina?"

We raced through the house, Charlie in the lead. A cloud

of pixies scattered and the dwarves groused as Charlie bounded right over their heads. Hudson and Nudd took the first floor and Lydia and Jenny took the second. Jackaby and I caught up to Charlie on the third.

"She was here," he panted. "I left her right here. She was watching the merpeople swimming in the lake." His eyes were wet and frantic.

"Who was?" came a voice just behind us. We spun around, and Charlie leapt to lock his sister in an embrace. "What is going on?" Alina demanded.

"You are safe," said Charlie, letting her go.

"Was there doubt?"

"Morwen," I said. "We were worried she might have made good on her threats."

"She may have taken someone else," said Jackaby. "We'll need to take stock of all of our visitors."

"Hostage or not, she has the blade again," I said. "Mr. Jackaby, there's something else I need to tell you. Hatun had another vision. It was one of her—I don't know—her prophesies. She mentioned the black blade. She called it the spear, but not the spear. Sir, she said the Seer would fall. Hatun said you would be lost."

Jackaby stiffened. "Did she refer to me by name?"

I blinked. "What? No. She just said the Seer would fall under the blade. Why?"

"She might have been talking about the one seeing the prophetic vision in the first place. Where is Hatun now?"

"She's been with us the whole–" I paused. "Does anybody remember seeing Hatun with us after we left the library?"

The eerie chill felt stronger than ever as we rounded the last bend to the Dangerous Documents section. Jackaby entered first, I followed, and Charlie and Alina crept behind us. The lamp-lit chamber stood empty and silent. The table was unoccupied, just as we had left it. Except . . .

"Is that blood?" I gulped.

Rough lines had been carved into the tabletop, and a pool of dark crimson spilled over the top of them, flowing into the cracks and giving the etching grim definition.

"It is." Jackaby's voice shook. "Hatun's. Her aura is unmistakable."

Silence reigned in the library.

"There's something in that chair," Alina whispered.

Jackaby's hand trembled as he reached for the dark shape. He picked up the knitwork lump. "Stubborn woman. I told her not to." In the flickering lamplight, his eyes looked somehow both full of tears and full of fire as he pulled the thing solemnly over his shaggy hair. It was a floppy heap, but with a little imagination, it was a hat. Hatun had knit him a new hat.

I turned away, my throat tight, and scrutinized the defaced tabletop. The gouges in the wood spelled out three bloody words: *COME GET HER.*

Chapter Sixteen

When Mr. Jackaby was in good spirits, he moved constantly, always fidgeting. I had learned to tell when
he was secretly afraid, because he moved more quickly still,
clipping along at a run and talking even more incessantly
than usual. When he was baffled–really, thoroughly flum-
moxed–he was practically a blur.

Now Hatun had been stolen away on his watch. Her
blood had been spilled in his house, under his protection.

And Jackaby.

Stopped.

Moving.

He sat at his desk, still as a statue, thunderclouds rolling
across his eyes. For hours, the only motion he made was
the slow rise and fall of his shoulders as he took measured

breaths. His jaw was set and his fingers steepled in front of his mouth.

Jenny hovered behind him. Hudson sat in the big armchair across from the desk. We had been taking it in shifts to try to draw him out. After an hour or so, Chief Nudd had gone, making the long journey to bring more of his horde back with him to assist us in the coming fray. Serif had been given permission to examine the rest of the house for any signs of Morwen or the twain, and Charlie had volunteered to clean up the library. It was not a task any of us felt ready to stomach. Jenny, Mr. Hudson, and I remained in the office.

"Jackaby." Jenny moved in to put a hand on his arm, but her translucent fingers found no purchase. Her hand dissolved away like vapor, reforming as she pulled it back. She bit her lip and looked as if she would like to cry.

"Sir?" I tried for the dozenth time.

"Why don't you all get some rest," Hudson suggested. "I'll wait up with our boy a little longer."

Jenny nodded silently and faded away into the shadows. I pushed myself up. "Thank you, Mr. Hudson," I said. It was very late already. "We will get her back, sir," I said from the doorway. Jackaby gave no reaction.

I reached the stairs just as Serif was coming down.

"Did you find anything?"

"I did not—but that comes as little surprise. I will need to report back to the Fair King that the twain is involved. Their kind do not leave a trace."

"But there were traces," I said. "The lock was opened from the outside. The chain was severed. Why would an all-powerful being bother with locks?"

Serif regarded me for a long moment. "You're human. It's a shame."

"A shame?"

"You've seen your share of pain and you've come out sharper. That scar suits you," she said. I touched a hand to my cheek, feeling the thin ridges. "I learned a long time ago that we do not survive because we're strong—we become stronger the more we survive. You're a survivor. You could be very strong someday. It is a shame that you will never have time to grow into your potential. Human life is fleeting."

"Yes, human life is fleeting," I said. "But that's what calls us to be strong now."

"Hm," Serif said, but she regarded me approvingly.

"You look as though you've seen your share of pain, as well," I said. "Where did you get your scar?"

Her expression cooled. "I became a lot stronger that day," she said. "I am leaving now. Good-bye, Abigail Rook."

I walked Serif to the door and doubled back up the winding hallway. Muffled voices reached me from Jackaby's office as I passed. I slowed to listen.

"Have a drink, chum." I could hear the clink of Hudson's flask flicking open.

"You already know I won't," Jackaby replied quietly.

"Yeah. I know ya won't, but hell if I know why." I peeked through the crack in the door as Hudson took a swig and then flipped the cap back up with his hook. "I never seen ya touch a drop, but I also know a lotta folks who would never stop drinking if they'd seen half the stuff you've seen."

"I don't like to be out of sorts."

"Don't know as I'd call yer usual state of affairs *in sorts*, but suit yerself."

Jackaby was silent as Hudson took another draught. "I'm not good enough," he said, at last. "That's why I don't drink. I can't afford to. At my best, my mind is only clever enough to keep me constantly aware that I am not clever enough. I can't keep up with the Dire King, let alone outmaneuver him. I don't know what I'm doing here. I never know what I'm doing. I pretend and posture and stumble through–and along the way I've somehow fooled a whole lot of people into thinking that I know what I'm doing. Now their lives depend on me being good enough. And I'm not."

Hudson rubbed his neck. He looked like he wanted to say something, then changed his mind. He took another swig instead.

"We're not behind you because you're good enough, sir," I said, pushing open the door. "We're behind you because you're *good*." Eyebrows lifted as both men turned to look at me. "You are a good man. I've never known you to pick an unnecessary fight just because you knew you could win it, just as I've never seen you back down from a necessary one that you knew you could not. You never ask for glory, you don't want people to chant your name—for goodness' sake, none of us even knows your real name. We don't need you to be good enough, sir. We just need you to keep being good. Because"—I swallowed—"because it reminds us that *we* can be good, too. All of us. This world doesn't need showy champions. It needs people who are good, people who *do* good, even if nobody will ever know."

Jackaby leaned on his desk and stared at me. At length he turned his eyes back to the trapper. "I've created a monster, Mr. Hudson. She won't even let me wallow properly."

Hank chuckled. "She sure talks pretty, though, don't she?" He pushed himself up. "I'll go ahead and give y'all the room. Should be gettin' on about now, anyway. I'll see you in the mornin'." He tipped his hat to Jackaby and gave me an approving wink and a pat on the shoulder as he headed out.

Jackaby slumped back in his chair. "She made me a hat, Miss Rook." The lumpy thing lay on the desk in front of him.

"Yes, she did," I told him. "And it is atrocious. It suits you."

He gave a halfhearted smile. "Bite your tongue," he managed, his brooding melancholy falling off him like heavy treacle from a spoon. "I think it's splendid."

"It may not have been woven with wool from a rare yeti, or dyes mixed by Baba Yaga," I told him, "but I'm sure it was made with love. And also with an ice pick. Hatun didn't come here for your protection; she came here because she believed in you. She believed that what you do matters. So, we're going to finish what we started, and we're going to save Hatun, and that's all there is to it."

"And if I can't keep you safe along the way?"

"You were never supposed to. I didn't take this position for safety, sir. I took it for purpose. Keep giving me that."

After a pause, Jackaby smiled in earnest. It was a tired smile, a slow smile, but it was good to have him back. "All right then, my sage young apprentice—what do we do next?"

"Something foolish, I imagine," I said. "Foolish and decidedly dangerous. That sounds about our style, doesn't it?"

From across the quiet house, three loud clanks echoed through the corridors.

"Was that the front door knocker?" I said. "Who would be calling at this ungodly hour?"

We both slipped quietly into the foyer. The giant's low snores rumbled, and the gnomes were piled on top of one another in the corner, sleeping like puppies. I looked up at the transom window. "Well. I'm not sure I like the look of that at all," I said. The transom read:

R. F. JACKABY:

REVENGE

Chapter Seventeen

B y all accounts he should be dead," Jackaby said, staring at the door. "But I suppose that is true about an increasing number of faces I've come across lately."

"Who is it?" I whispered.

"An old friend," drawled a muffled voice through the door. "Little pigs, little pigs, let me in."

My blood froze. Pavel. How was it possible? The last time any of us had seen the vile vampire, he had been leaving the premises very quickly through a closed window—into the sunlight—with a brick in his mouth. My own hands had done the banishing, although I had no memory of my actions. The Dire King had crept into my mind at the time, manipulating me, using me. How could Pavel be back? Why now? Had our night not gone wrong enough already?

"No, sir, don't–!" I began. Jackaby opened the door.

What awaited us on the other side was not the Dire Council's cold, confident killer, standing on the doorstep all dressed in black. What awaited us on the other side was barely standing at all. What was left of Pavel was draped in soiled rags. He wore a floppy hat low over his head, but I could see that his face and hands were a mess of angry scars. He had been badly burnt, and he was leaning heavily against the column outside. He looked small and thin and unsteady, and he smelled like a lavatory.

"Not going to just let yourself in?" Jackaby asked. "It went so well for you the last time."

"I thought I might give you the opportunity," Pavel managed, his voice slow and labored, "to make up for your poor manners during our previous encounter."

"You threatened to kill me," I said.

"I was making small talk."

"And then you actually tried to kill me."

"I get tired of small talk. You take things too personally."

"How did you survive?" Jackaby asked. "I watched Miss Rook drive you out into the direct sunlight. You should be ashes."

"Sorry to disappoint."

"The sewer system, I presume?" said Jackaby.

"I've had worse accommodations," Pavel said, closing his eyes. He looked as though the act of standing might prove too much for him soon.

"And you've been draining innocent people to regain your strength ever since?" Jackaby posited.

"Ungh. I wish. Pigs," said Pavel. "They taste almost human, if you close your eyes. And your nose. They were better than rats, at least. I found myself a quiet corner in the tunnels beneath that fat butcher in the Inkling District. I could go for a pint of the good stuff, though, if you're offering." He laughed a dry, hacking laugh.

"And now that you're back on your feet, you've come for your revenge, is that it?" said Jackaby.

"YES." Pavel's bloodshot eyes flashed up at me from blackened, blistered sockets. "Yes, I have. And you are going to help me get it."

"Help you?" I said. "Why should we help you avenge yourself on us?"

"On you? Don't flatter yourself," Pavel spat. "It was your hand that drove that brick into my jaw, but it was not you. I'm not stupid. I know who did this to me."

I blinked. The Dire King. Having that egomaniac trespassing inside my head had been the most disquieting experience of my life. I had lost time during his psychic transgressions. I had done things I could not remember. It was a violation I had told only my closest friends about, but Pavel knew.

"You want revenge on the Dire King," said Jackaby, his eyebrows rising.

Pavel nodded. "And you two want to save the world. We can help each other."

"Just because you've fallen out of favor with your mad monarch, we're supposed to believe you suddenly care about protecting the earth?" I said.

"The earth can rot," Pavel snarled. "I served that bastard for a century, and he cast me out the moment I was not of use to him. He cut pieces off me when he was displeased, he took my fangs when he was through with me, and then he threw me into the sunlight to die. I should have died—I would have died, if I had not reached that reeking grate in time. My whole body was burning in agony, greasy smoke pouring out of my lungs. But I refused to die. Not yet. The Dire King took everything from me. So, while I was choking down foul swine's blood, week after week, I began to ask myself, how do I make him suffer? How do I take everything from him as he did from me? I take the one thing he cares most about."

"Morwen?" I hazarded. "I'm afraid you've just missed her."

"No. He would let her die for his cause. He would let us all die. I want to rob him of his victory. He's waited so long—he yearns for it. It consumes him. I want to throw a wrench in the works of his grand plan. I want him to watch it fall apart around him."

"And how do you intend to do that?" Jackaby asked.

"You," said Pavel, "are the biggest wrench I know."

"That's a lovely thought," I said. "But we haven't come close to halting the Dire King, and it hasn't been for lack of trying."

"You didn't have me before." Pavel gave a crooked smile that pulled the scars all over his face in sickly contortions. "The rend. I will take you to it. The council's stronghold. The machine. The Dire King. He's yours. Everything you want is everything I want to give you."

My pulse quickened. Jackaby narrowed his eyes. "And what's in it for you?"

Pavel chuckled again. It sounded something like a badger being strangled to death. "That's the beauty of it. Your success is my success. I show you the way, and then I go my own way. Everybody wins. Except the Dire King, of course."

"If we accept your terms," said Jackaby, "that does not make us allies. The next time we meet, you will still be held accountable for the lives you have taken."

"Wouldn't have it any other way," Pavel replied with a courtly and rather melodramatic bow.

Jackaby's jaw was set. He glanced at me and I swallowed.

"Sounds foolish and decidedly dangerous," I said.

Jackaby took a deep breath, his face leaden. And then he made a deal with the devil.

"Come in," said Jackaby.

Pavel's eyes were half-lidded as he grinned drunkenly across the table at me a few minutes later. He swayed in his chair.

"Am I the only one who sees that this is a terrible idea?" Jenny said, hovering anxiously over us.

"No, no," I assured her. "We are all well aware. That's why we're moving forward at all. Obviously, only an absolute idiot would trust Pavel after everything he's done. The Dire King knows that we are not absolute idiots, so he knows we would never trust Pavel. Which is why we've chosen to trust Pavel. It has the element of surprise."

"So does a trap," said Jenny. "He shows up the exact same night Morwen escapes. That doesn't sound a little suspicious to you?"

"I don't bother with traps, love." Pavel smirked. "When I want someone dead, I . . . well, just ask your boyfriend."

Jenny's face darkened, and the air in the room dropped several degrees.

"Oh, ho, ho!" Pavel said, shivering a little in the sudden chill. "Very impressive. She must be handy to keep around in the summer. You're better than an ice chest."

"Jenny's right," Charlie said. "I don't trust him."

"Of course not." Pavel flopped his head toward Charlie. "But that's only because I would happily throw you to my least favorite wolves if I thought it might give them indigestion. See? Honest. *It must not be denied but I am a plain-dealing villain.* That's Shakespeare, love. *Much Ado.* Don't look so surprised. I like Shakespeare. Makes me feel classy. Classy *and* honest–I'm the whole package."

"We don't have to trust him," I said. "But we can trust his nature. He's a self-serving coward. He wouldn't have come to us this vulnerable if it weren't in his own self interest.

He wants something, and we can deliver it. That's what I trust."

"You're a shameless flatterer," Pavel drawled. "Compliments will get you everywhere, my darling."

"Please don't," I said. "We find the rend. We find the Dire King's war machine. We disable it. I am not your friend. I am not your darling."

"You think I enjoy slumming it with you lot? Misery acquaints a man with strange bedfellows, Miss Rook."

Jackaby strode back into the room. He had one sleeve rolled up past the elbow and a slim bandage tied tightly around his upper arm. Under his left arm was tucked what appeared to be a small bundle of firewood, and his right hand held something slim that clinked like glass. "All right," he said. "If we're doing this, we are doing it now, tonight, before word reaches the council; before we lose the element of surprise."

Pavel's nostrils twitched and his lip quivered. "Detective?" he said. "Is that what I think it is?"

"You get one." Jackaby held up three vials filled with a deep red liquid. "You will receive the next one only after you've shown us how to reach the rend and the council's stronghold. You'll get the last when I'm certain you haven't betrayed us."

"You've bled yourself?" Jenny exclaimed. "Oh, that's brilliant. Because you're sure to be at your sharpest right after a bloodletting."

"Pavel will need his strength."

"Of course he will." Jenny rolled her eyes. "If there's anything we should be doing, it's making the vampire you invited inside our house stronger. Nothing could possibly go wrong."

"Time is of the essence, Miss Cavanaugh," Jackaby said. "Pavel's vitality is fading. Pig's blood has done little more than stave off death. I cannot afford to have him collapsing on us, or shambling along until the sun comes up and it becomes too late."

He passed the first vial to Pavel. "I did not ask you for this," Pavel said.

"I would not have offered it to you if you had," said Jackaby. "As for the rest of you . . ." He shifted the bundle in his hands, and I saw that it was not firewood but sharpened stakes. He passed them out, one to each of us, and tucked the last one into a long, slim pocket in the lining of his coat. "These have been treated with garlic and silver dust for good measure. Add them to your traveling supplies. If Pavel gives you the faintest indication of duplicity, aim for his heart."

Jenny leveled her stake directly at Pavel. "The faintest," she repeated pointedly.

"Aww. It feels nice to be a part of the team, doesn't it?" Pavel said. He popped the wax stopper out of the vial with his thumb and clinked the glass against her wooden stake. "Cheers," he said, and downed it in an eager gulp.

Chapter Eighteen

I am going with you." Alina was adamant. She stood in the
middle of the hallway, blocking Charlie's way.

"You need to stay here," Charlie insisted. "I can't take
you where we're going. It's too dangerous."

"Oh, but the haunted house where people get stabbed
and kidnapped is safe?" she said.

"Technically, it won't be haunted while we're away,"
Charlie tried. "Because Jenny will be with us."

"Mr. Barker, may I have a moment?" Jackaby asked. He
was tucking a slim hourglass into his coat pocket.

Charlie nodded, gave his sister one more pleading look,
and then padded off up the hall after Jackaby.

"He cares about you," I said. Alina looked at me with
contempt. "He only wants you to be safe."

"You have no idea what it's like," she said, "being told to wait day after day, year after year, while your big brother goes halfway across the world and leaves you behind."

"No," I said. "Not exactly. For me it was my father." Alina closed her mouth and cocked her head at me.

"He was a paleontologist," I said. "Discovered amazing things all over the world. I was supposed to stay at home and learn the piano."

"And did you stay at home and learn it like a good girl?"

"I learned to hate it," I said. "I understand how you feel, I really do. But this is different."

"How is this different?"

"Because this isn't a dinosaur dig or a fancy conference you're missing. We're not searching for the bones of some long-dead monster—we're walking into a nest full of live ones."

"I don't see you practicing your arpeggios."

"What?"

"You're not waiting at home right now. Did your parents tell you to run off and fight magical beasts? Or did you finally decide to just stop listening when people told you to sit and stay?"

I considered her words. "Fair enough," I said. "I guess you're coming with us, then?"

"She's not coming," said Jackaby, swinging around the corner.

"I am not going to wait here while Kazimir goes and—"

"Yes," said Jackaby. "You *are* going to wait here. But so is he. Charlie will be staying."

"What?" Alina and I said together.

"Sir," I added, "we need Charlie."

"We do. We need him here. I have given the matter some thought. We do not need numbers for the mission in which we are currently engaged. We need stealth and subterfuge. You and I can manage that on our own. Jenny will come as well. An agent who can become literally invisible and physically intangible is an asset, but the more bodies we bring behind enemy lines, the greater our risk of detection."

"You can't seriously expect the three of us to defeat the Dire King all by ourselves?"

"No," he said. "Our role is not to defeat the Dire King, but to make defeating the Dire King possible. If we can undermine their defenses, we will leave the Dire King's forces vulnerable. I need leadership here. Charlie is my strongest general. Chief Nudd and Mr. Hudson should be back by daybreak to assist him, and the rest of our allies will be arriving throughout the day."

"And if we should fail?" I asked.

"Let's not, shall we? Whatever comes, the rest falls to Charlie."

There was silence for a beat, and then Jackaby clapped his hands together. "Right!" he said, and marched off down the hall again. "Let's go collect our ghost and vampire and get moving while we still have a few good hours of darkest night left ahead of us."

Charlie's eyes were locked on mine. "Come back alive," he whispered.

"That is the plan," I said, as gamely as I could manage. "And if I do . . ." I put a hand on his chest and tried to ignore Alina, who was watching intently.

"Miss Rook!" Jackaby hollered from the head of the stairs. "While it's still dark out!"

I caught up with Jackaby on the stairs.

"I think we kept that appropriately upbeat, don't you?" Jackaby mused.

"Upbeat, sir?"

"I am loath to dishearten Mr. Barker with the full gravity of our situation when he needs to remain optimistic. Of course, the reality is that we may be murdered by Pavel immediately, attacked by some rogue monster on our way to the rend, or assassinated by the recently liberated Morwen once we get there. Even if none of those things happens, reaching our destination still puts us squarely in the company of the most unfathomably powerful mage in the Annwyn, along with an army of the least savory creatures ever spawned. And that is only if we are able to cross the rend. Stepping through an unstable rift in the fabric joining parallel dimensional planes is stretching the definition of foolish."

"We're going to die," I said.

"Only probably."

"And you didn't want to dishearten Mr. Barker with that assessment?"

"Seemed cruel."

"Quite." I swallowed.

"Nobody needs that dread hanging over their head."

"No, certainly not."

"Ready?"

"My extremities might be numb. Is that normal?"

"I'm sure it is. Come along."

"But what does the machine *do*, exactly?" Jenny asked for the third time since we had left the house. Over her translucent shoulder was slung Jackaby's satchel. She had tucked within it the wooden stake and a handful of other protective implements and charms.

"I don't know what it does," Pavel replied. "It's big."

"How big?"

"I've never been good with all the technical nonsense—I just know that it is the crux of the Dire King's strategy. You should have seen him when his first one was destroyed. There was a lot of blood that night. He had been preparing for his rise back then, but he had to delay another decade just to get it right. The machine is his obsession. Without it, the veil does not fall."

"And you never bothered to ask how it works?"

"You don't ask the Dire King questions."

"It's fine," said Jackaby. "Based on our experience with Owen Finstern's device, the full-scale machine will probably have something to do with energies or vital forces." Owen Finstern was Morwen's twin brother, the king's bastard son. The king had been more concerned with stealing his son's unique device than he had been with preserving his son's life. "Whatever it is, we will just have to sort out what it is and how to sabotage it when we get there."

"Don't worry. You've got the eyes for it," Pavel said. "The Dire King wants those eyes. He had very strict rules about killing you because of those eyes. He never could get inside that head of yours to use them, though. It tickles me that instead of using your eyes to fine-tune his device, you will be using them to tear it apart. It's the little things, really."

"If the Dire King wanted Jackaby's sight to help him finish his machine," I said, "then it can't be operational, can it?"

"The Dire King always has alternative solutions."

"What sort of alternative solutions?"

"Hatun," Jackaby said flatly. "Hatun is the only other person I know of who occasionally sees things as I see them."

"That means she's more likely to be alive," I reassured him.

"They'll be amassing an army, too," Pavel added. "So, expect that."

"Of course they will," I said.

"Not just any army," Pavel continued. "The worst the

Annwyn has to offer. They will be waiting to flood into the human world as soon as the veil begins to crumble. This front line of monsters is supposed to prime the pump, wreaking havoc and leaving fear and chaos in its wake. The Dire King speaks often about balance," Pavel explained. "Order and chaos. He says creatures of chaos have too long been suppressed while their brethren are celebrated. The Unseelie fae eat it up whenever he talks like that. They get all frothy and wild-eyed."

"And you swallowed that maniac's nonsense?"

Pavel shrugged. "I swallowed fresh blood from fluted glasses. I have never hunted so often or lived in such luxury. Have you ever slept in a silk-lined coffin? Organized chaos is surprisingly lucrative."

"So, we need to sneak past an entire army undetected, and then work out how to disable an exotic technology that nobody fully understands," I said. "Anything else we should know?"

"That's about it. Oh, and try not to die too close to each other."

"What's that supposed to mean?" I said.

"We have a guy—I mean *they* have a guy," Pavel said. "He's very good with, how should I put this . . ."

Jackaby cleared his throat. "With the manipulation of the deceased? The dark art of necromancy?"

"I was going to say meat puppets," Pavel replied. "I mean, I am undead myself, but his little marionettes always give me the creeps. Dying makes your body fair game for his little trick, so if you happen to kick the bucket, just try to kick it as far away as you can in case he should raise you."

"Thank you," Jackaby said. "Very helpful."

We walked in silence for several paces. Jenny was worrying the strap on Jackaby's satchel as she walked. "Would you like me to carry it for you?" I asked her.

"Hm?" she said. "No, no thank you. I've been doing better with tangibility. I'm fine, really." She hung back as Jackaby and Pavel got a few paces ahead. "I think the only thing I can't seem to make contact with is Jackaby."

"You can't?"

Her shoulders sagged. "I don't know why. It's as though I can't give myself permission to."

"Do you think it's something to do with Mr. Carson?"

She looked pained, and I wished I hadn't spoken of her murdered fiancé. "Howard was a good man," she said. "But I finally had my chance to say good-bye. I–I don't know. I just can't."

I didn't press the matter. My ears perked up at the sound of a policeman's whistle a street or two away. I could hear faint voices, and in the distance a dog was barking. The streetlight ahead of us had gone out, leaving us in a pool of midnight black. I kept waiting for something to come leaping out at us from around a corner. We quickened our pace to catch up to the men.

"I've never liked being out in the streets this late," I

said, pulling my coat tighter around my shoulders. "New Fiddleham is not the same city after nightfall."

"You read my mind, Miss Rook," Pavel said, kneeling down by the curb. "The streets won't get us where we're going, anyway. From here, we travel below them."

He pulled up the heavy grate and dropped it onto the cobblestones with a clang. The tunnel beneath was even darker than the pitch-black streets, if that was possible.

"I am not going in there," I said.

"Suit yourself. Your boss is the only one I really need."

Jackaby lowered himself and dropped into the sewer. His feet hit the bottom with a splash. "Sir," I began. Pavel slipped in after him.

Jenny gave me a shrug. She slid gracefully after them, down into the darkness.

I stood alone on the street, my heart pumping. I had spent enough time in deep, dark tunnels to last a lifetime. I glanced back the way we had come. I closed my eyes. Deep breath. I could do this. I knelt down. I had not crossed an ocean just to take the safe path. Deep breath. I lowered my legs into the clammy air of the sewer. I had chosen this life. I had chosen foolish and dangerous and good. My feet hit the bottom with a splash. Deep breath. Oh good lord, that smell! I stopped taking deep breaths and held my sleeve over my face instead.

My eyes blinked open. The tunnel was not pure black. It was more of a hazy charcoal gray, punctuated every block or so by shafts of moonlight. I could see silhouettes slogging forward ahead of me. Pavel was leading the way, eager energy in his steps. The first dose of Jackaby's blood appeared to have brought him out of his languor; I hated to imagine what he could accomplish if he had drained the source completely. Jackaby was a step behind him, hunched over under the shallow ceiling, and Jenny was a shimmer at his side. I hastened to catch up.

If you have never had the pleasure of traveling by sewer, allow me to spare you the visceral details. This was not a space designed for comfort of either body or mind, and I found it distressingly difficult to gauge distance and time in those gloomy passages.

"Still an hour or so until sunrise," Jackaby said as we finally slowed to a stop. He was peeking out of a grate by his head. "We seem to be on the outskirts of New Fiddleham. Wait a moment. I know where we are!"

I propped myself up on the tips of my toes and peered out next to him. From my angle, I could see stars and dark trees and just the tips of the eaves of a few nearby buildings.

"Almost there," Pavel said. "This way." He braced his shoulder against a nondescript wall of the tunnel and pushed. With the grate of bricks against stone, a wide section of wall swung inward like a door.

"Where are we, sir?" I whispered as we followed Pavel through the hidden passageway. The door led to some sort of basement. The floor was packed earth, and the air was cold and dry.

"We are in the substructure of the last building our dear friend Douglas ever walked into while wearing shoes," Jackaby said. "Well, unless you count those little booties I had made for him so that he wouldn't drip pond water all down the staircase. But those didn't last a week, and they never fit well over his webbed feet."

I coughed.

"The church. We appear to be directly beneath Father Grafton's church. Several supernatural beings have been through here. They've left their traces like footprints. Pavel's aura is all over, and so is Morwen's. She definitely came through here before us tonight. She's hours ahead. There are hints of chameleomorphs, and I do believe—yes, that's a lingering residual imprint from the redcap we caught months ago!"

"But I was just inside the church," Jenny said. "I searched every room. I didn't see any secret passages or mysterious portals to another dimension."

"That sounds embarrassing," said Pavel. "I would be embarrassed. Are you embarrassed?"

Jenny glared daggers at him.

"There's a trace of someone else," said Jackaby. "A trace of someone who's been through recently—within the past week at least. A trace of someone . . . fae."

"That would probably be Tilde," Pavel surmised. "He's

not a lot of fun, but he does his job. He's not around right now, is he?" He glanced over his shoulder nervously.

"Tilde is a fairy?" said Jackaby. "But why would a fairy be sneaking through the rend when he could just use a veil-gate? Why is a fairy working with the Dire King at all? What I'm picking up is not monstrous; it's a Seelie fae."

Pavel shrugged. "I don't do auras."

"So how do we get up?" I asked, scanning the dusty planks above us for any sign of a trapdoor.

"We don't. We go down," smirked Pavel. "Obviously."

"There," said Jackaby, pointing at a small patch of absolutely nothing over in the corner. Pavel looked impressed.

"I don't see anything," I said.

"Neither do I," said Jackaby. "I do see something everywhere else, though. The whole ceiling is imbued with a tincture of religious faith, the walls have been saturated in history, the air around us has a fine mist of the mystical, and even the dirt beneath us is covered in trails and wisps of paranormal auras. Except there. It's as though there is a sinkhole right there, maybe ten feet wide."

Pavel knelt and dug his fingernails into the dust. "Cigar for the clever fellow." He pulled up a plank of wood the same color as the dirt and leaned it up against the wall. The earth below appeared to have been fractured like a broken mirror; crumbling fragments of dusty brown drifted around the edges, suspended as though floating in an invisible pond. The center of the cleft was a glowing pool of pale green light. "I do believe that's vial number two to me?"

Jackaby reached into his coat and retrieved a second glass tube of crimson blood. He tossed it to Pavel. "Fair enough. You were true to your word."

Pavel's eyes fluttered shut as he sucked down the sticky liquid. His whole body shuddered and he tossed the vial aside, licking his teeth. It broke against the rocky foundation. His face was still a mess of scar tissue, but by the light of the green glow it looked smoother already than it had when he first turned up on our doorstep, and it was fading to a pale pink and less of an angry red.

"Hits the spot," he said. "I'll have one more for the road, if you don't mind, Detective." His eyes looked dilated.

"You'll have one more when I am sure we're not walking into an ambush," Jackaby answered. "After you."

Pavel cracked his neck and gave Jackaby a smile that had gone rotten several days ago and probably should have been tossed out of the bushel before it spoiled all of the other smiles. "*Once more unto the breach*," he recited, and fell backward into the verdant glow.

Jackaby approached the rend.

"I don't suppose you can see what's waiting for us on the other side?" I asked.

"I see nothing beyond the point of crossing. I couldn't see the veil-gate in Rosemary's Green, either, although I knew it had to be right in front of me. I can register earthly auras just fine, and otherworldly auras are quite vivid—but I think the overlap of the two creates a sort of anomaly my sight doesn't know how to process."

"So, we're just going across blind?" I said.

"Looks that way." Jackaby nodded.

"Through a portal we know has been frequented by our worst enemies?"

"That's it."

"Because we're trusting a psychopath who has repeatedly tried to murder us?"

"Yes."

"Just so we're clear."

Jackaby stepped off the edge of the dirt floor and into the emerald light as though he had just walked off the end of a pier wearing lead shoes.

Jenny coasted in after him headfirst.

I screwed up my courage and took the crossing with a little jump, bending my knees as I dropped out of our world and into the next.

Chapter Nineteen

The world turned upside down. One moment I was looking down at the emerald pool beneath my feet as I fell into it—and the next moment I was looking at the sky, as I fell away from it. I scrambled to right myself as a floor of stone tiles leapt toward my head. My arms crumpled under me, but I managed to roll out of the landing just enough to cushion the blow. I pushed myself up and looked around.

We had traveled so far beneath the streets of the city, deep under the buildings, and deeper still into the earth, only to emerge in the biting-cold fresh air high atop a towering citadel overlooking a strange and foreign land.

I had visited the Annwyn once before. The first time had been a smooth transition, like stepping from one room into another. This was something else. I was standing on the rooftop of a tower on the corner of a castle wall. As I peered timidly over the edge, I blanched. Had the rend dropped us ten feet from this spot, we would have fallen half a dozen stories before we hit the ground.

I felt a hand on my shoulder and turned with a start. Jackaby held a finger to his lips and gestured for me to follow silently. Jenny was a few feet ahead. The tower on which we found ourselves stood higher than the castle's curtain wall. I looked where Jackaby was pointing just in time to see what appeared to be Pavel's soiled rags slipping over the edge of the rooftop and dropping onto the castle wall below.

We slid along the tiles until I could hear voices coming from just over the parapet. Jackaby held a hand up in warning. We kept our heads low as we neared the edge. I could not see Pavel anywhere.

"It's about the bits you carve off is what I'm saying," grunted a deep, gravelly voice right below us. "If I cut off some guy's arms and legs, you'd say he lost his arms and legs—you wouldn't say his arms an' legs had lost their torso."

"Yes, exactly," replied a second, scratchy voice, "but that's my point. If I cleave clean through some sap's neck, you ought to say that he lost his body, not that he lost his head. Body's just meat."

"Okay, but everyone knows that if you cut off a gremlin's head, its little runt body runs around for a good hour, causing just as much havoc as when it was whole. Sometimes more. You lose your head, not your body."

"That's just a myth, the gremlin thing."

"Isn't. Seen it myself."

"You have not."

"Hey! Who goes there?" the first voice suddenly grunted in alarm. There was a sickening crunch and then another, followed by a loud clattering and then two thumps like sandbags hitting stone.

Jackaby peeked tentatively over the edge, and then stood up. I followed suit.

The path that ran along the top of the castle wall was about six feet wide, bordered on either side by a short, crenellated wall. Two hulking bodies lay sprawled on the stones right below us. They were easily ten feet tall apiece. Poleaxes had fallen by their sides, and matching curved daggers hung on their hips. Their heads sat at unhealthy angles to their shoulders. Their necks had clearly been snapped.

"Such a waste." Pavel sighed, looking down at the slain guards as he dusted off his hands.

"Friends of yours?" Jackaby asked, dropping down next to him.

"What? No. I don't fraternize with the help. If I still had my fangs, I could have tucked into them before their hearts stopped pumping instead of just leaving perfectly good blood to congeal in their veins."

"That's terrible," I said.

"I'll get over it," Pavel said, giving the brute's head a kick. "Ogre blood is always sour, anyway. It's really best if you have a pixie chaser to sweeten it up. Theirs is like syrup, pixies."

"The Dire King will be none too pleased with you," said Jackaby.

"That is the idea," Pavel blustered, although his eyes were darting nervously up and down the wall.

"Where are we?" Jackaby asked, glancing out over the terrain. Surrounding the castle was a wide field bordered by tall pines.

"This is the Dire Council's stronghold," Pavel said. "Heart of the beast."

"Yes, but where is it within the Annwyn?" Jackaby said. "Arawn's finest soldiers couldn't find this place, but it hardly seems hidden."

"Heh." Pavel smiled. "That's because Arawn is an idiot. His own castle is beyond the trees there, not more than a few miles away. We're right under his nose. We're on his lands, technically. None of his subjects are allowed to hunt or travel these parts—not that they would, what with all the superstitions. This was Hafgan's Hold. Anyone loyal to Hafgan was killed or driven away after the last war, and then Arawn set his dogs to guarding the perimeter so they could never come back. It's supposed to be impossible to breach."

"But I see the Dire King managed to breach it."

"He didn't bother at first. Ten years ago, he tried to build a machine on the earthly side instead. After that one failed, I guess he opted for this old hold. The veil-gate here had been sealed after the war, of course, but the seam was still there. The church rests right on top of it. The Dire King didn't want to risk drawing too much attention, so he couldn't just destroy the church outright. We weren't even allowed to kill the clergyman. We broke through a couple of years ago and secured the rend right under his feet, though."

"The rend has been here for years?" Jackaby took a heavy breath. "Douglas and I scoured the church from top to bottom, but we never found anything. Arawn's not the only idiot. You've been under *my* nose this whole time, too."

Pavel giggled in a manner completely unbefitting an undead menace. "I know! Oh, you're fun. This has been fun. I'm going to miss this. Anyway, the Dire King's machine is in the center of the castle. The keep. See that tower with the domed top? That's it. You'll find sentries on every corner—every corner save this one, obviously. You're welcome, by the way." He leaned down and plucked one of the curved daggers from a fallen guard. He felt the grip and weighed it in his hands. "Waste not, want not," he mumbled. And then he paused and gave me a lascivious look that made my skin crawl.

"We would fare better with more of your help along the way," Jackaby said.

"Yeah, you would," Pavel agreed. "That's too bad for you." He was breathing heavily.

"I can see it rising in you," said Jackaby. "You don't have to be the monster."

Pavel dragged his eyes slowly off me and up to Jackaby. "I'll have that last vial of blood, and then I'll be on my merry way. Have fun making a nuisance of yourself, Detective."

Jackaby hesitated. He pursed his lips and drew out the vial.

"Thank you, Detective. Give her here." Jackaby did not toss it to him right away. His expression was clouded. Something was wrong.

"Come away from Miss Rook first, if you don't mind."

Pavel's eyes slowly crept back to me, crawling their way from my shoes up to not quite my face. It was a gaze I wanted to scrub off myself.

"You've gotten us in," Jenny said, sliding between us protectively. "You can collect your bloody payment and leave." She pulled out the wooden stake Jackaby had given her and let the bottomless satchel slip from her shoulder and drop to the ground.

"I know, I know," Pavel said. "But I have such a long way to go, and they are such small snacks. And, really, Mr. Jackaby doesn't need so much help, does he?" He leveled the dagger at Jenny.

She was not impressed. "And what exactly are you hoping to do with that?" she asked, pressing forward so that the dagger slid halfway through her chest. "You can't frighten the dead." She readied the stake, pressing it firmly against Pavel's chest. He did not flinch.

"Where will you go, I wonder?" Pavel asked, cocking his head to the side and smirking arrogantly.

"I–I'm not going anywhere," Jenny replied.

Jackaby slid his own stake out of the lining of his coat.

"If we were on earth, you would snap right back to that quaint old house of yours, wouldn't you?" Pavel continued. "But we've crossed a boundary. Will you make it all the way back there from here? Get lost somewhere in between? Or will you finally go where you should have gone all those years ago?"

"What are you talking–" Jenny began.

Pavel flicked his wrist, and the fine chain hanging around her neck snapped.

Jenny realized what was happening a moment too late. She made a desperate grab to catch the little pewter locket as it spun through the air, but her hand was already dissolving into wisps. Her wooden stake clattered to the ground at Pavel's feet, and beside it the locket struck the stones and clicked open, brick dust scattering across the top of the wall and blowing away in the breeze. Jenny's silver eyes flashed to Jackaby as she faded, frantic, desperate, pleading. And then Jenny Cavanaugh was gone.

Jackaby's eyes were iron. The stake in his hand whipped through the air, but Pavel dodged it easily.

Before I could even reach for my own, there was a blur of tattered rags and I felt icy steel against my neck.

My blood ran cold. No. We were here, on the brink of an actual victory against the Dire King. This was all wrong! Pavel's knife pressed against my skin.

"Wait!" Jackaby yelled. "Stop! Take it." He tossed the vial and Pavel caught it without letting up on the knife. "There. You can go. You don't have to do this!"

"I don't *have* to," said Pavel, casually. "But what did you say, Miss Rook?" He leaned in close and whispered in my ear, his breath cold and clammy. "It's my nature."

"Do you really think he'll still help you if you murder me?" I said, horrified.

Pavel snorted. "Do *you* really think he'll let the world burn just because you've died?" Pavel said.

"Try me," Jackaby growled.

"You'll finish what you've started," Pavel told him, "because the alternative is too much for you to stomach. Me? I win either way. I've sent your ghost friend scattering in the wind, and now I'm going to drain your lovely assistant right in front of you. After they're gone, if you die in a futile attempt to save your little world, then I'll have gotten my revenge on all of you. If you somehow succeed, I'll have gotten my revenge on the Dire King. Everybody wins. And by everybody, I mean me. I win. I'm pretty much the only one who wins."

"I gave you my blood so you wouldn't have to do this!" Jackaby yelled. "We struck a deal!"

Pavel popped the wax from the vial. "Yes, and I really have to thank you, Detective. I don't think I could have pulled this off without your little pick-me-ups. It will be nice to have both of you flowing through my veins as I make my exit." He tipped the last vial into his throat and threw the little glass off the tower.

The blade against my neck trembled. I felt it pierce the skin. I tried to think past my own pulse thrumming in my ears. I had nearly destroyed Pavel once before. True, it had been someone else inside my head, but my hands had done it. That meant it was just a matter of will. With every nerve in my body humming, I rammed my elbow backward and kicked away from the vile cretin. His knife sliced along my neck as I tumbled forward. I spun, ready to lash out and defend myself against his next attack, my neck instantly throbbing with pain.

Pavel dropped the knife.

His hands flew to his throat and he made a wretched choking sound.

I stared, confused and wary. I felt a sharp ache and hot blood running down my neck. Was he mocking me? No. Something was wrong with Pavel.

"Garlic," said Jackaby calmly. "And silver dust, and a drop of holy water, for good measure. I'm not much of a drinker, but I know how to mix a fierce cocktail."

Pavel's whole face twisted in agony. He stumbled backward, glaring furiously at Jackaby.

"Miss Rook." Jackaby had reached my side. He laid a hand gently on my shoulder. "You can end this."

I shook my head. I couldn't take my eyes off Pavel. He had collapsed with his back against the parapet. His legs kicked weakly as a convulsion shook his body.

"It's time to finish him, Miss Rook," said Jackaby.

"No," I breathed.

"You owe that creature no pity." There was a skin of ice over his words, but Jackaby's voice was shaking.

"No," I said.

Jackaby turned his gray eyes to me.

"He is already dying, sir."

"He died before. It didn't take."

"No. I won't become him," I said.

Jackaby raised an eyebrow. "He has no fangs. He couldn't change you into a monster like him now even if he tried to."

"He couldn't. But I could," I said.

"You don't understand the basic mechanics of vampirism. One must—"

"You don't understand the basic mechanics of humanity," I said. "I won't make myself a cold-blooded murderer, sir. Not for him. Not like this."

Jackaby met my gaze, and for several seconds neither of us blinked. Finally his eyes dropped. "No, you're absolutely right," he said. "I should not have suggested it." Jackaby knelt and retrieved the locket from the ground at his feet. He brushed it off and tucked it into his pocket. Then he scooped up Jenny's sharpened stake. "I will do it."

"Sir, don't—"

"The spear grips the hand," said a familiar voice very softly on the breeze. Jackaby's head shot up. The twain was sitting directly above Pavel on the parapet, his fluffy legs dangling over the edge.

"You keep saying that," said Jackaby.

"I do," said the twain. "It does."

"Well then," said Jackaby. "You're an unfathomably powerful being, and you've just caught us lurking about your master's stronghold, knee-deep in dead guards. So what happens next?"

The twain sighed. "Probably death," he said. "Usually death."

"The poem," I said.

"What was that?" Jackaby said.

The twain looked at me. The bushy whiskers around his chin twitched.

"The poem," I said again. "You keep repeating a line of it. I can tell it's important to you."

"It is important to you," said the twain.

"All right," I said. "Well, you've caught us red-handed, bodies left and right. We could fight. Somebody could die. Probably us, if we are to be honest. Or you could recite some poetry, instead."

Jackaby's eyebrow rose.

The twain rocked a little. Below him, Pavel's breaths were growing weaker. The vile vampire actually looked, somehow, peaceful. The twain pushed himself up until he was standing on the parapet. When he spoke, his voice was steady and softly intense.

"In the heart of hate is nothing dear.
The spear grips the hand that grips the spear.
Temper the armor, steady the shield.
The weapon to fear is the one that you wield,
for a Kingdom of Blood is a desolate thing,
a dire crown for a dire king."

"What does it mean?" said Jackaby.

The twain was silent.

"It means we're not going to kill him," I said.

Below him, Pavel's fingers twitched. The vampire was dying.

"You do not wish him dead?" said the twain.

"No," I said. "I don't wish anyone dead."

"He would not have any pity for you if your places were reversed."

"It isn't pity," I said. "It's . . . I don't know. Something else. Humanity?"

"Is that what humanity looks like?" said the twain. "Would that all humans possessed humanity."

His nose twitched, making him look even more like a hamster standing on its hind legs than usual. I felt a tingling sensation on my neck and then the sudden unexpected absence of a pain I had almost forgotten I was feeling. I clapped a hand to the cut Pavel had dealt me. It was gone. The front of my dress was still red with blood, but its source had been erased entirely.

"You–" I faltered. "Thank you. Can you help him, too?" I pointed at Pavel.

"I could," said the twain.

"But you won't," said Jackaby.

"He does not wish it," said the twain.

Pavel's mouth was now moving as though he was speaking, though no sound escaped his lips.

"What do you think he's saying?" I said.

"He, too, is speaking in verse," said the twain, listening to the silence. "I do not know it. Is it familiar to you?"

Pavel's voice was suddenly inside my head. ". . . *For in that sleep of death what dreams may come, when we have shuffled off this mortal coil . . .*"

Jackaby blinked, startled. I could tell the voice was in his ears as well. "This is the second-oddest poetry recital I have attended," he muttered.

"*Hamlet,*" I said, shaking my head. "He liked Shakespeare."

Pavel's lips gradually stopped moving. His muscles went slack. His hand twitched once, and then the voice in my ears was extinguished like a snuffed candle.

"He is gone now," said the twain.

"Well, that should make you happy. Save your boss the trouble," said Jackaby. "He was a traitor to all sides, that one."

"Death does not bring me joy," sighed the twain.

"You realize that more death will come?" Jackaby answered. "Hafgan is back! You saw to that, you and your other half, when you raised him from the dead. It won't only be soldiers and villains like Pavel, either. Thanks to your darling Hafgan, a lot of innocent people are going to die."

"No. That is not Hafgan's way. Hafgan's way is to do good."

"Tell that to Hafgan!"

"I cannot."

"How can you still believe in that lunatic?"

"My other half," said the twain, "gave herself to Hafgan during the last war."

"Yes. You told us. The twain's great sacrifice–bringing the dead back to life."

"The twain's gift can also be given to the living," he said. "The same power that can heal a broken body and retrieve a soul from the other side can be given to a body that yet lives. But for the living, it is a power that burns."

The twain's little round head sagged on his downy shoulders.

"Hafgan needed strength beyond anything the fair folk

were ever meant to possess," he continued. "My other half believed in him. She fashioned for Hafgan an instrument with which he might channel his power and a headpiece with which he might channel his will, the spear and the crown. When they were not enough, he opened himself to the full power of the twain. They accepted their fate together. Hafgan knew that it would destroy him. His need was dire."

"And so he became the Dire King," I said.

"But power corrupts," said Jackaby. "That's what the poem is about, isn't it? *The spear grips the hand that grips the spear.* In the end he failed because he became corrupted by his own power."

"Hafgan did not fail. He was victorious, but he succeeded at a terrible cost to himself. I cannot imagine the pain."

"Wait, what do you mean he was victorious?" I asked.

"He accomplished his goal. It should have killed him to do it, but I came to his aid as well. I forged for him an amulet to temper the power burning within him, to protect him, inside and out. I made it possible that he could not be killed by any mortal weapon, nor by flame, nor frost, nor even by the passing of years."

"The shield," said Jackaby. "It was an amulet. Your other half made him all-powerful, and then you made him invulnerable."

"Not invulnerable. I left a chink in his armor. Hafgan could be killed, but only by one who did not wish him dead. Only by one whose soul was pure and whose intentions were good."

"Enter Arawn," Jackaby said. "Don't go telling the Fair King he was pure and good, though. He's arrogant enough as it is."

"But, wait," I said. "If your other half sacrificed herself *before* the Dire King died—then who resurrected Hafgan afterward?"

"Nobody," answered the twain. "Hafgan is dead. He had borne the burden long enough. It would have been an unkindness to ask him to carry it again."

"If Hafgan is still dead," said Jackaby, "then who is wearing the Dire Crown?"

The twain opened his mouth to reply, but then abruptly vanished instead. The moment he was gone, an arrow glanced off the parapet with a spark, leaving a notch precisely where the furry figure had been standing. My eyes shot upward to a figure on the rooftop. She wore deep blue robes and was loading a second shot into a sleek crossbow. An ivory scar ran from her lip to the corner of her eye.

"Confused yet?" asked Serif.

Chapter Twenty

Y ou're meant to be confused," Serif continued. Her eyes were narrow and darting as she scanned the top of the castle wall. "It's what the twain does. They are creatures of confusion and chaos. A twain will make you unsure if day is night or up is down or friends are enemies."

Emerald light rippled across the spire above her and Virgule flipped out of the rend and spun to land in a crouch beside his general. The captain's entrance was far more graceful than mine had been. Virgule stood, his hand flying to the hilt of his own sword.

"Everyone seems to think so, but the twain didn't seem particularly malevolent," I said.

"They never do," Serif snarled. She lowered the crossbow.

I scowled. "What was Hafgan's original purpose?" I asked.

"What do you mean?" said Serif.

"The twain said that Hafgan was victorious. But Arawn told us that Hafgan wanted to destroy the barrier. He didn't. The veil still stands—for now, at least—so how was Hafgan victorious?"

"He wasn't. Hafgan failed. The twain lied to you."

"I don't think so," said Jackaby. "The twain wasn't lying. Or at least he believed what he was saying."

"Am I lying?" Serif asked.

Jackaby considered her. "Hm. No."

"There you have it."

"How did you two get here?" I asked. "If Arawn doesn't know about the Dire King's stronghold, then how did you two find it?"

"We followed you, obviously," said Serif. "We lost your trail briefly in the sewers, but Virgule connected the dots."

"Ley lines," Virgule said. "I knew we were close, so I plotted the nearest corresponding ley lines and found an intersection point very nearby."

"Ley lines?" I asked.

"Seams," said Jackaby. "A ley line is a seam along the veil wall. Our world has scarcely any functional magic compared to the Annwyn, but magic is always strongest along the seams. Sorcerers and witches throughout the ages have made use of these ley lines to strengthen their own natural gifts. It stands to reason the rend would fall on a ley line. Easier to pop a seam than to cut straight through."

"Care to explain why you were working with the enemy?" Serif asked. Her grip tightened on the crossbow, but for now she kept it hanging at her side.

"Better the devil you know," Jackaby answered. He nodded toward Pavel. "He got us closer to the devil we don't."

"It seems he outlived his usefulness." Serif raised an eyebrow. "Are you in the habit of killing all your informants?"

"Only those who are in the habit of trying to kill us," Jackaby said.

"Madam General," Virgule interrupted. "We're not alone."

The doors to a blocky guardhouse on the far corner of the hold flung open. In the doorway stood a lithe man with white-blond hair, his face shrouded in shadow. He was oddly familiar, but my attention was pulled from him to a pair of bright red imps who exploded past him, tails whipping behind them eagerly. They leapt onto the outer rim of the wall, vaulting the crenellations and chattering like monkeys as they galloped toward us.

Virgule's sword was out in a flash as he leapt down from the roof onto the wall. "Watch out, General."

Serif was unfazed. She stood her ground and leveled her crossbow at the nearest galloping imp. The bolt impaled the thing in midleap, sending the little red creature backward over the parapet with a pained squeak and then tumbling down the side of the wall. The second imp chittered angrily and continued forward in leaps and bounds. "If imps are the best they can throw at us–" Serif began.

She was interrupted by a wet groan. The ogres–the ones Pavel had dispatched for us–sat up. They pushed themselves heavily to their feet, their heads still hanging at an unnatural angle to their bodies. Their eyes were glassy like the late Mr. Fairmont's had been, right before the late Mr. Fairmont tried to eat Charlie and me back in the gardens.

If you are unfamiliar with the sensation of being surrounded by undead ogres, it is akin to the feeling of being lost in the woods. The shapes looming around you are simply too much to take in all at once. The difference, of course, is that trees are less inclined to murder you violently. Also, there is a smell.

The ogre corpses had reached their full height, their necks cracking sickeningly as they looked around to face us. My head barely came up to the largest brute's waist, my eyes roughly even with its meaty, swaying knuckles. I felt slightly dizzy as I gazed up.

Charlie and I had only barely survived one walking human corpse; I did not like our odds against this massive pair. Perhaps if Pavel had still been alive to help–and if he had not been actively trying to kill us himself–we might have stood half a chance. He had, after all, been strong enough to take on the two brutes by himself. But now–

Pavel sat up. The early morning sunlight washed his pale, scarred face. It was the first time I had ever seen him upright in the daylight. He did not look better for it. His eyes, like the ogres', were eerily vacant. The creature that had once been Pavel stood up clumsily.

"Lieutenant," barked Serif. "I've got the larger ogre; you see to the lesser. Go. Seer—can I trust you two to attend to your reanimated informant?"

"We've got it in hand!" Jackaby said.

Virgule had already advanced on the first ogre, sword drawn. The brute took a swipe at him, which he ducked easily, rising to bury the blade in the ogre's chest. The sword sank deep. The ogre glanced at the hilt protruding from his torso and then slapped Virgule with a blow that sent him skidding along the castle wall until he rolled to a stop twenty feet away.

Serif grunted as she launched herself against the other ogre, but my attention was quickly drawn to Pavel, who was advancing fast.

Jackaby gripped the wooden stake. "No hard feelings?" he said, and drove it into Pavel's heart. The forces driving Pavel had clearly changed. The stake sank into his chest, but to no avail. Pavel did not slow, but rather pushed into the attack, catching Jackaby by surprise.

Fortunately for my employer, Pavel appeared to have forgotten that he had no teeth. He buried his gums into Jackaby's neck. Jackaby cried out in alarm. The two of them were locked together, looking equally distraught for several seconds, until Jackaby came to his senses. He seized Pavel by the arm and flipped him around in an awkward tumble that sent both of them sprawling.

"Sir, look out!" I called. The remaining imp, still bounding along the parapets, was only a few leaps away. Jackaby looked about and grabbed his fallen satchel, which still lay atop the wall where Jenny had dropped it. He threw the entire thing haphazardly toward the imp.

He missed by a considerable margin. The sack flopped open on the ground about halfway between them. The beet red creature touched down one last time before he made his final pounce. Except, instead of solid stone, the imp encountered the inside of Jackaby's enchanted satchel. The thing about Jackaby's satchel was that there was considerably more of it inside than there was outside. The imp squawked in surprise and vanished from sight. Jackaby threw himself over the satchel and held it closed with his full weight.

Panting, he shot me a celebratory grin. "I've got this one," he said, then his eyes widened. "Watch yourself!"

I turned in time to see Serif's ogre, the larger of the two, stumble backward, nearly on top of me, as it recoiled from a blow. The brutes were slow and uncoordinated, but what they lacked in dexterity they more than made up for in sheer muscle. Crossbow bolts stuck out of this one like porcupine quills. The general had abandoned her bow in favor of her sword.

Virgule still had not managed to retrieve his own weapon

from the chest of the other ogre. It lumbered after him like a grunting, angry kebab. Virgule wove around its strikes, but he was moving stiffly, and the living dead showed no signs of slowing.

On the ground ahead of me I caught sight of one of the discarded poleaxes. I grabbed the pole–and nearly fell over. The weapon was stuck fast, jammed in place between the outer parapet and the inner wall. I abandoned it and snatched up the other, only a few feet away. The weapon was much too heavy for me to wield with finesse, but I hefted it with both hands anyway.

I glanced over my shoulder in time to see the largest ogre thundering furiously toward me, Serif on its shoulders, dodging its hands as it swatted at her. She raised her blade and swung down, landing a blow across the ogre's neck, but she had sacrificed her own defenses for the shot, and the ogre's thick hide was unforgiving. The blade cut a sickly cleft in the corpse's flesh that did not bleed so much as it leaked a dark, syrupy liquid. In return, the brute locked its teeth into her and tore a ragged bite out of her right shoulder. Serif's sword clanged to the stones, and her legs buckled as the ogre dropped her.

Serif defenseless beneath him, the brute went for the kill, and my hands acted on their own. Before I realized what I was doing, I had swung the poleax. I struck the ogre off-center, lopping off the wretched creature's ear and a goodly portion of its cheek.

My stomach lurched. I was going to be sick.

The creature turned slowly to face me. Well, it turned to three-fourths-of-a-face me. *Don't be sick. Don't be sick. Don't be sick until you're done fighting monsters.*

The ogre lunged, and I pelted toward the guardhouse in the opposite direction, slipping past Virgule and his own hulking opponent. I could hear my ogre slam into Virgule's as we passed, and I hazarded a glance over my shoulder. Virgule's impaled creature had abandoned its efforts to catch Virgule and was loping along behind us, glaring, instead. Splendid. Because what I needed was to have both brutes after me. Clumsy or not, they did not look inclined to stop anytime soon, and the heavy poleax in my hands felt more like an anchor than an asset.

An idea danced in my brain. I willed my legs to pump just a little faster, to put just a little more distance between the ogres and myself.

I could feel the thuds of both brutes now loping behind me along the wall. They were slow, but for every three of my strides they needed only one. When I was nearly to the guardhouse, I dropped to the ground and rammed the pointed tip of the poleax into the outer parapet and shoved the butt against the inner. I gave it a firm kick to wedge it between the two crenellated walls as tightly as I could. It stuck soundly, but I wasn't certain it would be strong enough. No time for certainty. I leapt back to my feet. *Please work. Please work. Please work.*

The first behemoth closed the gap, its disfigured face glistening and its lips snarling. I held my ground. Three more steps. Two. One. I dove aside, whipping around to watch the enormous ogre trip and tumble into the bricks. Its ankle smashed the pole into scraps. But it did not trip. It did not even stumble.

The brute paused. It craned its broken neck down to look at the remains of my useless trap. At that moment, Virgule's ogre, still barreling along behind the first, plowed straight into it from behind. The second ogre's momentum was enough to drive the first headlong into the stone wall of the guardhouse. The masonry was sturdy but no match for a battering ram made of ogres.

Virgule, who had been following close behind, came to a skidding halt as the guardhouse crumpled. Massive stones the size of writing desks collapsed inward, hammering the ogre with one blow after another until the colossus was buried from the shoulders up. The smaller of the two, the point of Virgule's sword still poking out of its back, was half-buried for a moment as well, but as bad luck would have it, its head remained fully intact. It shrugged off a few cracked roofing tiles and pulled itself free.

"I'll call that a qualified success," I breathed.

"Watch out!" Virgule cried, and in another moment we both were off again, racing back along the wall.

Ahead of us, Pavel had resumed his assault on Jackaby, who remained on the ground, clutching the jostling satchel.

With one hand, Jackaby was frantically searching his pockets, pitching whatever defenses he could find at the glassy-eyed attacker.

Jackaby swiveled his head in time to see us racing past him. "Here!" He had pulled something from his coat—it looked like a little medicine tablet—and he threw it haphazardly at the ogre's face. It caught the brute in the mouth and at once the ogre's jawline popped and shifted. Its teeth grew four sizes. They had been large to begin with, but at least they had been proportionately large. Now they jutted past its gray lips like enormous razor-sharp tusks. I ducked away as the ogre came at me with its new, horrifying jaws.

With one meaty hand, the undead thug grabbed me by the waist, pinning my right arm to my side. Its skin was cool and moist, like rising dough, and it smelled of wet rats and carrion birds. I struggled with my free hand and managed to pull the useless sharpened stake out of my pocket. I might not be able to take the thing's head off, but I would die fighting. I waited for the colossal corpse to raise its fist, but instead it did something far worse—it opened its mouth. Rancid breath washed over me, like rotten onions and spoiled death.

I did the only thing I could think to do before the brute could take a bite of me. I stuck my hand right in between those terrible teeth and stuffed the wooden stake into the creature's maw, wedging it between the roof of its mouth and its lower jaw. The thing halted, shaking its head. I could see the muscles of its jaw working. Pain did not appear to be an obstacle. With a final grunt of effort, it closed its great ugly mouth with a loud clack of gnashing teeth and a muffled crunch of something else inside its skull. The ogre's eyes widened. Its muscles went limp.

As the corpse swayed, I slipped through its grip. It managed to stagger a step or two backward before it stumbled over the edge and plummeted half a dozen stories to the ground below. The wall shook as the ogre landed. I breathed. That was both of them—we had done it!

Serif groaned, and Virgule hastened to her side.

"Don't trouble yourself on my account!" grunted Jackaby. I spun around. Pavel had him pinned to the ground. Jackaby was still clutching the satchel with one hand while the other held Pavel at arm's length. It was not really Pavel—it was a clumsy marionette of the treacherous vampire, but it was vicious all the same. The satchel flopped and bucked under Jackaby's grasp. The vampire clawed mercilessly at his arms and chest, and the detective's coat was in tatters.

Virgule was attending to Serif. Beside them lay her sword. I picked it up. It was heavier than it looked, but nothing compared to the poleax. The weight balanced comfortably in my hand. While Pavel tore at my employer, I raised the blade over my head. I swung my arms and felt the sword squish and click against bone. Cutting a person's head off is not like carving a slice of ham. There are tendons and vertebrae and . . . and . . . feelings. Feelings are awful. I was not the sort of lady who had been brought up to hack into the undead with a longsword.

Pavel's head turned ever so slightly, and I caught the faintest hint of that insufferable smirk he had been so good at before his un-re-dead-birth. His hollow eyes on me, Pavel caught Jackaby's wrist in one hand. Jackaby struggled, and I could tell the corpse had a grip like steel. He was now pinned. Jackaby had to either release his hold on the imp or leave himself defenseless against the vampire.

I hacked into Pavel with the longsword again. And a third time. And a fourth. I could feel his spine chipping with each blow. His head tilted rakishly forward. And then he caught the blade with one hand on the fifth. We all froze there for a moment, Pavel's left hand wrapped around the sword. It began to drip something thick and syrupy. His right hand was still locked on Jackaby's arm, and his head was lolling forward.

"Catch," Jackaby said, and opened the bag.

The imp catapulted out of the bag, and the effect was something like firing an angry red cannonball directly at Pavel's face. There was a crack.

We never did find the head.

The imp, having skidded and rolled to an ungainly landing halfway across the rooftop, went scampering away across the tiles.

"Should we stop him?" Virgule asked.

"Don't bother," Serif grunted. "He won't raise any alarms that throwing an ogre over the wall didn't already raise."

"You need to stay still," Jackaby cautioned as Serif attempted to push herself upright.

"I need to do precisely the opposite," snarled Serif. "Salamander gauze, Captain."

Virgule nodded. He produced a slim medical pouch from within his robes and took from it a roll of red-brown bandages. Serif gingerly slid the cloak from her shoulders. Her tunic beneath was saturated with blood.

Virgule bit his lip. "This is going to—"

"Do it now."

The captain swallowed and wrapped Serif's shoulder with the cloth. As he tied off the end, the fabric began to glow like a hot ember. The noise that Serif made was not a scream in the traditional sense, but something more animal, a roar of concentrated pain and fury. When the magic had run its course, Serif gasped and pitched forward, resting her head on the stones while she caught her breath, steam billowing from the bandages.

"Get her back to your castle," Jackaby said. "Tell Arawn to march on Hafgan's Hold immediately."

"I'm not going anywhere," Serif panted.

"The detective is right." Virgule swallowed. "We need reinforcements."

"Of course we do," Serif said. "Go, Captain, and tell Lord Arawn we need the elves and the dwarves and anyone else who will answer the call. They might not march for the Fair King, but they will march for the good of the Annwyn."

"You're staying here?"

"I do as Lord Arawn bids me. And you will do as your commander bids you. Now, go."

As Virgule leapt up onto the rooftop and climbed the spire back up into the rend, Jackaby pushed himself up. He tore off a particularly flappy bit of his tattered coat and sighed. One of the front pockets had been ripped halfway off, and a knot of yarn was protruding. Jackaby pulled it out. Hatun's hat. He regarded it with a somber look in his eyes and then stuffed it on his head. He looked as ridiculous as he had the day we met. "Somebody's got to keep the world in one piece until help arrives," he said, "and it looks like we're it."

Chapter Twenty-One

Had I been less secure in my own talents, I might have found it somewhat embarrassing to be the least graceful person in a group that also consisted of a madman wearing a lumpy tea cozy on his head and a grievously injured woman with only one functional arm. Jackaby and Serif moved through the stronghold like shadows, however, and I kept up with them as stealthily as I could.

Within the tall curtain walls of the hold stood half a dozen stout stone buildings with thatched roofs, all circling a fortified tower: the keep, the top of which had been replaced with a broad dome, like the roof of an observatory. Wooden scaffolding circled the outside of the structure, climbing halfway up the walls. Behind this, I could see thick metal tubes and snaking pipes that had punched their way out of the stonework and clung all over the tower like ivy. Here and there in the larger gaps between the metal and the bricks, I made out glimpses of what lay beyond.

It was like peeking into the inner workings of an enormous clock. If the Palace of Westminster were reduced to ruins and its great Clock Tower riddled with cracks, the effect might be similar. I could see bits and pieces of truly massive cogs revolving within the masonwork.

We made our way down from the wall along a very narrow, excruciatingly exposed staircase. With every step I was waiting for an alarm to sound and the entire compound to descend upon us. Miraculously, we reached the ground without incident. No sooner had we done so, however, than we heard the pounding of feet and the clatter of steel. Without a word, all three of us pressed into the shadows of the nearest structure, a rectangular building that smelled of hay and manure.

I held my breath as five, ten, twenty soldiers hurried up the narrow stairs we had just dismounted. Their ears stuck out like goblins', but unlike goblins, these troops were seven feet tall at the shortest. They were broad shouldered, with forearms as thick as a grown man's waist. Although leaner and faster than the mountainous ogres, they still looked as though they were bred for battle.

"Trolls," whispered Jackaby.

The troll in front stood at the top of the stairs and yelled something in a voice that sounded like a mixture of human vocal cords and untuned cello strings. I did not recognize the language. The rest of them split off evenly, half moving along the top of the wall to the left, the other half to the right.

"They're looking for us, in case there was any question," Serif hissed from her quiet patch of darkness. "They have noticed that someone in this castle is dropping ogres and pitching vampire heads off the walls. The commander just reminded his troops that they are under orders not to let the intruders get out of here alive."

"Well, that's good news, at least," Jackaby whispered. "They're worried about us getting out of here. They don't know we're still working on getting in."

"That is a great comfort, sir," I answered.

We kept to the shadows whenever possible, moving ever inward toward the domed keep in the center. For the last stretch, Jackaby found us cover by climbing up within the rafters of a long, thatched building. The crawl space was narrow and cramped, but better a claustrophobic attic than a claustrophobic coffin. From the chamber beneath us I could smell steam and blood and raw meat, and I found myself hoping very much that we were above a kitchen. We reached the end and peeked through the thatch. A court-yard lay directly between us and the tower, and in this space stood milling at least a hundred monstrous creatures. I recognized more trolls, imps, and ogres, but there were also swarms of fairies no bigger than locusts, great mangy wolves the size of bears, and wraithlike figures in tattered black robes who seemed to swim through the air, their rags trailing behind them like seaweed behind a trawler.

"Wights," Jackaby breathed. "Brownies, manticores, kaiju, jumbies, lobs, hobs—just about every Unseelie creature ever mentioned in *Mendel's Magical Menagerie*—and a few even I don't recognize."

"We'll go around to the back of the keep," said Serif.

"We'll need a distraction if we hope to get to the far side of the tower without being seen by that crowd," I said.

"Leave that to me." Serif reached into her robes with her good hand and pulled out a slim metal tube. She selected a dart from a little wooden box and slid it into the tube.

"Poison?" Jackaby inquired as Serif maneuvered herself painfully into a position from which she could see the throng through the thatch.

"Boxwood ash and mandrake root," she answered.

"That's a somnifacient, isn't it?" said Jackaby.

"We use it as a kobold sedative."

"Might be effective against the hobs, then, but even if it is, putting a single hob to sleep won't do much to improve our situation."

"This is not my first mission, Seer. It would drop a kobold, hob, or any lesser oddling. Against trollkin, however, it has the opposite effect," she grunted. "Increases violent tendencies."

"Best not to do that, then," Jackaby said.

Serif's cheeks puffed out and the pipe made a soft *thoom*. I pushed my head up to peer through the scratchy thatch. A muscular troll carrying a cudgel the size of a small child slapped at his neck as though bitten by a mosquito. He spun angrily, his lips curled back in a snarl.

"You missed," said Jackaby.

"I really didn't."

The big troll glared at the swarm of brownies fluttering in the air behind him and swung the cudgel through the cloud, which scattered and chittered angrily. The cudgel, finding very little resistance from the brownies, slammed instead into the back of a pale giant who sat hunched over in the dirt. The giant unfolded. He was so massive, he could have leaned casually with his elbow on the head of one of the ogres we had fought earlier. Beneath ice-white hair and pallid skin, he wore a simple tunic that might have doubled as the sail of a Spanish galleon.

"Oh. Oh my. That's got the jötun's attention now," Jackaby said. "This is the plan?"

"Wait for it."

The jötun rose to his feet. The troll clutched his cudgel and looked up. And then he looked farther up. The ground beneath the jötun began to glitter with spreading crystals of ice. The jötun raised one enormous foot and stomped. The building beneath us shook. In a circle all around the jötun, creatures were thrown to their backs and dusted by a glittering flurry of ice. Even from our hiding spot, I felt the wave of cold wash over us. There was now a cloud of sparkling mist surrounding the troll and everyone next to him. The monsters at the far end of the assembly were craning their necks to see the frost giant, who was only visible from the waist up. The sounds of scuffling and snarling were coming from within the icy mist at his feet. It was pandemonium.

"Now," said Serif.

Chapter Twenty-Two

As the sounds of the furious brawl came muffled through the thatch, Serif carved a hole at the back side of the roof and slipped out. We followed, padding as quietly as we could after her across the grass. By now the sun was high in the sky, and shadows were getting scarce. Part of me would have liked to tuck myself into a ball up in that attic and stay there until everything was over, but I gritted my teeth and forced my legs to pump, and we sprinted the last stretch. We were in plain view of the courtyard for only a few seconds, and even though the attention of the crowd remained fixed on the scuffle in the back, my heart was still pounding in my chest by the time we reached the far side of the hold, tucking ourselves under the cover of the creaky scaffolding.

"There's a charm on the whole building," Jackaby observed. He blinked at the stone. "It's strong."

"Defensive?" Serif asked.

"Protective. Hold on–" He pulled a series of little glass lenses from his pocket and peered at the stone through them. Serif glanced around impatiently. "The whole tower is held together by a net of magic. Probably necessary, by the looks of it. They've torn right through the support walls."

"Just a coherence charm, then?" said Serif. "No defensive hexing or barrier spells?"

"None that I can see," said Jackaby. "But there's all sorts of energy on the inside that I can't understand. Best proceed with caution."

"Hm. You're a bit useful after all, Seer," Serif grunted. She scrabbled up the scaffolding, holding her injured arm against her side as she pulled herself up one-handed. Jackaby and I followed. Halfway up the wall, we reached a cleft in the stones large enough to peer through. Jackaby pressed his face up against the gap, and when he pulled away he did not look happy. I slid up to have a look for myself.

The hold was a mess of copper and bronze. Somewhere down below, massive turbines were humming; I could feel the vibration of them through the stone. Clockwork ranging in size from carriage wheels to cogs took up an entire story of the tower. Somewhere above us, light crackled and popped, a golden-yellow glow with flashes of electric blue illuminating the bricks and metalwork. Heavy girders were bolted to the stone, and a staircase snaked up around the tower, following the curve of the wall. The remnants of a demolished landing were visible a few feet above us.

"I can't tell if the machine is at the top of the tower or the bottom," I said.

"I believe the machine is the tower," said Jackaby behind me. "There are unnatural energies running in and out of every inch of the building. The power it's generating is incomprehensible. Well, not *generating*, per se. Channeling. Directing. I think we've found our spear."

"Our spear?" I said, pulling my eyes away from the sight.

"Hafgan's spear was never a real spear. It was a metaphor. *The spear grips the hand that grips the spear.* Power takes hold of those who take hold of power."

"Do you suppose that's why Hafgan went bad?" I said. "Maybe he really did start out with the best intentions, but then power changed him? That would explain why Arawn had to kill him—why Arawn was able to kill him at all, even with the twain's shield protecting him."

"It fits. All this time we've been thinking of Morwen's sword as the new spear, but it's not at all, is it? The blade was just a tool. The Dire Council created a machine to do the same thing, to channel the sort of power no single soul was ever meant to control. The first attempt was destroyed a decade ago—Jenny's fiancé saw to that when he gave up his life to sabotage its construction—but it has been remade. And by the look of it, they've gotten it right this time."

"Up here," Serif whispered from above us. Jackaby and I clambered up on the swaying scaffolding to reach her. A thick pipe emerged from the brickwork where she stood. It ran up the wall several meters and reentered the building near the domed roof. The stones had clearly been knocked out to make room for the addition, and several of them were cracked and falling apart. There was space enough for someone very thin to squeeze through between the metal and the wall.

Serif plunged through the gap sword-first. Her lithe frame caught at the hips, though, and a cracked brick the size of my head began to slip loose. I grabbed for it before it could fall and crash down the scaffolding. It was lighter than I expected.

"What sort of stone is this?" I asked Jackaby. "It's like lifting a stale loaf of bread! Here, we can make the hole a little larger if we—" But the moment I pulled the brick away from the wall it wrenched my arms downward and smashed into the rickety platform. The scaffolding rocked perilously for several seconds.

"That would be the coherence charm," said Jackaby. "It's designed to prevent the building from collapsing by nullifying the material's gravitational burdens. Outside of the charm's range, gravity still exists."

We widened the gap, taking care to set the rest of the

stones down as gently as we could on the scaffolding, and then pressed our way into the building.

The keep was four stories tall. The floorboards on each level had been almost entirely knocked out to make room for the metal girders and myriad pipes and cables winding through the building. We found ourselves on what was left of the second-story landing.

On the ground level, just below us, a pair of rumbling generators sat against the wall. In the center of the floor, away from the cascade of coiling cables, stood three identical metal frames. Each was about eight feet tall, but they looked distinctly like empty coffins stood on end–albeit coffins constructed by an emotionally troubled metalsmith.

I looked up. Right ahead of us was suspended a curious contraption, hanging from a huge articulated metal arm. Its design was not unlike that of an enormous microscope: a brass canister as big as a bathtub with three smaller cylinders affixed to the bottom. Instead of lenses, each of these was capped with something halfway between a lightning rod and the nozzle of a fireman's hose. All three were attached to the larger canister by a series of interlocking cogs and joints, as though each could be finely adjusted. At present, they were aimed directly at the metal coffin-like frames below.

"My word," Jackaby breathed.

"What do you suppose it does?" I asked, but then I realized Jackaby was not looking at the brass device. I followed his eyes up. The landing above housed some sort of platform, although I could not make out what was on it from where we stood. Higher still, fabricated out of gleaming copper and burnished bronze, unfurled a mechanical marvel unlike anything I had ever seen.

It was twenty feet across, its framework butting against the walls around it on every side. It looked like a glorious rose made of living metal, every petal a polished disc, constantly circling in a pattern of inscrutable complexity. The discs on the rim glowed faintly, like an iron just pulled from the fire, and those in the very center were almost too bright to look at directly. It was beautiful, it was brilliant, and it was trying very hard to destroy the world.

Shadows danced in the dark tower as a pulsing beam of warm, golden light issued from the whirring discs. Sparkles of white light twinkled in the golden rays, moving upward, drawn in toward the center of the mechanical rose by the inscrutable forces of the machine.

Where the rippling light illuminated the wall, the tower shredded, stones ripping apart like weathered linen. Emerald light burst through the gaps, and through these I could see not the forests of the Annwyn, but a surprisingly pale sky and a simple country church. It made my insides feel strange—not only because it did not belong in this alien countryside, but because it belonged to a different horizon altogether. The spires of the church stood at a crooked angle, jutting off to the left, the trees beyond it doing the same.

Gears clicked and cogs spun, and the beautiful machine swiveled, its glowing light sliding down along the wall. As soon as the rippling golden beam passed, the rends between the two dimensions began to seal again. The stones knit together, leaving a few chips and spiderweb cracks as the only trace that they had been ruptured moments before. In the light of the pivoting machine, new rips began to form farther down.

"It's healing itself," said Jackaby. "The veil is healing itself faster than they can tear it apart. The machine still isn't powerful enough!"

"No machine is powerful enough to breach the veil." Serif scowled. She crept along the creaking floorboards until she had reached the edge of our broken landing. The newest split in the veil was only a few feet up from where she stood. Through it, I could see a stained glass window. The glass depicted the Blessed Virgin Mary, upside down, in a mosaic of cheery blues. It felt very out of place inside the grim tower. "This cannot be. The veil is the most powerful force on either of our worlds. This . . . this cannot be real." She stood on her toes and reached up toward the stained glass window with the tips of her fingers.

That's when everything went wrong.

The moment the wavering light touched Serif's hand, she shuddered. Jackaby leapt forward before I could see what was happening. Serif turned her head limply toward us just as her eyes rolled back in her head and her legs went limp. If Jackaby had been a moment slower, she would have tumbled over the edge and to the floor below us. He caught her with both hands and pulled her away from the ledge.

"Is she all right?" I cried.

"It's drained her," he answered, pulling Serif farther from the strange light. I helped him prop her against the wall. She was barely breathing. "She was in poor shape to begin with, but that thing sapped her in an instant."

"Will she live?" I whispered.

With a series of mechanical clacks and clicks above us, the machine stopped swiveling. Cogs whirred to a stop.

"She really won't," came a familiar voice from above us. Morwen Finstern stood at the crumbling edge of the landing above ours, black blade at her hip and a smirk on her lips. "And neither will you, in case you were wondering."

Chapter Twenty-Three

M iss Finstern," said Jackaby. "You're looking rather . . . villainous. Have you considered *not* destroying the world, though?"

Morwen sneered. "We aren't going to destroy the world, you stupid man. We're going to bring it back. We're going to make things the way they're supposed to be again. Your kind have spent far too long alone in an empty arena that was meant for blood. You've forgotten what it means to fight for your lives. You've grown fat and weak."

"So kind of you to look out for our best interests. Disseminating some nice pamphlets with advice on diet and exercise might be less trouble for everyone, though. I'd be happy to help you print them up. I know a fellow with his own press. He does marvelous woodcuts."

"Our kind have grown weak as well," Morwen continued, ignoring Jackaby. "They have dulled their blades with bureaucracy and diplomacy. They don't remember what it means to be wild any longer. They live their lives in chains and call it freedom. My father is going to return the worlds to a glorious new age of chaos."

"Where is that friendly father of yours? Off giving schoolchildren nightmares?"

"He is coming," said Morwen with a menacing smile. "He is setting in motion the next stage of his plan."

"And what might that be?" I asked. I was slowly moving toward Serif's sword. Morwen did not appear to have noticed.

"The final one," she said with sinister delight. "He will be very pleased you came to see it done."

"Will he be pleased about this?" I said. I whipped Serif's sword out of its sheath and swiped it at the pipe climbing up the wall beside me. It chimed like a church bell. My wrist throbbed with the vibration. The pipe was barely chipped.

"About your ineptitude?" she asked. "He might be a little amused."

Heavy footsteps sounded on the stairs behind me, and I turned to see a man with enormous muttonchop sideburns and wild eyes climbing up the second-floor landing. He reached the top and snarled. His teeth looked very sharp.

"Your assistance is not required, Mr. Loup," Morwen said lazily. The hairy man did not approach, but he did remain locked in place, effectively blocking any chance we might have had at making our exit down the stairs.

"Oh, come on!" I kicked at the pipe. It shifted and began to hiss from a seam a few feet up. I might not be able to take apart the whole building, but I would do as much damage as I could before she got to me. I kicked again, and a fine mist began to spray over us.

"Please, no," Morwen said in mock concern. "Don't ruin the cooling lines."

"Miss Rook, I think perhaps it would be unwise–" Jackaby began, but I drove one more kick into the pipe, and the metal split, a stream of water gushing out at once.

The fountain cascading over our heads did not splash down across the landing. It arced through the air and then defied physics to spin around us instead. It was a ribbon of whirling liquid, and then a wide band, growing thicker as more water fed it from the ruptured line. Mr. Loup chuckled thickly from the stairs. My eyes shot up. Morwen was spinning a hand lazily in the air as though stirring a pot with her fingers. I cursed inwardly. Nixie. Water spirit. I was an idiot.

"You know, I do enjoy a good evisceration, but it's been months since I properly drowned anyone," Morwen mused. The water was quickly spreading into a thick dome.

Soon it would be enough to encapsulate us in a complete globe of water. With all of those muscular monsters waiting right outside the door, I had not expected to be killed by a bubble.

"The window," Jackaby whispered. He nodded toward the rend, where, through the distortion of the gurgling wall of water, I could still make out the rip into our world. The hole torn through the fabric of the veil had ceased growing any larger, but the image of Mary all dressed in blue hung before us, dancing and bobbing on the far side of the wave. "We can make it if we move fast."

"What?" I whispered back. "Even if we could, the machine is still on."

"Three," said Jackaby.

"Wait, we can't—"

"Two."

"Sir!"

"One!" Jackaby grabbed me by the hand and leapt. I felt my body slow down as we crashed through the water. For a horrifying second I was afraid that I wouldn't have the momentum to escape its clutches, but then I was tumbling out the other side and Jackaby was pulling me to my feet. Soaking wet, we reached the edge of the demolished landing and jumped.

We leapt over the humming generators, through the glowing golden light, and into another world entirely.

Gravity shifted abruptly. Down became left and up

became right and then the Blessed Virgin was shattering into a million tiny pieces all around me and rows of pews were rushing toward me. I ricocheted into the first bench hard enough to send it tumbling into the second, skidded along the floor, and came to rest in an aisle. My head spun. From the sound of it, Jackaby's landing had been no smoother than mine.

I took a silent inventory of my injuries, wiggling my legs and arms and gingerly turning my neck this way and that before I sat up. We were in the church.

"So much for subterfuge," said Jackaby, climbing out from under an overturned lectern at the front of the chamber. "Are you all right?"

"I have felt better," I said, "but stiff upper lip and all that." I winced. "And stiff everything else while we're at it. I may have bruised parts of myself I didn't know I had."

I surveyed the room. It was a chapel like any other, with a large wooden cross on the wall above the dais, where Jackaby was now sitting up, and more stained glass windows around the room letting in colorful rays of filtered sunlight.

I looked back at the one through which we had made our explosive entrance. The dark tower was visible, its details hazy behind the bright green glow. I expected to see Morwen leaping after us at any moment, but the scene beyond the veil remained empty. Where was she?

Jackaby appeared to be having the same thought. "I doubt she wants to risk having her power siphoned if she comes through," he reasoned.

"Right," I said. "Why didn't that thing drain us the way it drained Serif?" I asked.

"It did," Jackaby grunted. He limped off the podium, moving toward the back of the church. "We're human, though, not beings of magic, so the effects were not as pronounced. It was definitely pulling at our vital energies, though. If we had hung about, it would have finished the job soon enough."

"Now that you mention it, I could use a sustaining cup of tea. Although that might come of being broadsided by a church," I said. "And cut by a vampire, and bullied by ogres."

"We also skipped breakfast," Jackaby added. "It's probably the breakfast."

The glow coming from the rend above us dimmed, and the gap began to seal over. I blinked as the sunlight from the earthly world crept through in its place. "She's shifted the device," Jackaby said. "The gap is mending itself again. The next one could be anywhere. Keep alert. We need to get out of here and back to the hold at once."

"Of course. We wouldn't want to leave Morwen waiting."

There was a flutter of movement from the shattered window above us. The gap was nearly closed when a streak of blue shot through it and came to land with a splash in the aisle next to me. I stumbled backward. The rend closed and unfiltered sunlight sparkled off the glistening figure rising in front of us. Morwen had ridden the burst of water into the church.

"I don't think she's the waiting type," said Jackaby.

Chapter Twenty-Four

Morwen took a deep breath, water curling up around her legs like a coiling liquid snake. There was nothing between us now but empty air. The church held its breath.

And then Morwen collapsed.

The nixie dropped to her knees. Her water whip fell, splattering into a damp smear across the floorboards.

"She must have drained her magic crossing the barrier!" I said.

"No," said Jackaby. "She turned the machine away from the gap so that she could make the jump. This is something else."

Morwen shuddered.

"It's the church," Jackaby said. "The last time you met,

she couldn't touch you when your scars formed the likeness of a cross on your cheek—now she's got apostles shining down at her from every window and that great big symbol hanging over her." He gestured up to the massive cross on the wall above the lectern.

Morwen was straining to rise, but her eyes screwed shut and she fell again.

"Luck is on our side for once," Jackaby added. "That's novel."

"Oh dear," I said. "I have a feeling it's not going to last."

"What?" He followed my eyes. Emerald light was playing across the surface of the enormous cross. A new rend was forming right on top of it.

"If the veil opens there, it's going to split the cross in two," I said. "If the sign of the cross is what's holding Morwen in place, I sincerely doubt it will be very effective in pieces."

"We need to get up there the moment it does," Jackaby declared. "That rend is our path back to the Annwyn."

Together we upturned the nearest pew. The bench was heavy and ungainly, but we managed to lean it up against the wall with its back side up, like a ramp. A tiny hole had formed in the center of the cross, and it was growing.

"It's opening," said Jackaby. He glanced back at Morwen Finstern, who was clenching her fists as if straining against an invisible weight. "Get up there."

I held my skirts and took the ramp at a run. I was nearly to the top when the base slid out and the pew dropped several inches. My feet skidded out from under me and I slammed hard against the wood, hugging it to keep from falling. Jackaby threw his body weight against the bottom of the bench to stop it from sliding.

I turned my eyes back to the cross just in time to see the rend rip through the wood completely. The bottom fell away, sending a wooden plank with one splintered end clattering to the floor below. The top of the cross swung apart as well, one arm swaying to the right and an L-shaped section dangling loosely to the left.

"Go!" Jackaby yelled. I heard the sound of Morwen's blade sliding free of its sheath, but I did not turn to look before I jumped back into the Annwyn.

I was met on the other side not by the dimly lit interior of the keep, but by intense sunlight and a startlingly long drop. The tower was four stories tall, and I had just slipped out at the top of it. From this dizzying height, I had an excellent view of the hundreds of monsters assembled in the courtyard thirty or forty feet below me. I yelped in alarm and clutched frantically at the wall, my hand unexpectedly finding purchase around a narrow copper pipe. I clung to it with both hands, feeling the metal sway.

I began to hear the shouts from below. The gruesome garrison had spotted me. I tried not to focus on the noise. My hands were shaking, and sweat trickled down my temple. It came as very little consolation that the fall would kill me before those brutes down below ever got the chance.

Jackaby burst out of the rend beside me, and I instinctively shot out an arm and grabbed him by his ragged, flapping coat. He clutched at my arm with one hand and at his ridiculous hat with the other.

"Pipe!" I managed, with remarkable articulation, given the circumstances. "Grab it!"

He slammed into the wall beneath me and my hand flew back to the pipe, which squeaked and leaned about six inches farther from the wall. I felt dizzy.

"This is not a measurable improvement from the church," said Jackaby.

The building rumbled and shook. I felt my grip slipping.

And then Morwen flew through the gap. She locked eyes on me for a fleeting second and swung the black blade hard toward me. The obsidian edge sparked against the stones and spun out of her hands, and then her eyes widened.

Morwen Finstern fell.

I closed my eyes, my breath coming in gasps and gulps. Below us, the crowd began to circle around the nixie's still body. A hundred eyes climbed the tower up toward us on our precarious perch.

"Back to the church," grunted Jackaby. "Sooner would be better."

The church was dark and cool and quiet as I hopped down from the upturned pew. My legs were about to give out.

My hands were throbbing. My chest was on fire. I collapsed onto the nearest bench.

Jackaby popped back through behind me and scooted down the pew to join me. For a long time he said nothing. We just sat there, breathing.

"She was holding back." Jackaby finally broke the silence.

"That was holding back?" I panted.

"Less so with you," he amended. "I don't think she likes you very much."

"I did put onions in her pie."

"She was holding back against me. She had a clean shot there, in the end, but she let me climb through after you before she took it."

"Why would she be holding back?"

"Pavel said he wasn't allowed to kill me. He said they needed me. Needed my eyes."

"Well, let's try to keep those in your head, shall we?"

I leaned back against the bench. The church was spinning slightly around me. I felt another shudder, like a faint earthquake.

"The whole fabric of the veil is strained in this church," Jackaby said. "The coherence charm is the only thing holding Hafgan's keep together. I don't imagine this parish can boast the same."

We sat there, gazing up at the stained glass apostles, catching our breath. It felt very much like we were sitting in the eye of a storm.

"Hm," I said. "That's funny."

"What's funny?"

"The apostles."

"Typically known for having been chummy with the Messiah and then dying torturous martyr's deaths," said Jackaby. "Hilarious."

"Not that sort of funny. There are only eleven of them here," I said.

"Well, we did make a rather dramatic entrance through the twelfth," said Jackaby.

"No, we came in via the Virgin Mary," I said.

"Oh. Perhaps they left Judas out," he said. "Traitor and all that."

"No, he's there, on the end," I said. Indeed, the duplicitous disciple was looking rather ashamed of himself, a stream of silver coins pouring from the pouch in his left hand. "And there's John with the chalice and snake. Matthew the tax collector. That one's Peter, there. Which one is missing?"

"Not really our chief concern, just at the moment." Jackaby sighed. He pushed himself up from the pew. "What we need to do now is find our way back to the sub-basement and through the original rend that Pavel showed us. That new one won't do us much good, unless you've sprouted wings." He paused. "Which, come to think of it, is exactly what Douglas did on the day that he visited this church."

I continued gazing up at the windows. Something was off about them, but I couldn't put my finger on it. I tried hard to remember my Sunday school lessons with old Vicar Peebles.

"That one must be Jude," I said to myself. Jackaby had already gone to poke his head into the rectory at the far end of the church. "And there's James the Elder and James the Younger. Andrew. Bartholomew. That has to be Thomas with the spears, and Philip with the basket. Who's missing? Paul?"

"Paul was never one of the twelve," Jackaby called, sweeping out of the back room again. "Aren't there any stairs in this silly church? We may need to chisel our way right through the floor. How they managed to pierce through in the first place and make a hole of that size without raising all sorts of attention is—" Jackaby stopped. He slapped himself in the face.

"Sir?"

"I'm an idiot," he said. "Of course they raised attention. They raised mine! They cleaved their way through a dimensional barrier—they produced a discharge of tremendous magical force. It would have left its mark."

"Like burn marks after a fire?" I said.

"Precisely. Except magic tends to have a more dramatic effect than flame. Untempered magic blasting out from a dimension full of ethereal energies into a veritable vacuum of the supernatural would wreak havoc on the earthly realm. Oh, I am an absolute dullard! I didn't just miss the scorch marks—I was there for the explosion itself! The day the council broke through, I was here! Douglas received the blast full force. I watched it happen, I just didn't know what it was! It's the reason he's a duck! I have been *living* with one of the scorch marks for the past three years, feeding him bread crumbs and paying him quarterly to keep my tax receipts in order!" He pulled off his hat and ran his hand through his tangled hair. "I thought that had been the end of a caper—it was just the start!"

The church shook with another tremor.

"Why this church?" he said, stuffing the floppy cap back on his head. "Why Father Grafton? How was he all mixed up in all this?"

A thought occurred to me. "Grafton knew about the shield because he *had* the shield," I said. "He must have had it for years. Maybe centuries. The twain said the shield was created to protect Hafgan against anything, even old age."

Jackaby nodded. "That would explain why I couldn't see a curse or a jinx on Grafton. He hadn't been attacked when we saw him; he had just stopped being protected. He had left the shield behind. We were watching countless years catch up with him all at once."

Another rumbling shudder shook the church. Dust trickled from the ceiling, and the lighting changed. I glanced around to find the source.

"But why leave it behind?" Jackaby continued. "Why give

it up? If Grafton was invulnerable, what would make him afraid enough to abandon his protection?"

There was another window. I blinked. There, on our right, a twelfth apostle had appeared. The other windows hadn't moved, their spacing hadn't changed—the missing apostle was simply suddenly among them.

"And if he did leave it behind," Jackaby rambled on, completely unaware of the window's appearance, "then where is it now?"

"Simon," I said, snapping my fingers. The window depicted a man with slightly wild eyes, a large saw leaning to one side of him. In his hands was clasped a book, presumably the Bible. Inlaid on the cover was the symbol of a ruby red fish. Vicar Peebles' voice echoed in my memory. "He was called Simon the—"

"He said it's in the Bible of the—" Jackaby began at the same time.

"—Zealot," we finished together.

I looked at Jackaby. Jackaby looked at me. We both looked at Simon.

"Oh," said Jackaby. "That window definitely wasn't there the last time."

"Something fishy about that fish?" I said.

"The quakes must have shaken loose a dimensional wrinkle." Jackaby's eyes were locked on the glass. The fish's tail and fins were of a slightly lighter shade of red glass than the body. "He hid the gem in broad daylight where none of us could find it," Jackaby marveled. "It was tucked halfway into the Annwyn. That meant even I couldn't see it. Human beings couldn't just stumble on it, and the Dire Council couldn't just march through a church looking for it."

The ground shook again. The building groaned, and another shower of dust sprinkled down around us. "I don't think the building's going to weather much more of this," I said.

"Whoever Father Grafton really was, the last thing he did with his very long life was enlist us to keep that gem from falling into the hands of the new Dire King," said Jackaby. "We need to secure Hafgan's shield before the Dire Council sends their army storming through here."

With another creative stacking of church pews, Jackaby and I erected a slightly sturdier ramp leading up to the window. I steadied the base this time while Jackaby ran up to the hidden gem. He pried it out with a little knife and held it up to the light. "This is . . . I can't . . . it's astounding, Miss Rook."

"Well, bring it down. Let's have a look," I said. Jackaby tucked it into his pocket and slid down to me, but before his feet were on the ground the church rumbled again. This time the quake did not ebb, but grew only more and more violent.

"Oh dear," said Jackaby.

"What's happening?" I said. "Did we cause that?"

"Oh dear," Jackaby said again. The rumble had built to a roar.

"What?" I yelled.

"I'm still an idiot! The gem wasn't just hidden, it was right where it was supposed to be—holding the veil shut!" The whole structure was shaking like a carriage on a rough road. "Grafton made it a part of the church. He set the stone dead in the center of the fraying seams of the veil. He protected his church because this church was more important than he was."

"Quick! Put it back!" I said.

As I spoke, Simon the Zealot cracked into two and then ruptured, raining colored glass down on us and all over the greatly abused benches. The walls fractured. Lumps of plaster crashed down, and Simon's fellow apostles began to burst.

The ground beneath our feet cracked, and I hopped across the break before I found myself trapped on the other side of the cleft from Jackaby. Emerald light poured up out of the chasm. Through the swirling mist, I could just make out Hafgan's Hold. I was looking down on the scene from across the courtyard. The medley of monsters was no longer milling about aimlessly. They weren't forming ranks, precisely, but they were clearly at attention. Someone was at the head of the group, addressing the crowd. Over the heads of giants and ogres and hairy beasts, I caught a foggy glimpse. There he was! The Dire King! Red eyes glowed in the shadows beneath his brow, and on his head sat a midnight black crown of tall, wicked points. Each spike was like a crooked talon clawing at the sky. Even the tallest giants bowed before him. The Dire King was readying his troops to invade.

And Jackaby and I had just unlocked the door for them.

Chapter Twenty-Five

I caught my breath and pulled my head away from the massive chasm. Maybe there was still time to fix this. Maybe the Dire King had not noticed that the enormous rift had opened. I glanced around. Daylight streamed down on us. The church had ruptured in two. The ceiling was split wide open and the back wall had largely collapsed.

"We need to get back there," Jackaby said, heaving a thick sigh. "We need to destroy that machine now. If the Dire King has found a way to manufacture a fraction of the power his acolytes seem to think he has, then this church is only a small sample of what's to come."

"We need Charlie," I said. "We need our reinforcements. We have support in the city, remember? They should be amassing as we speak."

"There isn't time." Jackaby's words were heavy. "Miss Rook," he said, "you should go. Be with Charlie. Bring them back. I will hold the threshold as long as I can, but I cannot leave now. The war has begun, and we are already losing it."

"You're losing it if you think I'm going to let you go marching into that mess alone! With all due respect, sir, you can't handle a hot breakfast without me—do you really intend to save the world on your own?"

"Miss Rook." He looked pained.

"Maybe Charlie is already on his way!" I said, stepping over the rubble toward the demolished wall to get a peek toward the street.

"Charlie doesn't even know where we've gone," Jackaby said. "None of them do. Pavel never told us before we left. He only showed us the way in. Even if they did heed our call, they would still be hours away on Augur Lane."

"Charlie is resourceful. He's cleverer than you give him credit for, sir. Maybe he worked out where we are." I reached the broken wall and looked out, the sun hot on my face.

I gazed at an empty lane. There was no Charlie. There was no Hudson or Nudd or even Douglas. There were no reinforcements. We were staggeringly, achingly alone against the end of the world.

"We're it," Jackaby said behind me.

I nodded. My throat felt dry.

"Virgule may come through," Jackaby said. "He may have reached Lord Arawn by now, and there's a chance the Fair King might actually take the threat seriously for once."

"Yes," I said. "Yes, I suppose that's true." I crossed back to Jackaby. "What's the plan?"

The building shook—the quakes weren't really stopping at all now, just ebbing and surging in intensity. A massive section of the back wall crumbled, rocks cascading and gonging off a toppled pipe organ in discordant tones. The enormous cleft running through the middle of the church had gotten larger.

"We stop the machine to protect the whole world—that's our priority. Next, we stall that army, as long as we can. They're preparing for battle, and we've just unlocked the gate for them. If we can delay the army, even for a minute, it gives Charlie more time to arrive, gives New Fiddleham a chance."

"All right," I said. "Let's save the worlds."

After examining the rends from our side, we determined that our best bet was not to drop straight through the biggest gap, but to slip through a small rip in the corner of the church. It deposited us sideways into an unoccupied space at the far end of Hafgan's Hold. Tall weeds and creeping vines had taken over in the centuries since Hafgan had last held power, and we crouched low among these as we hurried to take cover against the nearest wall.

The keep was ahead of us, troops lined up in front of it. The enormous tower had felt the effects of the quake as well. I stared at it. Like the church, the keep had been rocked and ruined—but unlike the church, the tower was held together by forces stronger than bricks and mortar. The base of the structure still stood intact, and the dome high atop the tower remained where it had been when we left it. In between, however, the building was effectively gone. Every floor was laid bare, the Dire King's device naked to the elements. Cracked stones orbited the building weightlessly, the remnants of the ruined tower spinning aimlessly around the massive framework of the machine.

I couldn't see the Dire King from this angle, but now and then the troops would respond to whatever he was saying with a roar of malicious excitement. The frenzy was building.

"Well, we've got excellent timing," Jackaby whispered. "They seem busy getting excited about the prospect of murdering humans with abandon. With a little luck, we can turn that distraction to our advantage."

"The evil warlord appears to be much better at pep talks than you are, sir."

"I have never subscribed to pep," Jackaby admitted. "Do try not to die."

We crept closer, peering around the corner of the wall. We were a stone's throw from the keep and the edge of the crowd. My foot struck something hard and I glanced down. The black blade lay at my feet.

"Sir!" I had seen Morwen's sword flipping away wildly when she fell, but I had not seen where it landed. "Look!"

"Who's back there?" shouted a voice from the other side of the wall we were using as cover. I froze.

Muffled footsteps began to tromp around the building. I snatched up the black blade and held it in front of me.

"You need to hide!" Jackaby whispered.

More footsteps joined the first. "Over this way!" the voice snarled.

Jackaby's eyes flashed. He rummaged in his pockets and pulled out a little pill. It looked like the tablet that had made the ogre's teeth grow back on the castle wall. That had worked so well the last time.

"They can't kill me," Jackaby whispered. "They're not allowed. But you . . ." The footsteps had nearly reached us. "Dentimorphic Engorgement. Might tickle," he said. And then he stuffed the pill in my mouth.

"Mmph! Sir, what on earth ar—ooomph!"

There was a sickening popping sound. I felt like someone had attached a weight to the bottom of my chin. My jaw immediately ached. Out of the bottom of my eyes I could see something pearly and realized I was looking at my own teeth.

"Whurph?" I managed. Jackaby ruffled my hair up just before a pair of trolls turned the corner.

"Fine!" Jackaby threw his hands up in the air, looking at me. "You caught me!"

"Good work," the first troll said, then looked me in the eyes. He jabbed a spear at me and leaned in to his comrade. "What's she?"

A strand of my ruffled hair drifted across my eyes. I blinked. "Uhm."

"She is the abominable brigand who just captured me," Jackaby declared dramatically.

"Er—yeff," I said through my enormous teeth. "Yeff, thaffs whu happeghed."

The trolls looked skeptical. "Yeah, but what are you?"

"I—uhm," I said.

"That's really quite offensive," Jackaby interjected. "Be careful. You'll make her mad. You really don't want to see her in her wrathful demon form. I've only just calmed her down as it is."

"I think she's one of them oni," the second troll whispered to the first. "You ever been to the Eastern Annwyn?"

The first shook his head, then turned back to us. "Your prisoner. What you think?" he said to me. "We bring him to the Dire King?"

My eyes widened. "Oh—I don' fthing thath a good idea. He'f righ in the miggle of hith thpeech to the trooph, and—"

"Obviously she's going to take me to the king," Jackaby interrupted. He nodded to me slyly.

"Yeth," I said. "You can go. I have thith trethpather under control."

The first troll's eyes narrowed. "We'll just come with you," he decided. "To be sure."

"Thath great," I said. "Good. Okay. Let'th go thee the Dire King. Right now. Together."

Chapter Twenty-Six

We marched through the center of the phalanx. Over the hubbub all around me and the pounding of my own heartbeat in my ears, I could catch snippets of the Dire King's voice.

"What was that?" Jackaby asked, cocking his head to the side. "What did he just say?"

"Unleashing glorious chaos on earth," grunted the troll on our right.

"No, before that."

"Rivers of blood?" suggested left troll.

"The bit about the machine," clarified Jackaby. "Something about the next stage?"

"Oh—don't you worry about that, human. It's almost fully realized," said right troll.

"Not fully realized now, then?" said Jackaby. "Seems to be chiseling away at the old barrier pretty well, all things considered."

"That's not all it's supposed to do," said right troll.

"It's not?" said left troll.

"No, stupid," said right troll. "The Dire King isn't even controlling the machine right now. Can't be doing what it's supposed to do without the Dire King, can it?"

"Can't it?" Jackaby prompted.

"Wouldn't you like to know," right troll snarled.

"Well, can it?" asked left troll.

"Of course it can't!" Right troll shot his compatriot a sour glance. "Do you read any of the notices? The Dire King, Unseelie of Unseelies, Lord of all Chaos, Bringer of Destruction, will make ready the road and he will make ready his warriors to travel it. Only then will he reach into the heavens to pull away the veil—for he alone can usher in the glorious Kingdom of Blood."

"What does that mean?" Jackaby pressed. "Make ready his warriors to travel it?"

"None of your concern, human."

"Buh the Dire Kigg warned againtht a Kiggdom of Blood in hith poem," I managed. "That doethn't make thenth."

We had reached the front of the line. At the head of the gruesome ranks stood two men. One was covered with thick, coarse hair and had sharp teeth. He was the man Morwen had called Mr. Loup. The other had white-blond hair. He had the sharp features of a fairy. In fact, he looked as if he could have been Virgule's brother, except that there was something eerie about him. His eyes were too cold.

"Where is the king?" the troll on the left demanded. "We've caught the Seer."

"The oni caught the Seer," corrected right. "But we were nearby."

Loup glared at them. "Quiet. It's starting," he said. His eyes wandered to Jackaby and to me.

"Starting?" Jackaby said.

I nudged him and nodded up at the keep. Through the spinning wreckage, a figure was ascending the tower. He climbed unhurried from one stair to the next, purposeful with each step, mounting stairs that floated in midair. Around his shoulders was draped a dark cloak and on his head was the wicked black crown.

"Hold on. That's the Seer!" Loup cried.

"That's what I said," protested the lead troll.

"The king has use for him," snarled Loup. "I'll take him from here."

"No!" I said. "Er–I capthured him. It'th my–erm–glory to prethent him to the Dire King, Lord of Chaoths." Loup leaned in closer to me. His nostrils twitched and he inhaled deeply as he looked at me. "Bringer of Dethruction?" I added. It was then that I realized the ache in my jaw was subsiding. The Denti-whatever was wearing off. My teeth were receding back into my mouth. I swallowed.

Loup's eyes narrowed. "You're no oni," he said. "What are you?"

"Oh. I don't think you can say that. It's offensive," the troll on the right said.

Loup looked as if he would like to have taken the troll's head off, but at that moment the massive gates of Hafgan's Hold shook with a thunderous blow.

Loup's eyes turned to the gate. "They're here," he said. He smiled wickedly, his teeth glistening. "To your places!" he bellowed. "It's happening!"

There was a scurry of movement as the phalanx of monsters braced themselves for battle. Swords and axes were drawn; claws scraped and glinted. The gate rocked with another echoing crack.

"Hold him until after," Loup snarled at me. "Time for my moment."

I blinked. We were in the center of the army. Monsters were rushing around us on every side, and none of them seemed concerned about us in the least.

Loup ran toward the tower. High above him, the metal dome over the roof of the keep was moving, tilting up like the lid on a sugar dish. Below it, the constantly moving flower of rotating discs was glowing brighter. It rose, aligning itself within the dome of the roof. The flower became brighter still as the curve of the metal reflected its golden light.

Just below the glowing machine, I could now clearly see the third-story landing. On one side, there was a seven-foot platform propped up at a forty-five-degree angle, and just above this was a stage bordered by a wall of switches and knobs with countless cables and tubes running up and down from the controls. At this control board stood the Dire King, his back to us as he threw levers and flipped toggles.

On the next landing down hung the cylinder device we had seen when we snuck in. Lights along this giant cylinder were now blinking to life.

Finally, down at the base of the tower, the generators were humming. Loup had reached the keep and stepped inside. Through the ruined masonry, I could see him walk across the floor to stand beneath one of the coffin-like metal frames.

The two other frames were already occupied—one by an imp, who danced back and forth on the balls of his little red feet, and the other by a woman who stood stock-still within her arched metal cage. She had wide, angry eyes and wings like an owl's that wrapped around her shoulders. Above their heads hung the lightning rod nozzles.

Out in the courtyard, the gate cracked loudly again, and this time I heard the wood splinter. The gate burst. A sea of fair folk swept into the courtyard, and there, at the front of the line, was Virgule. My heart lurched in my chest. He had done it! Arawn had listened! Something had finally gone right!

The Unseelie horde did not set upon the intruders at once. For a tense moment, the two forces faced each other across the turf. The fairies filed in, forming clean, clear ranks with practiced precision. Virgule stepped forward. "Hear me!" he yelled. A few Unseelie growled. "In the name of the Fair King, you are ordered to stand down," he declared.

The creepy blond man laughed, pulling on a pair of dark gloves as he strode down the center of the Unseelie army. "You really think you can stop us with Lord Arawn's *second*-best battalion?" he drawled.

Virgule locked eyes on the man and stammered. "You— we—" He took a breath and recovered. "It's over, Mr. Tilde. There is no need for further bloodshed. My Lord Arawn has sent for the dwarves from the South Mines and the elves from the North. Even if you stand against us, by now the whole of the Annwyn are riding to put an end to this madness. What you've done threatens us all. You've lost."

The blond man, Tilde, shrugged impassively. "We shall see, cousin."

And then the tower hummed. A beam of wavering light burst from the metal rose at the top, amplified a hundred times by the dome. It hit the fairy phalanx like a speeding train, and the whole courtyard was bathed in blinding light.

I blinked as my eyes adjusted. Virgule was on his knees. Several of the soldiers behind him had collapsed altogether. Beads of sparkling light rose from them like droplets of water falling from a tree after the rain, but upside down, spinning and circling and rising until they were absorbed by the machine high above them.

The blood drained from my face. All around me, trolls and gremlins and great hairy monsters were cackling with vile glee at the sight of the fairies collapsing to the ground. I looked to the tower. At the base of the machine, something was happening. The device that looked like a giant microscope whirred to life. From out of each nozzle suddenly burst an arc of concentrated light—white-blue and as intense as the sun itself, like writhing snakes of lightning.

The imp in the metal frame screamed. The owl woman groaned. Loup doubled over and growled. And then they changed. They grew.

As the eldritch energy washed over its little body, the imp began to bulge and pop grotesquely. Before my eyes it ceased to have a *little* body at all. It was a brute the size of a gorilla, and swelling larger still. Soon the thing was too large for the metal frame at all and it tumbled forward. Massive red horns had sprouted from its head where tiny nubs had been, and it let out a bellow like a lion's roar. Loup bent low as the arc of lightning blasted through him. His coarse hair thickened and his muscles groaned until suddenly there stood in his place a wolf the size of a workhorse. He bounded out of the ruined tower and shook his fur. The woman bared her teeth and clutched at the sides of the metal frame. Her wings grew wider and her feet became terrible talons. When the top of the frame began to press on her back, she burst out of the tower and flapped over the army.

The Unseelie horde parted. The owl woman soared across to the far end of the courtyard, where the enormous gap in the rend revealed the waiting ruins of the old church. Loup padded down the aisle after her, and the imp—now more of a demonic gargoyle—followed close behind. They trod past their brethren to approving cheers. More Unseelie creatures were already clamoring into the base of the tower to be the next soldiers to be *made ready.*

"He's draining them," I said. "The entire Seelie fae army. He's killing them!"

Virgule, his hand shaking uncontrollably, tried to lift his sword. It clattered back to the ground almost at once and he fell onto his side.

The fairy army was not simply dying. With every moment they grew weaker, the Unseelie were growing stronger. Inside the tower, new, wild-looking creatures were taking shape. Muscles bulged. Great thorns emerged from a dark spirit's arms and legs, and her hair looked like a briar patch. Next to her, a scaly man the size of an ox climbed out of his own frame. He looked like he could lift a carriage. "Miss Rook," whispered Jackaby.

"Yes, Mr. Jackaby," I whispered back.

"I think you ought to know. I'm about to do something very foolish."

"I had a feeling you might, sir," I said. "And I have a sinking suspicion I'm going to help."

Chapter Twenty-Seven

Make way! Move aside! Excuse us! Pardon me! Thank you!" The faces of the Unseelie soldiers wore a baffled expression as we cut through their ranks. Well, most of them looked baffled. One or two didn't really have faces at all, which made it hard to tell. There were hisses and murmurs and claws pointed in our direction, but the frank confidence with which my employer blustered his way through the thick of them was oddly mesmerizing. Apparently they had not expected a pair of unassuming humans to advance on their growing crowd of the nastiest, most powerful monsters in existence.

Jackaby was unarmed. I still held Morwen's black blade. I had it pointed, as I had been directed, squarely at my employer's back.

We reached the massive cleft in the fabric of the veil. The ruins of the quiet church stood on the other side. "That's it! Nearly there! I think that will do! Hello, yes, may I have everyone's attention?" Jackaby called out—entirely unnecessarily.

The crowd, already fixed on the pair of us, grew hushed. On the other side of the courtyard, Virgule and the fairy army were collapsing into stillness. The beam persisted relentlessly.

"I am R. F. Jackaby. I am a paranormal investigator and host to the immortal sight," he declared loudly. "As you all know, you cannot kill me. King's orders."

"I do not know that!" shouted a voice from the back.

"Shut your gob. I *told* you to read the pamphlet!" countered another voice.

"Well—as those of you who perused the literature are well aware," Jackaby continued, "your egomaniacal monarch has made it clear that he needs me alive in order to move on to phase two—which, as I understand it, has all the juiciest bits. Chaos and rivers of blood and all that."

The owl woman stepped forward. "So? He needs you. We already have you."

"Ah, right you are. But here's where it gets interesting," Jackaby went on. "Allow me to introduce my stalwart assistant, Miss Rook. Miss Rook, horrible mob. Horrible mob, Miss Rook."

I swallowed hard as their eyes rested on me.

"Like me, Miss Rook comes from the human world. She's grown rather fond of it. So here's the thing—the invasion is off."

The crowd erupted in barks of laughter and derisive scoffs.

"Or what?" asked the owl woman.

"Or," Jackaby answered, "Miss Rook will be forced to kill *me*. So, you can attack now, that's certainly an option. You attack—Rook kills me—maybe you kill her, and then you move straight to the messiest massacre you've ever imagined. You would have a grand old time, slaughtering humans left and right, stuff of legends—but, when the blood on your claws has dried, that's all it will have been. Phase one. By morning the veil will have mended and the Dire King's grand scheme for phase two will be ruined."

The monsters began to shift uncomfortably. Eyes darted up to the tower keep.

"You're not going to give up your life, just like that," said the owl woman. "You're bluffing."

"No. I'm not bluffing," said Jackaby. "What I am is tired. I have given up my life already. I have given it to the sight, and I have given it to my career, and I have given it to my city. I have given my life to protecting people I do not know from villains they do not know exist, and I am tired. If you think I will not give up my life to save the world one last time"–his brow cast heavy shadows over his gray eyes–"then you do not know me at all."

The black blade felt heavy in my clammy hands. I was rather hoping we were bluffing.

There was tense silence for several seconds, and then the machine up above us clicked off with a buzz. The light from the mechanical rose faded and the mechanism lowered. The fallen fairy army did not rise, although I could see signs of breathing from a few of the limp bodies. From high in the tower of floating rubble, the Dire King was watching.

"He's bluffing," snarled the owl woman. "Someone collect those humans. We're going through."

The horde stirred. Loup bared his fangs in a wicked grin.

"Stop." The voice that issued from atop the tower keep was deep and carried a note of finality.

The Unseelie army stopped. I breathed. It had worked. It should not have worked, but it had worked! We were safe, however fleetingly, poised in the eye of a hurricane. And then the Dire King spoke again.

"Kill the girl."

Almost at once, the throng leapt to obey the command. I scarcely had time to understand what he had said when a spiral-tipped javelin flew out of the crowd. Its aim was true–it soared straight for my chest. Too late, I ducked away. I heard a horrified gasp from the crowd, followed by a deafening silence. I peered out from behind my own hands.

Jackaby had stepped in the way of the javelin.

A jagged, twisted point entered his chest and emerged from the middle of his back.

Chapter Twenty-Eight

"Huh." Jackaby looked down at the javelin lodged in his chest. He took hold of the shaft in both hands and pulled. The barb slid free with a nauseating sucking sound.

"S-s-sir?" I managed.

"Huh," said Jackaby, almost to himself. "Ha! Oh! Yes, right." He dropped the bloody weapon to the ground. "They *can't* kill me!"

Jackaby pulled open his shirt front and prodded the spot where the javelin had entered, just left of his clavicle. He wiped the blood away, and aside from a small circle of young, fresh skin, he had not a mark on him. The gem. I had forgotten about Hafgan's shield!

"Well. All right." Jackaby addressed the crowd again.

"That changes the dynamic a bit, admittedly. But I can work with this. I appear to be immortal now. So there's that. The invasion is still off. You can't beat me. Couldn't kill me if you tried."

The Unseelie army was now abuzz with noise.

"Kill the girl," the deep voice repeated, echoing over the susurration of the horde, "and tear the Seer's limbs from his body. Don't be gentle. Death is no longer a risk, it seems. Bring whatever is left to me."

"I don't like that, sir," I said. The crowd swelled forward, all teeth and talons.

"Nor I. New plan," said Jackaby. "Run!"

He threw himself at me, grabbing my arm, and we tumbled backward through the rend. We hit the stones of the old church and rolled. Loup, the big bad wolf, was only a moment behind us. His sharp claws clicked and scraped the floor as he landed. I scrambled to get away, crawling for cover beneath the nearest pew. The owl woman swooped over me and the huge red imp was cackling savagely nearby. More monsters were piling through, like an unthinkably evil pot boiling over. I was scrambling across the cold floor, my heart thudding against my ribs, when a shot rang out like a cannon. The owl woman spun out of the air with a shriek and slammed against the altar.

"Sweet sassy molasses—that's a lotta ugly!" boomed a familiar voice. Hank Hudson unloaded a second loud shot, this time into the imp's face, and then tossed the pistol aside, pulling a fresh one from a bandolier across his chest. "Hey, everybody! In here!" he bellowed. "Looks like the war's on!"

From where I was crouched, half-hidden beneath the church bench, I heard a rapid pattering of footsteps from the front of the chapel, and then a mob of gray-green feet burst into my range of vision. They leapt up, swarming the giant wolf with almost gleeful whooping war cries. Loup howled in fury as half a dozen goblins attached themselves to his fur, pulling and stabbing and kicking furiously. Someone grabbed me by the wrist and I jolted, spinning around. "It's me," Jackaby said. "Come on!"

We raced past the broken cross and over the fallen bricks. Hudson had spent two more pistols, but he was in his element. He had another gun in his hands already and a pair of rifles strapped to his back, as well as an assortment of sharp knives and hatchets hanging from his belt for the moment his ammunition ran low.

A pair of centaurs vaulted over the broken wall just ahead of us, and I pulled Jackaby aside before their sharp hooves clattered down. The centaurs launched themselves into the battle, swiping with long spears and driving bone-crushing kicks into the monsters. I stumbled over the wall and out into daylight.

There, in the churchyard, was a glorious sight: pixies and spriggans and gnomes and goblins, Nudd shouting commands and cursing colorfully, bird-headed women and woman-headed birds, a man of living fire, and a smiling giant towering over the company. A battery of New Fiddleham police officers, along with Commissioner Marlowe and even Mayor Spade himself, fought with gusto. At the head of the field of uniforms stood Charlie Barker and, floating beside him, Jenny Cavanaugh.

Jenny spotted us, and her face burst into unmasked relief. She swept across the field and met me halfway with a firm embrace. Jenny felt solid. She also felt as cold as ice—but she felt solid, and as I threw my arms around her, I cried with unexpected happiness in the midst of all the horrors around us.

"You brought them? Oh, Jenny! We didn't even know if you—" I began.

"I thought for sure that you—" she started.

An arrow hit the ground beside us.

"Hurry, come on," she said, releasing me. She reached for Jackaby's hand to pull him along, too, but her fingers passed through his like vapor. Her face fell. She tried to hide it as she sallied on. "Come. Out of the line of fire!"

Even as she said it, a hulking gargantuan covered in scales crashed through the wall of the church and bounded out into the open in front of us. His skin was like a crocodile's, but he ran more like an orangutan, bounding forward using his legs and arms, balancing his weight on his meaty knuckles. He saw the phalanx of police officers and grinned hungrily. Those in the group who didn't scatter at his approach opened fire, smoke from their pistols rising thick over their heads—but the monster shrugged off the shots like they were pebbles. With a swipe of his gnarled hand, he sent one of the officers flying. The man landed on his back and did not get up. Mayor Spade stumbled backward, tripping over Lieutenant Dupin near the front of the formation and sending them both falling to the ground. Before the scaly colossus could take his next swipe, Chief Nudd screamed out a command, and a goblin swarm leapt onto the monster, scrambling onto its head and jabbing at its eyes.

The scaly monster threw the goblins off one at a time, but the distraction had been enough. In two strides, Mr. Dawl, our giant, was there, his massive hands clutching an enormous lance—a lance that had been the trunk of a nearby pine tree until very recently. He drove it straight through the brute's thick chest. Unlike Jackaby, the scaly monster did not survive being skewered.

Charlie helped the stunned mayor to his feet. Marlowe began barking commands, and the scattered officers formed into smaller units of five or six, fanning out and taking up positions all around the church.

Monsters large and small poured across the grass, the front line of the war spreading wider with every second. Our gnomes charged into a cluster of their angry hobs. A cloud of pixies met a swarm of brownies midair, tiny corpses dropping as they clashed. The bodies of Nudd's goblins began littering the ground as well. They had been the most fearless into the breach. From somewhere nearby, an ax whipped through the air and landed only a few feet from the already addled mayor.

"H-how can we even tell which ones are on our side?" Spade stammered, picking up the weapon and holding it out in front of himself with shaking hands.

"Iffin' they's tryin' tae kill ye," Nudd spat back at him sourly, "probably baddies."

Lydia Lee emerged from our crowd of allies with a litter. A stocky faun with horns that curled back around the side of his head and legs like a goat jogged over from the ranks behind her to help her maneuver the fallen officer onto it. The policeman did not look like he was breathing.

A bright burst of light and a wave of dry heat hit me from my left. I spun. Shihab had ignited a monstrous woman made of briars and thorns. She hardly seemed to notice that she was aflame as she lashed at the jinn with vines like barbed whips. A screech sounded behind me and I spun again. A gaunt figure with gray skin pulled taut over its angular bones leapt toward us from the melee. "Wendigo!" Jackaby cried out. It sank its yellow teeth into the faun, who dropped his end of the litter. Jackaby ran to help him.

"Behind you!" screamed Spade. I spun in time to watch the mayor hurl his ax at a hob who had trotted up right behind Nudd. The butt of Spade's weapon smacked the ugly elfin creature in the eye. It stumbled, dazed, and Nudd drove his own little sword into its neck. The hob dropped to the earth, very dead. Nudd and Mayor Spade exchanged a nod of tentative mutual respect.

Jackaby had pulled the wendigo off the bleeding faun. The wretched thing lashed out, and it was all Jackaby could do to hold the snarling creature at arm's length. It shredded his already tattered coat sleeves, but the skin beneath continued to heal as soon as it was cut. "I could use some assistance," he grunted.

I stepped up and took a swing at the wendigo's neck with Morwen's blade. It was like chopping through dry kindling. The creature collapsed, decapitated. I felt sick and numb watching its head roll to a stop.

Jackaby scooped the faun into his arms. Jenny leaned down and took the other side of the litter. I followed close behind them, watching over my shoulder for the next terror to come streaking through the fray at us. My hands were shaking. I couldn't seem to catch my breath.

And then I saw Charlie and Charlie saw me. It was just a moment in the midst of madness. In another instant Dupin would be clapping him on the shoulder, calling him back into action, and I would be rushing to keep up with Jackaby, Jenny, and Lydia. But for just that moment, Charlie's deep brown eyes locked on mine and my hands stopped shaking. He radiated calm. It was what made him an exceptional peacekeeper at the best of times–and what made him an exceptional leader at the worst. Charlie smiled at me, and in spite of overwhelming evidence to the contrary, I found myself able to believe that everything was going to be all right.

And then the moment was gone.

Voices were screaming, and the air smelled of gunpowder and blood. We made our way to the back of the allied forces, where Mona O'Connor had already set up cots for emergency triage. "First customer," Lydia Lee called out as we approached. Mona rushed to meet us and helped maneuver the unmoving policeman onto one of the makeshift beds.

Lydia looked at her grimly as she stood up with the litter under her arm. "I'm going back for more," she said. She swallowed. "We're going to need a lot more beds."

"We'll make do," Mona answered. Lydia hurried away. "His heart's not beating," she said.

"He's already dead," said Jackaby heavily.

Mona ignored him. She was at the policeman's head. She pressed his arms together into his chest and then raised them both up over his head, then repeated the motion.

"What are you doing?" Jenny asked.

"Silvester method. Artificial respiration."

"He's gone," said Jackaby.

"Do I tell you how to hunt fairy tales, or whatever it is you do?" Mona barked. "I've seen breath come back to those longer gone than him."

A series of shouts erupted from the battlefield, and the earth shook. The colossal Mr. Dawl had fallen. Over the heads of our allies I could see the Unseelie army's frost giant, the jötun, stomping into the fray. An orange blur darted across the plain just ahead of me. I glanced up. Bounding toward me was what appeared to be a miniature troll riding an orange tabby cat like a warhorse. I raised my blade as it raced toward us, but Jackaby caught me before I could swing.

"Not that one!"

I paused.

"Hammett." Jackaby addressed the diminutive figure. "Hatun would be proud of you."

The little troll barked something in a language I could not fathom.

"Not yet," answered Jackaby. "We still don't know where they've taken her."

The troll snarled and pulled at the reins, and the cat bounded away. Hammett sliced at the heels of his enemies as they disappeared into the mess.

Loup, his jaws red with blood, leapt across the clearing, snapping and snarling as frightened soldiers scattered. Lydia Lee was trying frantically to maneuver a bleeding gnome onto her litter. Her head shot up and she froze. She was directly in the wolf's path. Loup stalked forward, eyes bloodshot, growling. And then, very suddenly, a chocolate brown hound stood between her and the wolf.

Charlie had always seemed so large in his canine form. He did not seem large now. The wolf loomed over them, big and black and built of raw muscle and razor-sharp teeth. Charlie was half his size. The wolf did not slow as he neared them.

Marlowe yelled a command, and a cadre of policemen opened fire. Loup roared as the bullets ripped into him. When the volley paused, Charlie bounded forward and lunged for the wolf's neck, but Loup was too fast for him. He caught Charlie with a nasty bite that nearly tore his ear clean off. Charlie yelped and stumbled into the dirt.

Jackaby was holding me back before I realized I was lunging forward.

"Let go of me! He'll kill him!" I said.

"No, stop! Look!" Jackaby pointed.

Movement erupted at the tree line. A pack of great burly hounds burst onto the field. The lead hound was larger than Charlie, his fur patterned in rich browns and jet blacks with flecks of white about his muzzle. A dozen more raced behind them.

"Is that—?"

"The Om Caini," said Jackaby. "That's Charlie's uncle in the lead, if I'm not mistaken."

The Om Caini struck like lightning. Loup caught sight of a tawny hound closing in on his left and snapped at it, only to have Dragomir make the first attack from his right. Loup howled in pain and anger as another hound locked its jaws on his flank, and then a third at his throat. The dogs were merciless.

Lydia dragged the gnome away from the fight, panting. Mona O'Connor continued lifting and lowering the policeman's arms. He did not appear to be coming back.

As if reacting to my thought, the policeman took a sudden wheezing breath.

Mona fell over backward. "Ha!" she declared triumphantly.

The policeman sat up.

"Take it easy," Mona told him. "Stay down. You've got half a dozen broken ribs at least, you need rest."

"Get away!" Jackaby yelled.

"What are you talking about?" Mona began.

That's when I noticed the policeman's glassy eyes.

"Get back!" I cried, but the undead officer turned on Miss O'Connor. His pale hands shot out and he had her by the neck of her shirtwaist. Jackaby and I leapt forward as one, but Jenny shot past us both.

She threw herself at the reanimated corpse as if diving to tackle him, but instead Jenny's features sank into his, a swirl of silver mist fading away behind her as she vanished. The policeman froze.

Mona pulled away from him slowly, her eyes enormous, and the officer released his grip. He stood, moving clumsily, looking down at his own limbs.

"I–I have him," the man said hoarsely. It was hard to

hear the voice as Jenny's through the deep vocal cords, but something in the man's eyes told me she was in there. "It's not like a living body," she said. "It's just a shell. There's a voice in here with me. I don't think it's his. I can hear it whispering in the back of his skull."

"Look out!" Lydia cried. A spear came flying through the air, and Jenny slid out of the body half a second before the tip buried itself in the dead man's head.

The policeman toppled into the grass next to the injured gnome. Jenny hovered in the air. Lydia Lee was quietly sick in the bush behind her. She spat and wiped her mouth. "Enough gawking," she said. "Back to work, everyone."

And so the war raged on. The dead of both sides lay strewn across the battlefield. In the dust and smoke and stench, a man was emerging from the church. It was the thin man with white-blond hair whom Virgule had called Mr. Tilde. The battle seemed to bend around him, affording him a cushion of eerie calm. He held a small stone to his lips, and when he spoke, his voice carried over the din of the battle.

"Warriors. The Dire King has a message for you all."

The clamor of fighting ebbed and a tense hush settled over the battleground.

Tilde continued. "All of the otherworldly creatures currently taking up arms alongside these humans. You are free to go. Leave. Your new king has no need of your blood this day. Assist me in returning to him the human called the

Seer, and you can even earn yourself a place in his coming kingdom."

"Oi! Ye're supposed ta be one o' the good un's!" cried a disgusted voice. It sounded like Nudd's, but I could not see the goblin chief from where we stood. "Ye're nae one o' these Unseelie munters!"

"I am Seelie," the Tilde confirmed, smiling. There was a rumbling, like a roll of distant thunder, and the ground shivered. "Do you know," he said, ignoring the seismic interruptions, "that many Seelie fae are born with innate talents? Some control light and shadow. Some can make the plants grow. Some can even change the weather." The ground shook again, and this time one of the gravestones in the field behind us cracked in two. "We cannot control what gifts we are born with. They are a part of us. It seems wrong, then, to label some of these gifts good and others evil, doesn't it? Wrong to tell a child that he can never rise to his true potential, that he can never use his gifts." The soil within the graveyard began to churn. "The Dire King understands that we all just want our chance to bring something . . . beautiful into the world."

The first decrepit hand to burst free of its grave site was blue-gray, its flesh rotted and sloughing off its bones. It was pitted with stones and dark with wet earth from its journey up from the coffin. As the corpse clawed its way free of the topsoil, a second hand burst up behind it. And another. And another. The entire churchyard was rising.

"They are beautiful, aren't they?" said Tilde.

"You're not special," spat Lydia Lee. She stood with her shoulders squared as she faced Tilde. "You're a bully. I've met a hundred bullies just like you. You're afraid, so you poison the world into being afraid, too. There's nothing beautiful about that."

"You think I am afraid?" Tilde said.

"I know it. I know fear. And I know strength. Real strength comes from courage and compassion and hope. Never fear."

"You think you still have hope?" Tilde cocked his head at Miss Lee. "Well, I'll just have to see to that." He took a measured breath, and then closed his eyes in concentration. All across the battlefield, butchered bodies sat up, their eyes glassy. Imps, goblins, centaurs, even the towering figure of our once-loyal Mr. Dawl rose alongside the human dead.

Any illusion I had harbored that our motley volunteer army might have been a match for the Dire King's forces vanished. Hundreds of savage corpses had joined the fight, every soldier that had fallen plus a whole field of the properly buried—and with every new body that fell from here on in, their ranks would only grow.

We had lost. All that was left now was the dying.

Chapter Twenty-Nine

The noise of battle renewed itself with deafening intensity. The dead dragged the living to the ground. Screams of fear and bellows of anger and pain echoed across the parish. The air over the battlefield smelled rotten—worse, it *tasted* rotten, and I couldn't seem to draw a clear breath. The sound of gunfire pierced the air less and less often as the last futile rounds left the barrels of their guns.

I swung the black blade for all I was worth. The recently unburied dead, at least, were brittle and far more easily decapitated than the freshly slain, but for every one of their ranks that I felled, I could see two more of our own being overtaken.

"We can't keep this up," Jackaby grunted as he felled another shambling corpse.

"I know a way," came a woman's voice behind us. We both turned.

Alina stood there, flinching at the sounds of the battle all around her. "I found it," she said. "You can't stop this fight from here, Detective. You need to do what you came here to do in the first place. We need to get you back to that machine. I–I can take you there."

Jackaby eyed her curiously. "Lead the way."

Returning to the Annwyn through the church would have been unthinkable. Within the ruins, the dead had fallen and risen again angry–but Alina had found a smaller rend around the back of the church, near the tree line. Jackaby went first. The sounds of the battle faded as we crossed into the Annwyn. We emerged to face a familiar landscape. After the deafening clamor, Hafgan's Hold was unsettlingly silent.

Alina's path had led us almost directly behind the tower. Stones littered the ground all around the keep, but just as many remained suspended in midair by the power of the cohesion charm. As silently as possible, we climbed through the spiraling, weightless debris into the ruined keep. The generators hummed loudly. An Unseelie soldier, a troll, had climbed into one of the metal frames at the base of the tower for his chance to become a great and power-ful Dire Warrior, but something had gone horribly wrong. The wretch's arm had become stuck in the metalwork. The process had made him larger still, and thus more inexorably stuck. Unable to pull free, the troll had warped to a grotesque parody of his original shape.

"It is a power that burns," Jackaby recalled.

The Dire King was up there, I mouthed. Alina bit her lip and looked as though she wanted to run. She took a deep breath and kept with us. The stairway, although supported by nothing but empty air, held our weight without crumbling. Several of the stairs were badly cracked or missing entirely, but we were able to negotiate them without incident. None of us said a word in the foreboding silence as we ascended. When we reached the third floor, Jackaby again took the lead. He crested the landing gingerly, and then rose to his full height, peering around. The machinery hummed loudly, a thrumming, rhythmic buzz.

"Where is the Dire King?" Alina whispered, her eyes darting back and forth.

"Mysteriously absent," answered Jackaby. His brow was furrowed as he peered around the landing.

"He could be back any moment." I swallowed. "We need to be quick. This is where he controls it all. Can you see how it works?"

Jackaby climbed up onto the raised control stage. "I can see—hold on. I can see an aura, over there. Human." Jackaby stepped to the edge to peer down. An inclined platform was set at an angle just below the control panel. A smile broke Jackaby's brooding face.

"Hatun!" he yelled over the thrum of the machine. "You're alive! And we've come to rescue you!"

"About time!" Hatun called back. She was strapped to the platform by her wrists and ankles. A series of tinted glass discs like giant magnifying glasses hung over her head. "Hey," she said as Jackaby leaned his head around the lenses to see her clearly. "Is that my knitting?"

"It is!" Jackaby beamed.

"Why are you wearing my new sundries bag on your big head?"

"It is a hat!" Jackaby hollered back, proud and defiant. "And I love it!"

Hatun shook her head. "Are you going to get me out of this thing or not?"

We climbed out onto the ledge. The platform on which Hatun was strapped hung over the demolished edge of the landing. Below us I could see the wretched, deformed troll. Its head twitched. Jackaby undid the straps on the far side, while I got those on the near. Her arm bore a long, deep cut, although the blood was already mostly dry. Very carefully, we helped her off the device. Her steps were shaky.

"This place doesn't have its walls attached," she said. "Just a bunch of floating bricks."

"That's true," I told her.

"Hm—you see it, too?" Hatun said. "That's probably bad. I was hoping that it was just me. Did you see the man with red eyes and the big black hat?"

"The Dire King," I said. "Do you know where he went?"

Hatun shook her head. "I'm sorry. I feel like a damn fool," she said. "I came to help, not to be bait locked away in a tower."

"You're not a fool. We were all just worried about you," I said. "Even Hammett came looking for you."

"You should take Hatun back through the barrier," said Jackaby. "I'm going to try to see what I can do with this."

"Can't we just tear it apart?" I said. I raised the black blade.

"No! No, no, no. Definitely no. That would be exceedingly bad right now. Do you see that metal tank down there? That is a containment reserve. The vital energy of an entire army of highly magical creatures is collected in there. Some of it got pumped into the Unseelie soldiers, but it still contains a massive reserve of power. Releasing that energy now could set off a dangerous blast of untempered magic."

"Enough to turn someone into a duck?"

"Enough to turn New Fiddleham into a duck," Jackaby said. "It's a magic bomb, and it needs to be defused and dismantled."

"I'll leave the supernatural science to you, sir. Do be careful."

I helped Hatun down the floating steps. Her legs were shaking terribly all the way.

"Hammett will be happy to see you alive and well," I

said. "I met him face-to-face for the first time today. He's actually a little bit cute."

Hatun smiled. "Don't go calling him cute to his face, though. He will eat your toes."

We reached the rift behind the tower and slid through. "The road is just along there," I said.

"You go," Hatun said. "I can find my way well enough."

I nodded and climbed back through the rend. Just as I slid back in the Annwyn, a flash of something pale flicked in the corner of my eye. I whipped my head to see it disappear behind the ruined tower. I blinked, unsure if I had really seen anything at all. There was another flutter of movement and I definitely caught sight of something white disappearing around the corner of a squat stone building next to the keep. Cautiously I walked around the side of the structure, the black blade drawn, but when I came around the corner there was nothing to see. The hair on the back of my neck prickled. I was not alone in the courtyard.

I looked up at the third-story landing. Alina was pacing the floor, her dark hair bobbing in and out of view. I had a good view of the control stage from where I stood. Jackaby was tracing a wire to its source through a handful of cables. All manner of switches and toggles and little red lights appeared behind him. My blood froze. Two red eyes moved forward out of the darkness. The shadows took shape. A dark cloak. A black crown.

Jackaby's back was to the figure. I screamed, but the buzz of the machinery and the droning of the generators drowned me out. I felt like I was in a nightmare.

Alina saw him. She grabbed Jackaby by his coat, but he pulled away from her. Alina stumbled backward. There was a flurry of movement and the shadowy figure struck Jackaby at the base of the skull.

For just a moment, a glimmer of hope hung in my mind; Jackaby still could not be harmed. Perhaps the Dire King did not realize the power of the gem? Perhaps this would be Jackaby's chance to snatch the upper hand!

My hopes crumpled with Jackaby's body. He collapsed to the floor of the control stage at the feet of the dark king. My head reeled. It wasn't possible! How?

And then Alina stepped forward. Her shivering, frightened affectations had ceased. She sank down on one knee in front of the Dire King and held up her hand. In it was clutched the gleaming red gem.

I felt sick as realization struck, and the world spun. Alina had betrayed us.

Alina hadn't been trying to pull Jackaby out of harm's way. She had been stealing Hafgan's shield from his pocket. The gem glinted as the Dire King accepted her offering. He put a pale hand on her shoulder as he held the stone up in the light. It was a perfect match for his ruby red eyes.

Chapter Thirty

I ran numbly to the edge of the tower, where I would be out of the Dire King's line of sight.

I closed my eyes and tried to slow my heartbeat. Jackaby was down. Our army was losing. Alina had betrayed us. And I was alone. I could believe in multiple worlds, but perhaps not in a world in which I could take on an invulnerable evil king and his minions all by myself.

I opened my eyes slowly. I was going to be as good as I could be, even if I was not good enough. I gripped the black blade in my shaking fist.

Every step up the exposed stairway was agonizing. Every flurry of rock dust that trickled down to earth felt like an avalanche. Every shadow felt like the Dire King looming over my shoulder.

By the time I reached the upper landing and summoned the courage to peek up over the top, the Dire King had already latched Jackaby into restraints. I could see my employer's battered coat rising and falling with shallow breaths. The knit hat–or possibly sundries bag–lay in a lumpy pile on the floor.

"Sir," I whispered. He did not react.

Darkness swept past me and I froze. The Dire King stepped up to the controls. From where I was hiding, I could see only the sharp peaks of his wicked crown. "Welcome back, Seer. I know that you are awake. You can stop pretending. I can sense your mind."

Jackaby groaned.

"Everything is in place, Seer. The world is ready to be whole again. Your eyes are all we need."

"Ungh," Jackaby croaked. "Thanks, but no thanks. I'll pass on the multiglobal cataclysm. Eschatology was never my favorite subject anyway. The apocalypse always seemed a bit grim."

"I said we need your eyes, Seer. Not your permission."

Jackaby turned his head, attempting to get a good look at the king, but couldn't seem to manage it. "You couldn't break Eleanor," he said icily. "You won't break me."

"Ah, but that is the glory of science. You humans are so inventive. The things you've dreamed up to circumnavigate simple spells and common curses. I've studied. Eleanor's death taught us more than you can imagine about the nature of your special gift. I have corrected. You will find my noumenoneum expedites the process marvelously now."

"Well." Jackaby sniffed. "That is a terrible name. It sounds as though you've got a dab of peanut butter stuck to the roof of your mouth. *Noo-meh-nom-nom-nom.*"

"Feel free to keep talking." The king pulled a switch, and the wide lenses over Jackaby's face realigned. "It makes no difference to me."

"Fine. Okay." Jackaby swallowed. "You might crack my egg. You might not. Even if you do manage it, you'll have to find your way around. Bit of a mess up there. It will take time, and the armies of the Annwyn are on their way as we speak—"

The Dire King chuckled. "The Seelie army is destroyed," he said calmly. "And I am not concerned about dwarves and elves. Hold on tight, now. This might tickle."

"Unnngh." Jackaby shuddered. His eyes clenched. The Dire King was digging into his mind.

Fight him, I thought. *Fight him.* I recalled too well the periods when the Dire King had infiltrated my mind. I woke up dizzy and confused, learning only afterward about what I had done—what he had done in my skin. Anger rose hot in my chest.

Jackaby suddenly lay still. He took a deep breath and opened his eyes.

"Amazing," said a voice that was not Jackaby's. "Truly breathtaking. I can see the patterns, the powers at play.

I can see how the veil was made. I can see how it can be unmade. Alina."

"I am here." I heard her voice from above me, but I could not see her behind the control bank.

"The fluctuator controls. Are you ready?"

"I'm ready, my lord."

"The large dial at the top, turn it ten degrees."

The hum of the machine changed pitch ever so slightly.

"No. Back two degrees. There. Now the fine adjustor below it. Five degrees. One more. Stop. Yes—it's aligning! It's beautiful! Now the polyphase alternator—that's the controls on the opposite panel."

I could hear Alina throwing switches and adjusting dials. The thrum of the machine was louder now, pulsing in my ears.

"It is done," said the voice out of Jackaby's lips at last. And his head sagged. The Dire King had left his mind. "You performed well, little dog," he said from his own body. I still couldn't see his face, but something about his voice was familiar. "Now move aside."

Alina stepped abruptly in front of me and I panicked. I tried to slide out of view before she looked down at me, and my foot slipped on the step. I was suddenly standing on nothing at all. I fell. Before I could get my wits about me enough to even scream, I was caught hard in the gut by a thick stone, floating weightlessly in midair. I clung to it desperately. The stone trembled and rolled, but it held my weight as it continued to drift, floating silently under the landing.

"Did you hear something?" Alina said above me. I held my breath.

And then gears ground into motion and the tower was filled with noise. The device below me, the metal tank, began to swivel upward on its massive arm.

"I saw you," Jackaby moaned. "You looked inside my head. And I looked inside yours."

"Tsk, tsk," chided the king.

"I saw a battle—from a long time ago. A rift between factions of fair folk."

"There were many."

"This one was a duel between kings. I was watching it from a distance. I saw Arawn and Hafgan, the Fair King and the Dire King. Hafgan was wearing the black crown and holding a black spear. He lost. Arawn killed him. The crown fell to earth."

"This is history. It is well known," said Alina.

"Did you know that Lord Arawn hesitated?" said Jackaby. "When it was over, he looked mortified by what he had done. His face—there was something very human about his eyes. As the Dire King lay dying, he beckoned Arawn close. He whispered something to him. He pressed something into his hand, which Arawn tucked away with a shaking hand. The crowd rushed in and soon Lord Arawn was pulled away. His people were celebrating, but he did not look proud. He looked sad and frightened."

"Why should he not look proud?" Alina asked.

"Why indeed?" the Dire King asked.

"I saw what happened next," Jackaby continued, "in the darkness of the tower keep–this tower keep. Lord Arawn was approached by a cloaked figure. Do you remember who was under that cloak?"

The Dire King did not answer.

I had drifted close enough to the edge of the landing that I was able to reach a hand out to catch hold of the platform. I pulled myself up. On the far side of Jackaby now, I crouched low, keeping out of sight with my back pressed up against the control panel.

The machine above us clicked, settling into place. Its mechanical arm had raised it high into the air, and now the mechanism whirred as it rotated to face the control stage. The nozzles at the end buzzed and clicked as they realigned, their apertures swiveling to focus on a single point. The device was directed now squarely at the Dire King.

"It was you," said Jackaby. "You raised a hand out of your cloak, and with a motion the glamour covering Lord Arawn dropped away–but of course he wasn't Arawn, not really. The victor who killed Hafgan all those centuries ago, the good and righteous champion who wore Arawn's face and claimed victory over the Dire King, was not Arawn at all. He was a man. A mortal. I recognized him. He was much younger in your memory than I had ever known him. You called him Pwyll, back then, but I knew him as Father Grafton."

"A very plain name," the Dire King drawled. "His aliases always were."

"Grafton never wanted to kill anyone," Jackaby continued. "I think that might have been why Hafgan gave him the shield. Hafgan recognized goodness in him, even after Grafton had delivered the killing blow. Hafgan lay dying, but he knew that Grafton would keep the gem safe. He knew Grafton would keep it out of the hands of his sworn enemy. Out of your hands, Lord Arawn."

The Dire King chuckled darkly from behind the panel. That was why his voice had been so familiar. It was deeper, rumbling like an echo caught in a tunnel—but that voice was Arawn's. The Dire King and the Fair King were one and the same! "I didn't know about the gem back then," he snarled.

"In your memory, Grafton asked you to honor your side of the agreement. You nodded. What was that agreement, I wonder?"

"I promised him that I would leave him in peace for as long as he lived," the king answered. "He cheated, obviously. He wasn't supposed to have the gem. Wasn't supposed to survive so long. But I couldn't kill him, so I made life interesting for the people all around him. He didn't like that. I lost track of him, to be honest, around the seventeenth century. He resurfaced a couple hundred years later in New Fiddleham, and by then I had found humankind a bit of a fascination."

"You don't deny it?"

"What should I deny?" Arawn said. "I am in the right. When humanity split from the otherworld, you left magic behind. But humans are good at surviving. Humankind had to get creative in ways the fair folk didn't fully understand. Look around you! Nothing like this device exists in the magical world—it doesn't need to. No one in the Annwyn could have dreamed it up. I do not hate humanity; I want to bring out its full potential. Idle, you humans become complacent. Threatened, you become vital. You bring order to chaos, and the process is beautiful. But you have no concept of true chaos. You are like children born in a desert who can only dream of the ocean. You are thirsty for it, and you do not even know it. What you need is a ruler who will bring the chaos to you."

Lights flashed to life on the machine, and Lord Arawn's face was fully illuminated at last, maniacal and proud.

"The ocean," Jackaby said, "is salt water. It isn't fit to drink."

"What?" said Arawn.

"We don't want your new world order, and neither do your own kind. You know that already, though. You've lied to make it happen. Your people all believe Hafgan was trying to destroy the veil. The opposite is true, isn't it? He was the one protecting it."

"Not exactly. He wanted to punch a few holes," Arawn replied. "Create rifts in the veil to mend the rifts between our people. Bridges. He wanted to allow easier passage between the worlds. Hafgan wanted us to live among mankind as equals. Can you imagine it? He talked of laws, endless rules to protect his impossible harmony. His oppressively regulated coexistence would not have been peace; it would have been prison. I am not the villain here, Seer. I am giving my people freedom, not tyranny. I will give them chaos—real, natural freedom—and I will rule over this chaos as my forefathers once did. This is the natural order."

The device was vibrating now, and the hum was getting louder. Arawn stood in the center of the control stage, his arms spread out, welcoming the burst.

"There's nothing natural about this," Jackaby said. "If you do this—if you *become* this—there will be no going back."

"Alina," said Arawn. "Throw the switch."

Chapter Thirty-One

Energy cracked out of all three channels like whips of golden light. Arawn took the blast full in the chest. He bellowed as the bolts surged into him, sparkling tendrils of light writhing around his arms and legs like snakes.

Arawn grew. His features did not warp or stretch. He was not replaced by some grotesque version of himself, as his warriors had been. He simply grew. He was eight feet tall. Ten. Fifteen.

I tore my eyes away from the transformation and pulled myself up, hastening to loosen Jackaby's bindings. "Sir!" I said. "I'm here."

"We've failed," Jackaby said.

"Maybe if we can keep him distracted, slow him down. You said yourself, the armies of the Annwyn—"

"Aren't coming. It was Arawn who promised to send for them."

"It isn't over, sir!"

"It's over. The veil is like a great big lock. Arawn had a clumsy hammer—and I've made it into a key for him. He has all the power he needs, thanks to me. The crown affords him the focus to control it. The gem ensures he has the strength to survive it."

"So jam the lock!" I said, pulling off the strap around his wrist.

"What?" Jackaby said.

"You've given him a key, fine. How do we stop him from turning it?"

The machine above us whirred louder and louder, until its hum became more like the deafening absence of noise. My ears rang terribly in the ensuing silence.

Arawn raised his arms and the power burst through them.

The hovering stones orbiting the tower keep flew in all directions, hammering into the walls of the hold like cannon fire. The torn places in the veil swelled and stretched, meeting each other to form great gaping clefts. A sound crept slowly back to my ears. Cries. Growls. The clang of steel. The clamor of battle was seeping through the thinning barrier as a muffled echo. Down in the courtyard, I could see shapes—clusters of fighters here and there, like shadows behind an oilcloth. Arawn gave a broad wave of his arms and my vision rippled. The courtyard and church-yard were suddenly one. There were no gaps, no holes–Grafton's Parish and Hafgan's Hold were now the same space. The earth and Annwyn were one, and the din of the fight was all around us.

"I have an idea," said Jackaby.

High atop the windswept landing, I helped Jackaby pry loose a copper panel. It came free with a loud squeak. We froze.

"Charge the mechanism for a final drain," Arawn commanded. His voice echoed like a kettledrum. He hadn't heard us.

"Yes, my lord," came Alina's voice. I gritted my teeth. She had had the audacity to accuse Charlie of turning his back on his people. "Where shall I direct the pulse?"

"Full breadth," boomed the king. "All of them."

"All of them?" Alina said.

"All of them."

Jackaby eased the panel onto the ground silently. "He's exhausted the reserves," he whispered. "He's going to drain his people and ours for the final push."

"The final push–then the veil isn't down yet?"

"Only locally. It's unfathomable, the power that must have taken. He's driven the wedge. Now he's summoning the force to drive it through. The first drain, he targeted the Seelie army, but they were never going to be enough.

We played right into his hands. The monsters, the undead, the occult nonsense—he was planting fear and strife. He wanted this war. He knew from the start he would need to take power from the Seelie, the Unseelie, and everyone in between."

"But you can stop it?"

Jackaby took a deep breath. "Not exactly," he said. "But like you said—I might be able to jam the lock." He pulled a coin from his pocket and began using it to turn a screw inside the panel. "A full burst would almost certainly kill me, but I can siphon the flow. It should take less energy to hold the veil in place than Arawn will require to split it open."

"You're going to channel the energy through yourself?"

"I may be the only one who can," said Jackaby. "That's why Arawn needed my eyes. His noumenoneum brings into focus the imperceptible."

"His what?"

"The lenses, here. When he was inside my head he had them in place and the veil became visible. I can see it. I can repair it. Not a perfect job, but I should be able to manage a few crude stitches—and you're holding the needle."

I glanced down at my hands—the black blade. "The original spear!" I said.

"Yes, with a little luck, it should help me channel power through myself, imbued with my will, into the fabric of the veil. With more luck, I might even survive the process."

With that, he wrenched a cable from the panel and light burst out of the end of it, a thin ribbon of electric blue snapping, buzzing, and writhing up his arm as it danced along his skin and through his body.

He held out his free hand, twitching and shuddering under the strain. I fumbled to hand him the sword. As he took it, the shivering, dancing tangle of light smoothed into a single curve. It fed from the cable straight into his left arm and back out his right, crackling faintly around the hilt of the weapon. Jackaby pointed the blade, his face screwed tight in concentration.

At first, nothing seemed to happen. Then, starting with the farthest graves, the churchyard began to fade, like fog rolling in. The veil was pulling back over the earthly side. It was working—with agonizing slowness, it was working! Jackaby was mending the veil!

And then the black blade shook violently and spun out of Jackaby's grip. He grabbed for it, but it fell, spinning down to the bottom of the tower. Jackaby cursed. He looked at me, pained, ribbons of energy dancing across his chest once more.

"Hold on!" I said, and leapt into action.

I raced down the crumbling stairway as quickly as I dared. My feet hit solid ground, and I scooped up the black blade. From ground level, the raging battle felt overwhelming. The echoing clatter of steel and the screeches and shouts of combatants were deafening. Worse still, the groaning snarls of the undead horde seemed to have coalesced into a constant, terrible drone.

Through the ruins of the wall, I could see Lydia Lee and Hank Hudson in the distance, fighting madly, back to back. Blood was streaming down Hudson's temple. Jenny's silvery form darted from corpse to corpse, slowing the tide, but it was little use. From all sides, Tilde's reanimated army was closing in. We had to end this.

I gripped the blade tightly, but before I could steel myself to race back up the tower, my heart lurched. A huddle of ragged allies had pulled free of the crush and was crossing the courtyard toward the hold, right ahead of me. Commissioner Marlowe and Lieutenant Dupin, their uniforms torn and ragged, flanked Dragomir and Charlie, both of whom had slipped back into their human forms. Dragomir's thick furs were wet with blood, although I could not tell if it was his or that of his enemies. Charlie's ear was a red mess, and he was limping slightly, but his face was a mask of determination.

They were not twenty feet away when a streak of white fur shot across the courtyard and Dupin spun and yelped, clutching his arm. A moment later another blur of motion cut his legs out from under him. The lieutenant hit the ground with a cry of pain. Commissioner Marlowe ran to his aid.

"No, wait!" I called, but I was too late.

A pack of a dozen of Arawn's milk white hounds materialized in front of the hold, growling and braying. Another flurry of motion, and the commissioner was on the ground beside Dupin. Dragomir howled in pain as the beasts forced him to his knees as well. They were everywhere at once. They moved like lightning.

"Stop!" Charlie screamed.

The hounds, against all expectation, stopped. Marlowe began to push himself up, but the growls resumed at once. He sank back to his knees and the growls stopped. The dogs clearly were not releasing the men, and yet they had listened to Charlie.

Dragomir grunted. "They recognize your place, Suveran, even if you do not," he said.

"It was Alina!" I called across the gap at Charlie. "Alina and Lord Arawn. They lied to us! Arawn is the new Dire King! He tricked us all! He's going to destroy the veil. I need to get back up there before–"

Above us, Arawn's voice boomed. "Trigger the actuator."

"No!" I cried. "I need more time!"

All of us. Arawn was about to drain all of us. The life force of every friend and enemy alike on the battlefield was about to be stolen, only to be spent unraveling the entire world as we knew it!

"I–I challenge Lord Arawn to single combat!" Charlie yelled.

I stared.

From high above, a pair of ruby red eyes and a crown of midnight leaned over the edge of the ruined tower.

Arawn scowled down. "You have no kingdom on earth or in the Annwyn, mutt. Do not delude yourself. You're no king."

"They seem to disagree." Charlie pointed. The snow white hounds were parting, giving Charlie a path into the tower. "And this is not the earth or the Annwyn anymore, is it? It's something else. Something older."

Dragomir smiled, his face awash with pride, as Charlie pressed forward. "I was wrong about you, Kazi," he said. "You are every bit the Suveran your father knew you would be."

High above, amusement danced in Arawn's red eyes. I would have preferred rage. What was Charlie doing? He couldn't possibly defeat the king. Nobody could defeat him! He had the gem!

Charlie swallowed. The broken sword in his hands looked sad and short. The hounds dipped their heads reverently as he passed.

I stood, frozen, as he reached me. Gingerly, he brushed his hand across my cheek. "Don't waste it," he whispered.

"Well, King of the Dogs? I'm waiting," Arawn called from above. Charlie mounted the steps. I waited until he was halfway up the tower before I slid silently up after him.

Arawn regarded Charlie calmly as he finally reached the third landing. Even from below, I could see that Arawn was twice Charlie's height. I crept up another stair and suddenly the king's red eyes darted to me. My stomach turned.

"You were not invited." Arawn waved a hand casually, and the hovering stone stairway suddenly remembered what gravity was. I screamed and scrambled frantically to catch hold of anything solid. My flailing hands found the machine's nearest support beam, and I clung to it with all my strength. The heavy stones crashed and cracked as they fell to the ground below and I hastily found my footing on one of the metal struts, but the landing was on the opposite side of the tower and half a flight above me, much too far a gap to jump, even if I had dared.

"So?" Arawn said evenly, turning back to Charlie. "Are you going to kill me, King of the Dogs? You haven't even got a real weapon."

"I have enough," Charlie said.

"Hm. A broken sword for the broken king of a broken kingdom," said Arawn. "Can you even use it?"

"I intend to try," answered Charlie. He sounded as though he meant it. Oh, God–Charlie didn't even know about the gem!

"Well then," said Arawn, leaning his face down close to Charlie's. "Try."

Charlie swung suddenly, taking Arawn by surprise and raking his cheek. The king spun backward. The obsidian crown tumbled from his head to land at his feet. He straightened as a ribbon of red healed itself along his cheek. The ruby glow faded from his eyes.

"You're new to this," Arawn said conversationally, "so

allow me to offer you a little advice." Charlie leapt at the king again, this time slicing Arawn's arm with the blade. Again, Arawn shrugged off the attack. He glanced at the fresh split in his cloak, making a point to brush an imaginary speck of hair from the dark fabric before turning back to Charlie. "Never pick a fight you're not prepared to finish." Another slash. "Nor one you can't afford to lose." Slash. "Nor one in which you're not willing to do what it takes to win. Now, really. Is that the best you can do?"

Again and again Charlie came at the king, and again and again Arawn took the blows with dispassionate irritation. He raised not a hand against Charlie in return. There was no anger on his face, only cold, calculating patience. He was toying with Charlie.

I could see Alina on the side of the control stage closest to me. She flinched and turned away from the fight, her face wan and her eyebrows knit with concern.

Charlie's next blow drove the king to the ground. I gasped. Had the gem failed? Arawn did not stand up. He lay motionless, barely breathing. Charlie's chest was heaving as he padded around the king's body.

"Yield," Charlie said, standing over Arawn.

Arawn's back shook. He pushed himself up to one knee. He was laughing. He raised his head and appraised Charlie. "There it is," he said. "That look in your eyes. I know that look. Standing over your foe, his life in your hands. You want to kill me, I can tell. You've never looked more regal."

Charlie did look regal. His jaw was set and his eyes were hard. Even in his tattered rags, Charlie looked every inch a king. But none of this felt right.

"I don't want to kill you. I want the killing to end." Charlie turned his eyes to the battleground. "Stop this—all of you. Yes, we are different. Deeply, fundamentally, we are different, but being different doesn't have to mean a decision between separation or confrontation. I have to believe there's a third path. I have to believe that we can walk that path together."

The hush spread gradually over the battlefield, swords and clubs lowering hesitantly as men and monsters and all manner of magical beings looked up. Even the shuffling undead slowed their shambling attacks as Mr. Tilde turned a disbelieving eye toward his kneeling king.

"Not a bad speech, Dog King." Arawn's voice was a purr. "But what is a king without a crown?" Obsidian glinted in Arawn's hands.

"NO!" I screamed.

The jagged spikes of the Dire Crown pierced just beneath Charlie's ribs, burying themselves deep in his chest, biting into him like terrible black teeth. Arawn raised Charlie up by that horrible crown, held him there until the blood ran down his arms in rivers, held him up until Charlie's eyes— which had always been Charlie's eyes, no matter what form he took—were no longer Charlie's eyes.

Arawn dropped what was left of Charlie ungraciously

to the stage and placed the bloody crown calmly back on his head. Wet streams of crimson ran freely down his face.

The whole world shuddered and darkened. There was no sound. Only when I found myself out of breath did I realize I had not stopped screaming. Some part of me would never stop screaming.

Charlie was dead.

Chapter Thirty-Two

A rawn threw the switch.

My vision swam. As if from deep underwater, I took in what was happening. The flower of metal disks up above us burst into light like an enormous beacon. All around the tower, soldiers staggered to the ground. The undead were the first to fall, sustained as they were by Tilde's magic. I watched numbly as Shihab's blue flames flickered and dimmed. Bird women fell from the sky. The earth shook as the giants collapsed under their own weight. For a moment, the confused humans watched the otherworldly creatures crumble around them and allowed themselves to hope that their salvation had come—but then they, too, began to weaken and fall to their knees. The containment reserve above us trembled, lights blinking to life as it filled, gorging itself on the life force of friends and enemies alike.

Jenny hung in the center of the field, helplessly watching as they fell around her. She, too, was fading, thinning.

Charlie was dead. Help was not coming. The veil was falling. The Dire King had won.

I trembled, and the black blade nearly slipped from my grip. I held fast. Why was I holding on?

I lifted my eyes and saw the pain I felt inside my soul playing out on another face. Alina was slumped on the floor of the control stage.

"Alina," I called out to her. "Please, Alina. We can still fix this if we act quickly. You need to believe me!"

"Kazimir is the only one who ever believed in me," she said. Her voice sounded as numb as I felt. "All my life, he told me I could become more than what I was. Now? I don't even know what I've become."

"You're the choices you make, same as all of us. Good ones, terrible ones. It's never too late to start making better ones. Please."

"You don't know the choices I've made!" she snapped. "I believed in Kazimir, too! He always said he wanted more from life than to run away, but then he ran away! That's what he chose! He was my light, and then one day he wasn't there, and I was alone in the dark."

"You're not alone now, Alina. Please. Help me. If I can get this blade to Jackaby–"

"My kingdom is dead. My father is dead. My brother– I don't know what to believe anymore."

"Believe in what your brother believed in," I said.

Alina wiped the tears from her eyes and glared at me. "In what?" she spat. "In you?"

"No," I said, tossing the black blade to land at her feet. "In you."

Alina blinked and wiped her face on her arm.

"I'm believing in you, too. I'm trusting you. For Charlie." She picked up the sword. "Give that blade to Jackaby. Hurry!"

A dark resolve had come over her face. "A new sun is rising."

Alina turned. She stepped up the platform–in the wrong direction. Jackaby was still crouched behind the panel. Alina took the blade directly to Arawn.

She held the sword high, offering it to him. I felt a sickening weight in my gut. After everything she had just witnessed, she was still serving the Dire King. *Don't waste it*, Charlie had said. His last words to me. I felt dizzy.

Arawn pulled a lever and the light dimmed. The device hummed to a stop. The reserve had filled to capacity. In the field below, soldiers from all sides lay barely moving, barely breathing.

"I gave that blade to my daughter," Arawn said, eyeing Alina skeptically.

"I know," Alina breathed. "When you sent me to unlock her from her prison, I used it to cut her bonds."

Arawn was dispassionate. "I have no need of it, little dog. I have my machine."

"The Seer has need of it," Alina said. Her jaw was set, but her eyes were glistening with tears. "At this very moment, he is seeking to usurp the power that is rightfully yours. He's there." She pointed to the panel. Jackaby's eyes went wide.

My blood froze. How could she? I began edging along the metal strut, inch by inch, until the platform was nearly within my reach.

Arawn took the black blade. Tears streamed down Alina's stony face. She broke. "Please, my lord," she said, suddenly, clutching pitifully at his robes. "Forgive the disloyalty of my family."

"You seek a place in the coming kingdom?" the king said.

"I do." She straightened.

Arawn nodded. "So be it," he said. He turned. "Our friend the Seer would like to share my power?" My eyes shot to where Jackaby was hidden. The thin snake of blue light was still dancing across his arms. His face twitched involuntarily.

"Let it not be said that I am not a reasonable king," said Arawn, turning a small dial, "a generous king." Arawn flipped a switch. "I will let him have his share."

There was a massive burst behind the control panel. The feeble ribbon of light dancing through Jackaby became a thick bolt of lightning. Jackaby was lifted off his feet, his whole body convulsing. His eyes clenched as the blast crackled violently through his chest. No! Losing Charlie had been too much. Jackaby could not die–not like this.

His spasms calmed for a fleeting moment, and Jackaby's eyes opened. I held my breath. He locked his gaze on me, desperate and intense. His lips parted and he mouthed two words. *I'm sorry.* And then his eyes rolled back in his head. Arawn switched off the device. Under the light of the humming machinery, Jackaby's lifeless body fell from the tower.

Ice rippled across the battlefield. The wave of cold hit my chest. I couldn't breathe. A shimmer of silver danced around him as he fell, and Jenny Cavanaugh coalesced.

Some part of me saw her catch Jackaby. Some part of me saw her hold him, limp in her arms, saw her lower his body to the frozen earth. Some part of me saw the furious icy gale whipping around her as she lifted his unmoving arms and pressed them against his chest. Compressions. Jenny had always been a quick study. Some part of me saw the mad, manic, furious hope in her eyes as she pressed. Another part of me knew it was too late. Jenny's efforts were in vain.

Jackaby was dead.

I knew, because the moment his life was snuffed out, a blaze was lit behind my eyes. It was as though I had been stumbling through the darkness my entire life and somebody had just flicked on a light. It was everything Jackaby had ever described. Halos in hues I had no names for bloomed in front of me. They were the colors of pain and courage and distress. There were tastes of the air my tongue could not name. The smell of turmoil. The feel of distress. I looked out over the fields below, and the bodies piled across the frosted earth took new forms in my eyes. They were brighter, more vivid, but also more broken. The visions were beautiful and mad and they were true. I knew that they were true. I knew.

The sight had been Jackaby's beautiful burden and his terrible gift. And now it was mine.

"It is time," Arawn said behind me. "Alina, give me their power. Give me the worlds and I will give you your kingdom."

Alina's hand trembled as she threw the switch, and the triple bolts shot out once more, hammering into the waiting king. This time, the light was more beautiful than I could describe. It was magic and science and love and hate and the beginning and the end. It was pure and raw. It was life.

Arawn was more brilliant than a hundred suns. I could now see it, roiling beneath his skin, bubbling inside him. The energy of countless lives, their power and potential. He held the black blade as the energy crackled into him. It looked small in his hands as he aimed it toward the sky, and my mind reeled as I looked up. I could just make out the threads of the veil above and all around us. If I concentrated I could see the intricate charms that spun together to hold our two worlds apart. I could also see them rupture under his will. Tears streamed down my face.

And then Arawn stopped. The powers within him were churning, red hot. Something was wrong.

"Rrrrrraaaaaargh!" Arawn bellowed. "Turn it off!"

Alina's hand did not tremble. "No," she said.

The king's eyes grew wide, blood red and enraged.

"Let it not be said I am not a reasonable queen," said Alina. "A generous queen. I am Alina Cane. Suverana of the Om Caini."

Arawn shuddered. The energy was burning him apart.

"You—" He shuddered, unable to escape the torment. The crackling energy streams would not release him. "You . . . bitch!" Arawn whipped the black blade through the air. It sank into Alina's chest.

Alina looked down, startled. Slowly, she pulled it back out and dropped it beside her. The injury had already vanished.

"Hafgan's shield," I breathed. She hadn't been groveling to the king after all—she had been pickpocketing him. Alina had the gem.

Arawn made a tortured sound that was neither human nor animal. He was beginning to glow so brightly I could hardly see him. My eyes watered. The metal beneath me shook. In another moment there was a sound like a hundred crystals all shattering into dust, and my vision went white. When the blinding light dimmed, the king was gone.

The Dire Crown lay on its side in the center of the stage. Alina turned off the machine.

"You," I panted, climbing the rest of the way up onto the platform beside her. "You did it."

"No." Alina sank to the ground. Her eyes were on the body lying at her feet. "I ruined everything."

I sat down beside her. Charlie's body lay still on the platform.

"You wanted purpose," I said quietly. "That's what your brother wanted, too—something to run toward instead of running away. The Dire King made you feel like you had found your purpose—but his purpose was never really yours. You found your own way, in the end."

"Too late." Alina's shoulders heaved. "So many people are dead. My family—" Her voice cracked. "And now the veil is crumbling around us."

"The veil can still be mended," I said. "Jackaby—" I stopped.

"The Seer is dead," said Alina.

"No," I said, swallowing hard. "She's not."

Chapter Thirty-Three

My insides churned as the machine burst to life. I held the gem in one hand, and the black blade felt heavy in the other. The hardest part had been the crown. Neither Alina nor I had wanted to touch the terrible thing, but in the end I had put it on. Crown to focus the power. Blade to direct it. Gem to survive it.

I pointed the sword to the farthest edge of the unraveling veil and concentrated. The crown felt like a band of ice around my forehead as my mind cleared of all thoughts but the one. There was only the veil. I followed the patterns with my mind, willing them to knit together. I had no idea what I was doing. Bit by bit, the threads slid together and the two worlds slid apart. The veil was healing.

It was like drinking boiling water. The earthly trees

slipped behind the curtain, and the rolling fields of the Annwyn stood alone once more. The heat rose in me until it felt as though my blood had been replaced with fire. The ruined walls of Grafton's church faded away, and soon Hafgan's Hold was Hafgan's Hold once more. I willed the last frail ends of the veil to come together, pulling the rend together from a gap of one hundred feet across to fifty. I didn't know how much longer I could stand it. Thirty. I closed my eyes, but the visions still hung in front of me—there was no respite for the Seer. Twenty. The world swam. My whole body burned. Darkness closed in.

And then the pain was suddenly—not gone, exactly, but someone else's. I felt it as though from far away. I opened my eyes. A stranger clad in purest black stood over me. A memory. A shadow I had seen only once before in the depths of the underworld.

"Hello, Abigail Rook."

I could not find words to speak. My mind turned to Charlie and Jackaby, both dead on the battlefield. Had I joined them?

"You have not gone to the other side," said the stranger. "Not yet. But you may, if you choose to. I wonder. Will you? It's a very human thing to do, after all. They're always writing about it. Pyramus and Thisbe. Romeo and Juliet. You and I both know that you have nothing to fear from the other side, little mortal. Only old friends. Will you join him? You love him. I can see it."

My body felt both weightless and very heavy all at once.

"Very well," said the stranger.

I opened my eyes. Jackaby's face hung in a halo of light above me. I caught my breath. I hadn't chosen this. More faces appeared beside his. Jenny. Hudson. Lydia. All of them were swimming in their own glow, lit by brilliant auras. They radiated love and pride. The one face I wanted most to see was not among them.

My head throbbed. "I'm not dead?" I said.

"We didn't know for sure for a while," said Jackaby. "Very odd thing, not knowing."

"But you, sir!" I said. "You were dead. I saw you! You're . . . alive?"

"That's Jenny's doing," said Jackaby. "And it was physical science, no less. No magic involved."

"Well, I did reach inside your chest when the compressions weren't working," Jenny admitted. "But otherwise, good old-fashioned medical care, yes."

"She saved my life," said Jackaby. "No—I guess that isn't right. She brought me back. Which, I suppose, makes me undead as well, now, doesn't it?" He sounded a little too tickled at the notion. "I was definitely briefly dead, after all—as evidenced by the sight leaving my body." His expression sobered. He looked into my eyes. "I had no right to do it, Miss Rook," he said. "I am so sorry. It was the only thing I could think to do, the only way to give you a chance at mending the veil after I had gone. It should never have been your burden to bear. I just couldn't imagine it falling to anyone else. I couldn't imagine anyone else understanding."

"I expect that's how Eleanor felt when she willed it to you," I said. "It's fine. It's done." I looked him in the face. He looked positively destroyed. Except his eyes. His eyes looked, somehow, younger.

"They're blue," I said. "Your eyes have turned blue."

"They always were," he said. He allowed himself a soft chuckle. "Yours went red for a while there. They've turned gray now. They're like storm clouds."

I pushed myself up. We were still high atop the machine. Down below, there was a circle in the center of the court- yard twenty feet wide. Through it, human and inhuman soldiers were staggering toward the keep, gazing up at us on the tower for answers. "The rend isn't fully closed," I said. "I still need to finish this."

"No. Wait." I turned at the sound of another voice. Alina was hunched over in the corner. She stood. "This should never have happened. I was wrong. I was stupid. This war was never the answer—but a wall is not the answer, either. We don't need battles or barriers; we need bridges. My brother was right. We do not need hate; we need hope. We need to leave it open."

"We need nothing of the sort," said Jackaby.

"We need to learn how to coexist," Alina insisted. "The Dire King did not invent hate and fear; he only used them.

They were here all along. The wall just preserved them. Isolation preserved them. You think he's going to be the last to cut through that barrier? It will happen again. We need–"

"I do believe you've lost the right to tell us what we need," Jackaby said.

"No," I said. "No, she's right. And she has earned the right." I picked up the crown from beside me. "It was Alina who stopped Arawn. The king is dead." I reached the crown across toward Alina. "Long live the queen."

Alina stared at the crown. She didn't take it.

"Not me," she said. "I'm not a leader like Charlie."

"That's the first thing you've said I fully agree with," Jackaby replied. I raised an eyebrow at him and he sighed. "Miss Rook may have a point," he went on. "The Seelie and Unseelie alike have lost their king. There will be a void in Arawn's absence. That can get very messy if it goes too long without anyone presenting a legitimate claim."

Alina still looked hesitant. She took the crown tentatively, staring at it in her hands. "Things will not be as they once were," she said.

"Maybe they're not supposed to be," Jackaby said heavily. "There are times from which history does not bounce back. This feels like an end, but maybe also a beginning."

"If there are to be bridges, there will need to be guardians, as well. Sentinels to safeguard the peace," I said. "Someone with one foot in the world of magic, and one in the world of men. Keeper of the Veil is quite a role for someone look-ing for her purpose in life."

Alina looked from the crown to me. "I can't. I don't deserve it."

"Of course you don't," I said. I took a deep breath. "That's not how responsibility works. It is a gift and a burden in one. You don't deserve it, but I think you'll rise to it. Charlie would have thought so, too."

"If you're looking for a contractor to fix up this old cas-tle," added Jackaby, "I know a few people who are very good with creative use of space. Might be nice to have a place to call home again."

"Suverana of the Om Caini. Keeper of the Veil." Alina seemed to be trying out the idea. She lifted the crown to her head. "You're sure?" she said.

"Never." Jackaby gave her a weak smile. "Good luck, your majesty."

Alina sent the surviving warriors away. There would be no reparations. There would be no prisoners nor punish-ments. They all obliged.

I don't know what I expected, exactly. No one questioned her right to rule. They did not put up a fight. The Unseelie were more than eager to scatter into the forests and back to their homes. Those who cared to tend to their fallen kinfolk were free to carry them away. The goblins tended to their dead, as well as anyone else's leftover dead, especially ones with expensive-looking weapons or full pockets.

Bit by bit the battleground cleared. Charlie's body remained. We had brought him down to ground level, to be among the ranks of loyal police officers who had gone down with him. I found Alina standing over him.

"The city will honor him," I told her. "This time, the people will know. Marlowe will see to it. I will see to it." My throat was dry.

"He never cared about being honored," said Alina.

"I suppose not. But New Fiddleham was his city–and he was their peacekeeper. I think they should know." I stared at Charlie's body. His expression was sad. It didn't feel real. "Will you come to the funeral?"

"We have our own rituals," she said.

"Abigail." Jenny's soft voice was behind me. "Are you ready?"

"Wait," said Alina. "Before you go." She held out a hand and I reached for it. She pressed something into my palm. "This was our mother's," she said. "Kazimir wanted you to have it. He wanted–" She broke off.

I took the ring. Its aura shone in my hand, and the glow was full of Charlie. He had held this ring, fidgeted with it, kept it close to his heart. My chest ached.

"You were already family in Kazimir's eyes," she said. "I have been so blind. I don't expect you to fully trust me, but know that you are kin to the Om Caini now. If you ever have need of our help, you need only call on us."

I nodded. "Thank you," I said. "For what it's worth– I think he would be very proud of you."

"He always was." She sniffed. "For once in my life, I think it is time I begin giving him a reason to be."

The trip back to Augur Lane was quiet. I don't remember getting into the carriage, or who was driving it. I remember Jackaby watching me with pursed lips and saying nothing for several long minutes. I was glad he said nothing. I did not want to talk. I did not want to be comforted. The war was done, and now I wanted to mourn.

Mourning, however, did not come easily. The sight was relentless. All around me, the air was filled with lights and colors and smells and tastes more intense than I could handle. It was as though I had wandered into the middle of a mad parade and could not get out again. The world as I had always known it was there, but it lay perpetually underneath a wild nightmare. When I closed my eyes it was worse; only the mundane blinked away, leaving nothing but the fantastical. The whole experience was overwhelming and exhausting.

We arrived at Jackaby's house, and I had to stop at the front walk to take it all in.

"Miss Rook?" Jackaby said, a hand at my elbow.

"I-it's just too much," I said.

"Oh, yes," he said. "The salt and sage, the knots and

carvings. This house must be aglow for you with all the protective charms. I'll miss that."

I nodded. "It's all that and more. It's like the color of a worried father's hug mixed with a mother cat's bite. It's other things, too. Flowing all through the house and down the walk is a river of lighter auras. It's a kaleidoscope of feelings and intentions and potentials."

"Our recent guests," Jackaby confirmed. "Their presence will take time to fade. You will grow accustomed to it over time."

All of this had been easier when we had been on the battlefield. There, at the end of the war, on the threshold between realms, the visions had seemed almost normal. Now that we were at home, they felt like an assault. I tried to breathe evenly as we walked up the step. At the front door, the magic of the transom window swirled.

"Huh," said Jackaby.

"Oh my," said Jenny.

I glanced up.

ABIGAIL ROOK:
PRIVATE DETECTIVE

"What?" I said. "I'm not—"

"Makes sense," Jackaby said in a tone I found offensively rational and even. "I hadn't even thought about that. I'll stay on, of course, if you like."

"*What?*" I said. "You'll stay on? I'm not the investigator here! I'm your assistant. I don't know what I'm doing. I don't even know what I'm *seeing*."

"You'll be marvelous," Jackaby said earnestly. "You're already more keen than I ever was about putting together clues and looking in dustbins and questioning people and all that. Besides, you have something I never had when I was first starting out."

"Oh? What's that?"

"Me!" His smile was incorrigible.

"It would be really wonderful if all this could be a dream," I said.

"Come now, you'll get there. Focus on one aura at a time; that helps. What do you see when you look at me?"

I took a breath. "A kind of idiosyncratic bluish with a happy patch of crimson right around your middle. You're a bit dark—but also very light in funny little ways." I blinked. "There are also notes of a sort of rosy color hanging all around both you and Jenny. No, not rosy, exactly. How would you describe it—a buoyant sort of flush?"

"Buoyant is not a color," said Jackaby. "You sound ridiculous. But an excellent start! The sight will take time to understand. I'm here to help."

"I'm here for you, too, Abigail," Jenny assured me, putting a hand on Jackaby's shoulder as she glided forward to join us. "We can practice together and take it slow. It's the least I could do after everything you've done to help me figure out my own abilities."

I nodded. "It's nice to see that you're not having any more trouble in that area," I said. Jenny's hand was still on Jackaby's shoulder. The flush around their auras increased when I mentioned it.

"I'm not even sure how it happened," Jenny said. "I just needed it to happen, and it did."

"Not surprised about it at all," said Jackaby.

"Not surprised?" Jenny said. "Yesterday I couldn't so much as brush a hair out of your eyes, but today I reached inside your chest and held your heart in my hands–and you're not surprised?"

"Not at all. My heart was always yours," said Jackaby.

Jenny leaned back and looked at him, startled. "That is about the sweetest thing I think you've ever said."

"Was it good?" He gave her a goofy grin. "I was trying to work out how to phrase it the whole ride over."

"Not good at all, no," she said, trying unsuccessfully to keep a smile off her face. "It was sappy and maudlin and positively terrible. Sweet, though. Excellent effort."

"You're just jealous because we're both technically undead now, and I'm clearly so much better at it."

"Jealous? I'm not jealous. For the first time since I've known you, I have the power to shut you up." She leaned in and kissed him right on the lips.

Chapter Thirty-Four

J ackaby slept. It was the first time I had ever seen him do so. He nodded off in the library's comfortable armchair while we were talking. He looked peaceful, so I let him rest as I gazed around the room.

Sleep would not come so easily to me. I tried to settle my nerves. I slipped out and made myself a cup of chamomile, only I couldn't tell if I had used the wrong tin, or if now that I was the Seer, chamomile really did taste like riding a hot air balloon in the mist on a nondescript Saturday afternoon. I was plagued by visions and sensations and emotions I could not put into words, and worse, looming right behind all of this was a cold, swelling ache.

I took the ring out of my pocket. I turned it over and over, watching the glow that was Charlie leave little trails of light in my third eye. I focused, as Jackaby had suggested, until there was nothing in my world except that aura. And nothing changed. And Charlie was still dead.

Jackaby's head bobbed back up a few minutes later.

"I–wha? Who did? Was I sleeping?"

"You were, sir." I put the ring back in my pocket.

"Mmm. Delightful. I'm looking forward to a lot more of that. What were we saying?"

"Not important," I said. "I was just looking at all the books. I could never see it before, but they really are meticulously shelved. It's an elegant gradient of auras."

"Thank you," said Jackaby. "Nice to be appreciated."

"Yes. I can see the magic in them now. All of them. Even the ones out here with the beige auras. Your whole library is magic, isn't it?"

"Of course it is."

"Would a book without magic have any aura at all?"

He considered the question. "I have never found a book that did not have at least a little magic in it," said Jackaby. "They can't help it. They're made out of words and sometimes even pictures."

"The ones toward the back are beautiful," I said. "They're so intense."

"You should go look in the Dangerous Documents section sometime, now that you can really see them. I've got a few on thaumaturgy that glow like hot embers, a tome on invocations that pulses like a heartbeat, journals by an artificer that vent magic like hissing steam."

"Have you any about the afterlife?" I asked before I realized I was thinking it.

There was silence for several seconds. "He's gone," Jackaby said.

"I wasn't—"

"I don't need to be the Seer to see some things."

I swallowed the lump forming in my throat. "It isn't fair," I said.

"No, it is not."

"You can't tell me it isn't possible for a person to come back," I said. "We met the boatman—the underworld is a real place. There are souls there—"

"Not his," said Jackaby. "Charon told us last time. Half humans can't enter his underworld. They go—well, someplace else. Mag Mell, perhaps? That might just be fairies, though."

I let that sink in.

Jackaby and I sat in silence for a long while. "Well, I think I'd best be off to get some rest now," Jackaby said, pushing himself up.

I nodded. "Of course, sir. You have spent twenty years earning it."

He nodded and patted my shoulder as he left. "Just remember—you're stronger than you think, Miss Rook. And you're not alone."

"Good night, Mr. Jackaby."

When his footsteps faded up the stairs, I took the ring out again, holding it between my finger and thumb.

He was right. Charlie was gone. Not only was Charlie gone, but when the time came for me to go, Charlie wouldn't be there waiting for me. He would be–somewhere else. The swelling ache in my chest finally burst, and the lights and auras in front of me blurred with hot tears. A door in my chest quietly closed and locked itself forever.

I don't know how long I remained in the library–nor whether I had slept at all–but the sky through the window was full of stars when I heard a voice above me.

"Why did you say no?"

I looked up. Perched on the bookshelf was a squat little man all covered in fur. Through my new eyes, I could see the twain's power and potential spinning within him.

"You could be with him," he said. "He is your twain. You were given the choice. Why did you say no?"

I wiped my eyes. "You mean, why didn't I join Charlie in death?"

He nodded. "I often think about my twain. I miss her, every day. I am incomplete without her. I am . . . I am–"

"Lost," I suggested.

"Lost." The twain leaned against the inside of the bookcase. "That is love, though, isn't it? Sacrifice."

"No," I said, after a pause. "All due respect to Romeo and Juliet, but I don't think love is sacrifice at all. Real love is when you let another person make you better. You don't lose yourself in love–you find yourself there."

The twain lifted his head.

"Charlie made me feel like a better me," I continued. "And he made the world better, day by day. It was his gift. And now he's gone. I can let that gift die with him, or I can make it my gift. I can keep making the world better, day by day. That feels more like love to me." I wiped my eyes. "Charlie's gone, and I'm not all right. Not yet. But I intend to keep making myself better, day by day, too."

I looked up again. The twain had vanished. The sky was already warming to a rich plum outside the window. The sun was rising.

Supplemental Material

The funeral was held at Rosemary's Green. There were more caskets than I had expected, and some of them were very large. A heady glamour hung over the crowd, although no one else seemed to notice it. Human beings, I realized, made up only half of the mourners at the event. In my eyes, the various otherworlders' true faces were coupled with the human masks they were presenting and were underscored by their unique auras, as well as wave after wave of heavy emotions. The sensory overload was beginning to make me nauseated.

Marlowe stood at the front and said something, but I was having trouble focusing on his voice. Everybody began to sit down. I felt a hand on my arm, and Jackaby led me to an open chair. Someone else was talking now–something about many faiths and noble sacrifices. I think the sermon had begun.

Suddenly, a tiny figure materialized in the aisle ahead of me. The twain. I wiped my eyes, trying to catch a clear breath through the fog of glamour. I looked at the faces in the crowd, but nobody else appeared to see him. The twain gave me a solemn nod, then he turned away and began walking toward the front of the crowd.

I stood up. Faces all around me turned to look, and a medley of concern and irritation bubbled up from the crowd. The twain reached the front, and then, in the next moment, he was standing on a casket—on Charlie's casket. I pushed my way past several sets of knees until I was in the aisle. Somewhere in the back of my mind I realized that the speaker had halted his sermon. I was disrupting the ceremony, but I could not have been less concerned about how it looked to any of them. They could not see what I was seeing.

The twain turned to face me one last time. "Make the world better for being in it," he said. "And make each other better for being in it together." And then he sank down into the wood.

There was a blinding light within the coffin. The twain's greatest gift. I couldn't breathe. I couldn't move. The sun was rising inside my chest. In my pounding heart, a door that had been locked was opening.

Acknowledgments

I would like to thank Katrina, without whom this entire series would have never been more than a collection of playful notes; Lucy, who took a chance on a ridiculous idea and rode with it to the end; and Elise and her entire team, who have helped turn a lump of clay into something beautiful. I am unspeakably grateful.

I would also like to thank my mother, for providing moral support and technical advice, and Rita Moore, for being my Slavic languages consultant.

Finally, I would like to thank so many amazing readers who have given my strange little stories space on their bookshelves and a place in their hearts. You are always welcome in New Fiddleham.

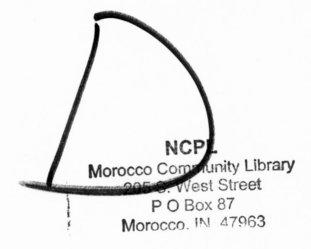